LIFEline

by James Belmont

To Marina, for being the prime reader. Thank you for making this journey incredible.

CONTENTS

Chapter One

Murder is too easy to get away with in this world. Especially when you have confidence, he thought, as he walked past a couple walking hand in hand in the opposite direction. The black straps of their LIFEline trackers around their wrists rubbed together as their arms swayed in sequence with each coordinated step. He set his face so it beamed a happy smile, and sweetly said "Goodnight", as he shifted the heavy duffle bag from one shoulder to the other. It was harder to get the body into the bag than it had been to do the deed.

"Do you require assistance, sir?" the man asked. Now that he had a good look, he noticed he was quite large and muscular, definitely built of stronger stock than him. This was obviously one of their first dates; the young lady was gazing at her prospective partner with approval, admiration, and the merest spark of love, something that would no doubt flourish given the right time and attention.

He laughed to himself; *this man has very nicely offered to become an accomplice to murder.* As tempting as his offer was, he profusely declined the help, thanking the stranger all the while as they went on their way. An extra pair of arms to carry the body would have no doubt been of help, but an extra pair of eyes watching as he dumped the body off the bridge and into the cold waiting waters below would have been a hindrance, to say the very least. The woman's compliments to her partner followed on the air as he kept his pace crossing the bridge.

He saw paintings, photos, and even videos of this iconic bridge with the large clock tower in the background, standing sentinel over history itself. A beacon of hope. A sign of strength older than nations and a reminder of the power of a great Empire. In all these clips from history, there were crowds of people at its feet, even in the dead of night. Not tonight though.

As the clock face chimed off on the thirty-minute marker, marking time as it did so dutifully throughout the decades, there was nobody here to witness it. Everyone was plugged in. It wasn't even a choice anymore. All choice was taken away in the worst way possible. Democratically. Just as the freedom was taken away from the girl in his large duffel bag. She didn't know, that as she sat in the restaurant awaiting her true love, that her demise was sitting outside, patiently watching, stalking her every move as keenly as any prospective partner would on a first date.

Their date was just as intimate. Just as tense, and just as permanent. He watched as she arrived. Her hair, an unnatural shade of red that made her slightly pale face glow. She opted to wear a black dress that dipped down far enough to show that she had a woman's body, but no further. Her clothes were picked to showcase the layers of her, an outer skin that showed a professional woman that was not afraid of her looks. As she took her long coat off and draped it over the back of her seat, her eyes flickered around the room.

From his spot, he could see that her eyes betrayed a hint of shock at not being met by her LIFEpartner. He made the reservation for seven, and she did not show up until five past to ensure that he could get a good look at her as she approached. This was textbook LIFEline protocol. She touched the black strap on her wrist. She held it up to her face and smiled. A small flash came from the device, and she sat down, pulling out her sleek phone as she did.

He watched her as she typed away, and he pulled out his own phone to check.

Her post, photo, and check-in had all been confirmed by LIFEline. Her hair looked much nicer in the photo, and her smile looked genuine, a little nervous, but real. Not the masks worn in countless photos across the platform, smiles that never truly reached the eyes. The post underneath the photo said it all. *Waiting for Mr. Right! #firstdate #love #LIFEline.* It also listed the location, time, her heart rate, her present mood, and if he wanted to check, a link to her full profile which would tell him everything about her. He locked the phone and continued to watch her.

There was a song he remembered from his youth, an old song even then, that his mother played often. There was a line that stated, "and the waiting is the hardest part". This was not his experience as he lay in wait. The waiting made him feel alive. He could feel his heart beat as if it was almost connected to this world, not the online fake plugged-in reality that was imposed upon him, but the real world. The soft breeze outside, whistling against the closed window of his vehicle, the smell of the air, the casual passers-by not paying him any attention. It moved majestically around him as he watched. As he waited.

She had a glass of wine, white, just like her profile said she liked. He liked her more and more, she seemed real. Her manner became more agitated as the minutes slipped by, and eventually she picked up her phone and dialled a number. Phone to her ear, she looked annoyed, but he noticed from his vantage point that there was also a hint of concern. The phone in his pocket vibrated. He just left it to ring out against his leg. She would get sick of waiting. He saw her slam the phone down, stand up, put her coat on and storm out. She jumped into a car outside the restaurant, and it drove her home. He followed at a safe distance.

She lived in a nice area in Kensington, not too far from where some of the royal family once lived. He knew where she lived, and on more than one occasion as he followed the car through the streets of London, he was tempted to take a more direct route than the smart driverless car. He decided against the risk. She may deviate from his plan, go to a bar, and blow off some steam. But the car took her straight home and drove off the second she stepped onto the pavement.

She stomped up her steps, opened her door, and slammed it shut behind her. Now was his chance. It had to be as soon as she posted the photo. If he waited too long, her actions would seem suspicious. After the photo and post that followed, LIFEline would expect one of two things to happen: she would either drown her sorrows and go to bed, which would give him the time he needed, or they would expect her to post her update on how the date went now.

He checked his phone - a new photo of her, make-up running alongside her tears, down her cheeks, red hair now tossed as if she pulled at it. The post read, *Stood up! Thanks for nothing @MrJMLong! #heartbroken #furious #alone #LIFEline.* She used the name, but that wasn't too bad. He would be the first suspect when she didn't post tomorrow. He walked calmly from the car, keeping his head tilted, across the road and up her steps. There were some cameras up ahead and some drones fluttering overhead, their lights travelling like twinkling stars. His measures should protect him but there was a shadow of fear niggling in the back of his mind.

One thought chased itself around his head: *do not post or publish anything else*! He knocked raptly three times and kept an eye on his phone. Other photos and posts were being shared by London all around him, like a steady stream of the city's consciousness. Smiling children sleeping, dogs chasing things in their dreams, drunken adults at house parties, and even some nude photos that would be gone in a couple of seconds, no doubt. LIFEline was good at ensuring only the best of humanity's traits were left online and nudes were a no-go. The light behind the door came on. Good, still no posts.

She had a small smile on her face. He was late, desperate to chase her down and explain, she convinced herself as she walked down the stairs. She played it out like a romantic comedy in her mind: the nervous sweating face as he flusters through his apology, her playing bad cop before quickly softening, the smiles as she hugs him, the forgiving kisses, the story they will tell their grandchildren.

The door wasn't even fully opened when the smile dropped.

He could see her mouth starting to form the words as she lifted her wrist out of sheer habit. She was going to take a photo of him. *Stranger at door. #fml #wrongnumber.*

He kicked forwards, slamming the door into her face before her hand even moved past her midriff. She fell backwards and he was on her. He shut the door with his foot and dragged her upstairs.

He brought himself back to the present, as his shoulder ached again.

The bell was no longer chiming, not that it really was to begin with. They replaced the actual bell with a recording when everything went online. More reliable that way. Authentic life was hard to come by these days.

The only time people are truly themselves, he mused, was when they became aware of their demise. He had witnessed it before tonight. He unplugged other people. He helped them move on. Their eyes looked so free. Not like the blank smiles and eyes of the churning photos they put up for everyone to see throughout their lives.

Those gazes, those stares, were for him alone. Just like she had one for him tonight. They all eventually stopped going for their wrist, for their slim phones, and started to fight; realised that their only real lifeline in this situation was not a piece of technology.

They always discovered it too late. They all thought LIFEline would save them. He chuckled to himself as he hoisted the bag onto the edge of the bridge, unseen by all but the clock face. The bag bulged as the pieces inside spread out, pushing against the fabric walls, her final resistance. He pushed it off the edge.

He watched as the water greeted her like an old friend. Swallowing it into her depths with just a minor disturbance to the running river, as if he did nothing more than skim a stone in a vast ocean. *I'll need more bags*, he thought.

Above, the clock tower stood sentinel to this scene. It couldn't pick and choose the historical moments that happened at its feet.

◆ ◆ ◆

Rachel pulled off her virtual reality glasses, massaged her dark brown eyes, and carefully placed the glasses on her living room table. The VR classrooms always made her feel slightly dizzy, especially when she was walking around adjusting work, when in reality she was sitting in her one-bedroom London apartment in her pyjamas, ironically suffering from motion sickness from her couch.

Rachel taught English and the Classics, which was basically the Greek and Roman myths and heroes that she loved as a child, to Certificate Level teenagers. She loved her job and the freedom it gave her. Between classes, she liked to rest her eyes so VR entertainment, which was the main way to keep occupied, wasn't an option after spending hours teaching through it. Rachel loved to read - not posts, publications, or blogs, but real books.

She collected hard and paperback books and even owned some rare and valuable copies of some vintage pieces that dated as far back as Shakespeare.

Teachers and students were given leeway when it came to posting times, so Rachel took a quick photo and posted an update: *First Class of the day down! #teachinginVR #breaktime #booktime.* She had a cursory check to see if she had any instant messages - she always turned the sound and vibrate off during work; it was distracting when something vibrated on your wrist mid-class. She brushed her long dark hair out of her eyes and took her latest book to her reading spot, an armchair by the window. Like her books, the chair was well-worn and well-loved.

The book was a bestseller in the late nineteen nineties and gave the printed word a last push into the next century. A push that unfortunately didn't get the boat all the way to the other shore, but briefly rejuvenated reading.

Rachel felt a slight pity that not everyone read this way, feeling the paper, smelling the pages, and hearing them flick over as you dive deeper and deeper into the story and the storyteller's mind. The empathetic lurch as you watch the character you love, in your mind's eye, as they go through innumerable trials and tribulations. Feeling physically connected to a story that you didn't star in, a story totally outside of you. With the inception of VR and multiple online film formats, the pages of all these books have been transcribed to other, more easily consumed media.

As the magic of the written word engulfed her, Rachel only had time for one other object in the room. She stopped every few pages to update her LIFEline. Photos of her with the book, posts on her thoughts on the character arcs, and even a whole publication on why the main character was not the "main" character.

All this almost made Rachel late for her next lesson.

She quickly made herself the second coffee of the day, picked up the glasses, and found herself back in the classroom. The room was huge, with tiered rows of pupils all around her, modelled off the ancient Greek Senate. Some pupils were still popping into existence as she stood there, patiently waiting. LIFEline's teaching association suggested a wait time of three to five minutes before officially starting a class.

Rachel turned to look at her screen. The class name and topic were already projected there. In the top left corner of the screen, there was a little picture in picture that showed all attendees' postings and checking in. It was like a steady flow of thoughts flickering in and out of existence.

The screen blinked: *Class present and 100% attendance recorded, Miss Fox.*

Rachel turned back to the class.

"Good morning, I believe last lesson we were debating George Orwell's *1984* and the effect it had on some sections of society when we accepted the LIFEline initiative. Who would like to start us off? Phillip?Okay, go ahead."

The debate was a good one, Rachel reflected as she took off her glasses sometime later. The class had clearly done the assigned reading and understood the complexity of *1984* and the small factions around the world who opposed the LIFEline initiative. There was even a very strong argument, led by Phillip, on how we were now effectively living in this "Orwellian" world, of our own free will.

"We made our own Big Brother, strapped this enemy onto our own wrists and to make matters worse, we strap it onto our children freely so they can be born with this shackle attached. Never getting the merest hint of real freedom," he said, inflamed with the power of youthful justification. "We have our every move monitored. We have all our thoughts logged and how do we combat our oppressors? We make sure we stay up to date. We can't help ourselves! We are driven to let everyone know everything about us. We can't use the toilet without posting a picture. The little flashing notification must be answered!"The argument against was just as strong, if not stronger, as it was based on facts and statistics, and without too much blooded emotion.

"We are now self-policing," Amber called back standing, although Rachel couldn't help but think that she was probably also sitting at home comfortably in pyjamas, using the glasses controls. "Crime is down year on year, and it's at a low of two percent worldwide. That is just taking into account petty crime. The major crimes are almost none existent, below zero-point one percent worldwide. Education is now accessible to all, no matter how far away from their local school. Ninety-nine percent of the population is educated to degree level in some specialism or other. Poverty and hunger? Obliterated, thanks to the most highly educated farmers, transport managers, and storage experts we have ever had, and this increased reliance and trust in technology.

"Life expectancy is higher than ever, with more doctors, nurses, and health workers than at any other time in recorded history. Sicknesses that at one time would have stopped our society for months, if not years, are now contained in seconds with the best health tracking. Quality of life has surpassed all expectations, now that individual wealth has become a thing of the past. Now that all governments have been disbanded, which I will remind you was our democratic decision, and LIFEline lead, the world has changed for the better! If this world was like Orwell's *1984,* we wouldn't be able to have this debate at all. #Thoughtcrime!"

There was great applause. But still, Rachel thought, picking up her book, as much as she agreed with everything Amber said, it was hard to argue with statistics. The book in her hand served as a reminder that not all changes were for the better.

The LIFEline device on her wrist vibrated and she took out her connected phone. An instant message from Jake. Her heart leapt as she opened the message.

HEY ZEUS, HOW GOES THE CLASSES?
MANAGING TO SHAPE YOUNG MINDS?
JAKE

HI, APHRODITE. CLASSES ARE FINE.
I WASN'T EXPECTING TO HEAR FROM
YOU UNTIL MUCH LATER. YOU FINISHED
FOR THE DAY ALREADY?!?
RACHEL

His font was blue; he said it was his favourite colour when they started to get to know each other, so she changed it to reflect his choice. He promised to change hers to a bolded and italic black, but she wouldn't know if he did it until they finally met. He gave her the name Zeus when he found out her specialist subject. She returned the favour in kind, giving him the most feminine name possible. Although, the meaning of love behind the name was becoming more prevalent the more they got to know each other.

A buzz at her wrist.

YEAH. WAS ON A NIGHT SHIFT, JUST
FINISHED. MANAGED TO GET SOME
SLEEP THOUGH, WHICH WAS HELPFUL.
WHAT PLANS HAVE YOU GOT FOR THE
DAY? X
JAKE

I'VE GOT A COUPLE OF
LESSONS LEFT. THEN I'M HAVING
DINNER WITH MY PARENTS.
AFTER THAT IT'LL BE CURLING
UP IN BED WITH A BOOK.
RACHEL

They have been texting for over eleven months now, LIFEline rules stated that they were not allowed to meet face to face until they had been talking for a full year. This, LIFEline said, gave the highest likelihood of success in matches - getting to know someone's personality before getting to know them physically. Rachel was curious about how they were matched. It was said that the Partnerships department had some of the best matching algorithms in the world, and that they took everything, from educational performance to genetics, into account. They didn't physically meet yet, but she had multiple photos of Jake and he had lots of her too, they were all over LIFEline.

OH, I WISH I WAS IN THAT
BED WITH YOU TOO! DON'T
THINK I'VE EVER BEEN JEALOUS
OF A BOOK BEFORE! X
JAKE

OH, BEHAVE YOU. YOU KNOW
THE RULES. NOTHING NAUGHTY
IS PERMITTED. AT LEAST,
NOT UNTIL WE MEET.
RACHEL

She sent a short video of herself winking to him. LIFEline monitored all activity between prospective partners. Any nude photos would be almost instantly deleted, and a very strict warning message would be sent to partners, reminding them that they could be unmatched just as quickly. Jake and Rachel knew this first hand, having already been reprimanded on more than one occasion.

We can't help it, she thought. *We are perfectly matched! Those damn computers know what they are doing.* Jake was a tall, muscular personal trainer, she saw his VR videos. He had a great smile, a sense of humour, and was intelligent. He read just as much as her, although he did most of his reading on screen.

*I WISH I HAD SOME FRIENDS
IN LIFEline, BET THEY CAN
GO AROUND THE RULES!*
JAKE

*NOPE, I TOLD YOU BEFORE,
A FRIEND OF MINE'S BROTHER
WAS RECRUITED BY LIFEline.
RIDICULOUSLY INTELLIGENT.
PART OF THE CONTRACT IS
THAT YOU'RE NOT ALLOWED
TO BE A PART OF LIFEline.
I GUESS THEY'RE AFRAID
OF THEIR OWN EMPLOYEES
TAKING ADVANTAGE OF THE
SYSTEM. HE COMES HOME FOR
HOLIDAYS SOMETIMES BUT STAYS*

OUT OF PHOTOS AND THEY CAN'T
POST ANYTHING ABOUT HIM.
WON`T TALK ABOUT HIS JOB.
IT'S ALL TOP SECRET STUFF!!
RACHEL

SO THEY CAN`T HAVE
A FAMILY? A LIFE OF THEIR
OWN? THAT'S PRETTY
RUBBISH! ESPECIALLY SEEING
AS THEY DO SO MUCH. BIG SACRIFICE.
JAKE

I GUESS THAT IS WHY IT PAYS SO
WELL. THANKS TO THEM THOUGH
WE ARE ABLE TO LIVE.
RACHEL

Rachel remembered the topic of debate in her classroom - the emotional arguments against LIFEline. It was easy, given the technology on your wrist, your phone, and all around the world, to forget that real-life people were behind every one of those innovations.

IT`S SO EASY TO FORGET
THEY BROUGHT US
TOGETHER.
JAKE

WE OWE THEM.

She looked at the clock and groaned. She hated being the one to have to end their chat. She was also glad he couldn't see her struggling to end the conversation, like a teenage girl unable to hang up.

> *I HAVE TO GO. TALK LATER?*
> RACHEL

> *SORRY ZEUS. I'M ON AGAIN*
> *TONIGHT. INTERNATIONAL*
> *CLIENTS. GOOD PAY, TERRIBLE*
> *HOURS! CHAT TOMORROW?*
> JAKE

> *DEFINITELY. CAN'T WAIT*
> *FOR TWELVE MONTHS!*
> *BYYYEEEE X O X*
> RACHEL

She sent him a video of her blowing a kiss. As she got ready for her last class, she wondered where they would meet. It was only two weeks away and they discussed so many different places over the last eleven months. Paris even was mentioned, although he may have been just trying to show off. *But still*, she thought as she raised her glasses to her eyes, *a girl can dream.*

❖ ❖ ❖

The room was so dark that it was impossible to tell if it was day or night, but with no real windows anywhere, it wasn't a problem that was ever going to be solved. The man that entered cleared his throat. He knew somewhere in this darkness there was a huddled lump lying in a bed fast asleep. He also knew that the huddled lump would not wake up at a throat clearing.

Russell "Rusty" Styles, the London Area Manager for LIFEline, was a heavy sleeper, which Dan knew because he was sent in here on other occasions, exactly like this. Well, maybe not exactly. Occasions where being the newest member of the team, even though he was here for three years already, meant that you stood in front of the boss and delivered the bad news.

Don't shoot the messenger, Dan thought, as he said quietly into the darkness, "Mr Styles, sir?"

The words were swallowed greedily by the mocking darkness, as if it wanted him to have to do the inevitable, get further into the room, grab Rusty's slumbering shoulder and shake it. *What the hell*, he thought, and did it. He jumped back straight after, as if expecting a bomb to go off. He was right, too. An old motto popped into his mind: *don't poke a sleeping dragon.*

Rusty exploded up and groggily looked around the room. He rubbed his eyes and muttered something that sounded exactly like "Shit".

There were only a few reasons why they would've sent the kid in here. *Some shit has hit the fan*, Rusty thought, as he rubbed his eyes. "What is it, kid?"

"They want you in the L.O.O.P, Mr Styles."

"Tell them to give me five minutes," Rusty said, staring around the dark room for his trousers and his prosthesis. He knew better than to waste time asking the kid too much. He would get nervous, splutter and stutter, and just waste valuable time. If they woke him up, time was probably something he didn't have a lot of to spare. The sliver of light darted into the room like an unwanted guest, throwing its light onto the bed and the jumble of clothes, food boxes, and the high-tech prosthetic leg, as Dan left the room.

Five minutes later, he was in the London Operations Observation Post, affectionately known as the L.O.O.P, with his team around him. He had fresh clothes on and splashed some cold water onto his face. He hoped that he looked better than he felt. From the clock on the monitors, he knew he slept five hours.

"Explain what I am seeing," Rusty said, as he looked at a huge screen that had a blinking solitary light on a constellation-like map of white lights in the shape of London.

"It seems that this girl, Natasha Anderson, has gone missing. Her last posts have her at her address at twenty-fifteen. Then all goes silent for the night until now, that is. She's offline," Ciri said, eyeing Rusty as she spoke. "She was stood up on her first date."

"Did you send someone to the address? Make sure she hasn't just broken her gear out of frustration? Wouldn't be the first girl to blame us for a poor match. Sure as hell won't be the last." Rusty knew the answers before he asked. Ciri was no novice. She had the experience, and she knew that, if she woke him up for no reason, he would chew her up and spit her out for such a rookie move. Even the kid was here long enough to know that the boss is only woken up if God can't help. It went: one - try to fix it yourself; two -pray to God to see if that improves matters; three - kick it, punch it and swear at it until you're blue in the face; four - wake the boss.

"Yeah, Rusty. First thing we did. QRT are at her place, live link is on that screen," Ciri said, gesturing towards a twenty-two-inch monitor displaying a small apartment room. Rusty followed her gesture.

"Holy shit." The room looked like if a child got into the finger paints and decided it was time to give the place a bit of colour. Red being the colour of choice. There was blood everywhere along with chunks, of what Rusty assumed, was Natasha Anderson. Anyone who lost that much blood was not going to be sharing any photos tonight, *#yolo*, he thought. There wasn't much he could ascertain from the screen, but it looked like there were rough gouge marks in the floor, possibly from where whatever made this mess struck. *After going through Miss Anderson*, he thought.

"Dan, get the London Director on the line. Ciri, who have you got from the Quick Reaction Team down there and where the hell is this all going on?" Rusty asked, looking around the room to see who he had at hand.

"I sent the Harris twins as soon as the light went. They are down in the Kensington area, not too far from the Royal Albert Hall," Ciri replied, "Do you want me to get more bodies down there?"

"Hell no, we need to keep a lid on this for as long as possible. Having an entire team down there will just draw in a crowd. We may be able to catch whoever did this before morning posts. Tell Jonas to stand at the door as casually as possible. He's the politer of the two." Rusty knew that the Harris twins had very relaxing and trusting faces, it was their mouths that were the issue, and something he hoped they wouldn't have to use. "You said she was on a first date?"

"Yeah, guy never showed up. Her last post tagged him, so we are trying to pin his last known location," Ciri replied.

"Trying..." Rusty started, but he was interrupted by Dan.

"I've got Director Carter, sir. He is not happy at being woken up."

"Well, that's the least of his problems. Put him through," Rusty said, picking up a headset the size of a thumb and hooking it on his ear.

"Rus, you better have a God damned good..."

"Sorry to cut you off sir, but you will want to hear this. We've had a murder." As he said it, Rusty felt the weight hit him and could physically see it impact the team around the room. Dan outwardly grimaced at the words, from the other end of the phone there was nothing but silence. The monitor that was splashed with red seemed to be the only thing in the room. The team had boots on the ground, but it wasn't live, it didn't feel real for anyone until he uttered the words. The penny was spinning precariously, wobbling as gravity tried to take over, but the boss slammed his hand down and it dropped for everyone.

"Are you sure?"

"Yes, one hundred per cent, sir."

"Definitely not a suicide?"

"Not unless the victim killed herself and then disposed of her own body. I know this is far from ideal, sir, but we are already chasing some solid leads," Rusty said, eyeing Ciri meaningfully, "and her last post was from twenty-fifteen, so we are not far behind."

"How... How has this happened?" Director Carter asked, and Rusty detected fear in his voice. Unlike all the men and women in this room, Director Carter was not involved with LIFEline's inner workings. He was in the system. He had a wife, a family - his life was still online – online, and extremely close to London.

"I don't know, Carter," Rusty replied, looking down at his unshackled wrists, "but we will find out."

Rusty hung up the phone by pressing at his ear, and addressed Ciri straight away, "What do you mean 'trying to pin' the guy? You said she tagged him in her post. Just follow that to his profile and check his last login. Get a location from his wrist tracker. Track him down."

"We did, his profile's down. He hasn't done anything since just before the date. Traffic on his page had only Natasha send him some messages, try call, and search his page. She obviously was seeing if he would stand her up online, as well as in public. We think there are some..." Ciri's voice trailed off, and Rusty could not blame her. Not two in one night. Not two in London. That haven't happened since LIFEline's global acceptance. Since the world signed on that dotted line.

"Send a team to his last known place of residence. If he's alive, I want him here for questioning. Damn it, we are going to need an external investigator on this," Rusty swore, and put his head in his hands for a brief second, shutting out the team, the light, and the flicker of the screens. Five hours away from those screens was not enough if he wanted to keep his sanity.

The team were silent as he raised his head. "Call everyone in. I want to brief the entire building on this. Have all heads of departments in this room in an hour. The rest of you, keep LIFEline running in London, and keep an eye out on any online traffic that mentions unusual activity. If you see any posts on this murder, shut them down straight away. I want to control how we get this out. We cannot afford London to panic."

The room emptied of all the other departments, leaving just the skeleton crew of the L.O.O.P. The office was open plan, and everywhere the eye could see there were computer monitors and screens. They were built into the walls, the desk faces, and traditional computer terminals were set up in rows. Cameras from lights, driverless cars, drones, and buildings were relaying the story of a dark London night to the team. Dan was fidgeting at his desk as Rusty approached.

"You slept yet, kid?" Rusty asked, looking down at him, arms crossed over his chest like a teacher reprimanding a pupil.

"Yeah, I got a few hours."

"Go get a few more, you look as terrible as I feel. We got a long day ahead of us. That, by the way, was not a request." Rusty said, as he made to argue.

Dan stood up and walked off towards the rooms. The L.O.O.P team had a shift pattern covering three hundred and sixty-five days a year, twenty-four seven, like most teams at LIFEline, but here, in the big city, it was more of a drain. The observation teams needed to be omnipotent. They needed to know when you'd been bad or good. Tonight, someone was bad, and what was worse, they weren't on the naughty list.

The Anti-Terrorist Unit's, role in LIFEline was to check that list twice. On the last review, yesterday morning, there were no red flags on that list. The list was another algorithm, like everything in LIFEline, it was simple math. Well, not simple, but just a simple case of the right math, and previous case study evidence to have the correct formula. Thanks to the increased criminal and terrorist activity online in the early two thousands, the formula was created. We had all the profiling we needed. Effectively, all the make-up of a criminal, all the effective ingredients: broken home, religious extremism, even people's grades and dissertations, were used. The recipe for our homo criminalis. The DNA that spelt trouble.

It became only a matter of time before it was possible to pinpoint when someone was going to join a terrorist organisation. A matter of time before someone dropped a bag with more than just your weekly groceries at a national event. Add all of this to the monitored usage of the internet, and you have a safer world - a world where things are not supposed to go bump in the night. Hell, a world where the thing that is about to go bump in the night gets knocked on its ass until morning, and the light at the end of that particular tunnel, not a pleasant place for the bump maker to be.

Preventative measures were put in place to stop these kinds of people from existing. LIFEline had almost abolished crime, but there were still some bugs that needed fixing. And now it seemed there was a bug, a glitch, in London.

Chapter Two

T
he L.O.O.P filled steadily over the next hour. There were looks of concern on sleep-deprived faces, which quickly turned to shock, sadness, and, inevitably, fear as those present relayed the news in whispers to their teammates who were off duty. Most members of the L.O.O.P stayed on site or close by when off duty. Working for LIFEline was not like a typical job where you could clock in and out as easily as turning on a computer or putting on a pair of VR glasses. LIFEline was a way of life. Colleagues became family, the only other people in the world that truly understood what it was like to not be online. The only other people on the outside. Well, almost.

Seven teams were responsible for the regular operational running of the Greater London area: the Observation team led by Charlotte "Ciri" Iris, A.T.U, Q.R.T, P.R, Learning and Development, Technical Support, and Partnerships. Each team an important cog in a well-oiled machine, like a clock. A slight hiccup could cause a chain reaction that would be seismically worse than showing up late to a party.

As Rusty watched his entire operation walk in, he realised that it was very seldom that everyone needed to be in the same room at the same time. Teams had different objectives, sometimes different working shifts which lead to him usually briefing teams separately. Partnerships, led by Evan Levvett, never needed to know what was going on in L&D. Their role was to match LIFEpartners, ensuring to keep matches inside a ninety per cent chance of success. No need for them to know how many people passed or failed the latest accountancy examination.

Addressing the room like this, standing at the front, one of the only people in the room authorised to pass on relevant information, reminded him of his military days. And just like those days, it was totally up to him what he decided to share, or, more importantly, what not to share, with the mass of people around him. It wasn't that he didn't trust his team, Rusty told himself, it was just some people in this room had family and friends plugged into LIFEline. When it comes to loved ones, people tend to get a little crazy and a whole lot of stupid. Rusty has seen the biggest, hardest men in rooms break down and cry and seen shy, meek women lash out aggressively, both verbally and physically, when restrained by duty.

When the room was finally buzzing with activity, Rusty called the Heads of Departments to the front and addressed the whole crowd. "By now you are all aware that there has been a murder. Time is still on our side, but we need to act quickly. There will no doubt be an external investigator on this…"

"Why do we need an external? This is our city. Who better to track down this guy than us?" The question came from one of the monitors, from one of the Harris twins down at the scene. There was a general murmur travelling steadily around the room that clearly agreed wholeheartedly with the confidence and conviction of the twin.

"It's protocol. It is not a question of competence. The external is here to add their expertise in this field to our team. For example, let's not jump to the conclusion that it is a 'guy' just yet. External investigators are tasked with investigating all murders worldwide. It has been a long time since anything of this scale has happened here in London," he shifted his weight from leg to leg, not to spare the prosthetic, which was built to relieve any pressure points, but because internally he felt the same as the Harris twin; unfortunately, he had to voice the party line. "Damn, some of you in this room haven't seen anything worse than a domestic dispute."

"Some have seen much worse," the quiet comment travelled well in the screen-filled room. The words came from Evan Levvett. He spent a lot of time in his early LIFEline career as an Investigator. He was, at one time, considered to be the best the company had ever seen, until he requested a transfer. A few job changes later and he found another true calling; Partnerships. From catching murderers to ensnaring lovers together, a change Evan wore well. He looked up at Rusty grimly.

"I'll help out as much as I can on this boss, but don't expect me to get hands-on," the pleading tone was extremely evident to everyone. Some of the newer team members, who, obviously, didn't know Evan, even looked at the Head of Partnerships as if he was a coward. Rusty responded with a nod.

"Now, back to time being on our side," he glared at the monitor, where the Harris twins were. "I want the P.R team to draft the news straight away, so, liaise with Ciri on all the details. Nothing too gruesome, but don't leave out the facts. Reiterate to the public to keep their activity trackers on and posts up to date. They are their best weapons in these situations. I also want to know the best time to get this news out."

"Just before dinner is best, if we can hold off that long for bad news like this, boss," Lindsay Morgan, Head of PR, spoke up as she scratched her head. "It will prompt people to talk about it at dinner and relay their fears, making it much less likely for there to be any major issue going viral. A side effect of the timing of the message will be that any scheduled dates have a high probability of being cancelled. People don't like meeting new people during these kinds of incidents. Message-wise, I'd suggest we get an Influencer to announce. Someone calming, controlling, and a reliable voice."

Lindsay worked her way up in the communications team through a great ability to be able to pinpoint precise timings, content, and media sources that would elicit the response that LIFEline was looking for and make it, most importantly, seem organic.

During a particularly poor period for the Learning & Development team, when test scores were low and admissions suffering some of the worst numbers since education went online, Muhammad Chopra, Head of L&D, enlisted Lindsay's help. Thanks to some amazing advertising content, some elaborate, yet subtle product placements, and a variety of campaigns, tailor-made to the struggling subjects, L&D reported their best figures ever.

"Good idea. I'll leave the details to you. Partnerships, get ahead of the curve on this cancellation of dates. Let's cancel any scheduled for tonight, but try to organise an event to appease the backlash. Something like an old school party or organised ball in a week or two. That'll serve both purposes of fulfilling dates and having a large crowd to discourage any violence. I also want you to pull up all the stats on the couple, our victim, and this Long guy. I want to know if it was their first rodeo or either have been matched in the past. Focus more on this Long character. He's our unknown entity in this. If he's dated others in the past, I want to know where they are now. We may need to question them."

"No problem, boss," Evan replied, folding his arms across his chest as he sighed.

"Good. L&D, I want a report on all Londoners who have expressed an interest in any violent course content or courses that are similar. I also want a report of any behavioural issues in classes from London pupils. Anyone openly rebelling or being outwardly vocal about their contempt of the LIFEline systems. If a pupil has even made a wisecrack about murder, I want to see the profile. Tech Support, I need your two best with Observations to track this guy. We seem to be having a technical issue with his tracker and the activity on his page. Cut through the noise quickly and, hopefully, we will have this wrapped up before the end of the day. A.T.U, I want a list of all LIFEliners on your records..."

"Boss, you know we can't do that. It's privileged information. We can give you Amber alerts or above. Nothing more without Director approval. Sorry, Rusty," the Head of A.T.U, Pender said, taking off his glasses and rubbing them against his shirt. Rusty could see he was feeling the pressure. His team dropped the ball somewhere on this, and it was now bouncing around causing mayhem. *We've all dropped the ball here*, Rusty thought. A head may roll for this, more than just Miss Anderson.

"Amber and above will do, for now. I will speak to the Director if we need the rest. Ciri, get footage of outside the scene for the entire day. Use whatever you need, driverless cars, drones, people's devices, I want to see how this happened. How our murderer got in, how they got out, the entire show. I don't want to miss anything. Better get us the feed for around the date site too. The murderer may have stalked her all the way home.

"When the external gets here, I will build a team to assist us on this," Rusty looked at Evan and Lindsay in turn, they both knew from the stare that they have been fielded. He wished he could give Evan his wish, but he used to be an Investigator, and the quicker this mess was cleared, the quicker he could get back to playing Cupid. "The rest of you will continue with your regular job and make sure that LIFEline stays unaffected by this. Any planned leave is cancelled. I shouldn't have to say this, but I will, none of this information leaves this room without my say-so. We can't afford any type of panic. We can't let London go dark."

People started to disperse. Moving back to their stations and slowly, but extremely surely, the life and noise of the working office swept everyone up. Rusty moved to Ciri's desk. She was sitting in one of the main central hub positions, around her at every angle was a screen. Rusty sat beside her and watched her effortlessly pull up all the locations and camera angles they would need across the tapestry of screens, like a seasoned conductor coaxing music from all around them, each scene like a soloist waiting to be called on.

Ciri looked at Rusty, "Shouldn't we wait for the Investigator?"

Rusty sighed, the book said wait. Sometimes, you have the tear the book up, "No, he could be hours. Evan?" Rusty's voice carried across the room easily, and when Evan looked over, a slight tilt of the head told him that he was to join them.

As he sat, Rusty turned to him, "Where do we start here?"

"Rusty, you're more than qualified to..."

"Save the shit for the pot, Evan. I am also more than qualified to pull up these feeds, but, by comparison, Ciri would make me look like an ape trying to play the piano. Brush off the cobwebs and show us what you can do."

Evan did not respond, he just lent forward, brought his hands together, his left a fist covered by his right, with fingers drumming the knuckles as he observed the screens. After a moment, he pointed with his right index, "Show me that one."

It was the restaurant's camera. It showed the inside of the room, it was brightly lit and there were some dates already taking place. There was one empty table, a small white sign on it said reserved. As they watched Natasha walk in, Evan's hands were close to his face, his right index now tapping a slow rhythm on his nose, as his eyes watched the screen intently. Rusty noticed the annoyance on Natasha's face briefly before she shook it off, sat down, and took out her phone.

"That didn't take her long," Ciri remarked.

Evan looked at her, "Standard date procedure, the first one in should check them in. Although, in heterosexual couples, we see a much higher percentage of males being the first to show up. We tend to advise that, if one party is late, you do not wait longer than ten minutes without checking in with them. It is extremely uncommon to have a no-show for the first date, but it does happen."

On the screen, Natasha had already picked up her phone, held it to her ear, and slammed it back down when she received no response. She stood up and stormed outside.

"Bring that camera up," Evan said, with the efficiency of a surgeon. They were now a passing drone, hovering above the street, watching Natasha rush out of the restaurant and make her way into a car. The car took off the second the door closed.

"There." Evan did not need to elaborate for either Rusty or Ciri. The car moved off slowly enough, but it was very clear that it was following the driverless vehicle home. As Evan asked for different video feeds, dancing from one to the next, they watched as Natasha was being stalked all the way home.

"Ciri, is that car on the grid?" Rusty asked, looking at the monitor. There was a time when he would have known just from glancing at the screen. He would have been able to pull up all the details he needed in an instant but, with the last few years spent leading the entire city, he was more of a generalist than a specialist given the sheer volume of technological advancements.

"No. It seems to be a self-drive, old car. No registration and very low tech," she responded, "practically invisible to us. We can have the system follow the car automatically though, if you'd prefer?"

"Stop there. No, let's follow manually for now. We will move to systems if we need them," Evan interrupted, as the following car came into a good area of view for a camera and the lighting was good, "Zoom in."

Ciri manoeuvred the camera and zoomed in as far as possible. The LIFEline cameras were top-of-the-range equipment. They had the highest specifications possible and were constantly updated and maintained. The best technology in the world does not stay on top without constant upgrades. As the picture zoomed in, the face seemed to become more and more distorted. When it eventually cleared up, the face was still indistinguishable, a mere mask of pixels.

"What is going on?" Rusty asked Ciri.

"Seems we are not the only ones with good tech at our disposal. Our murderer knows their way around," Ciri responded. "We have seen this before, remember that graffiti kid was going around on the old South Bank, writing up profanities, and tagging "The Dead Shall Rise" everywhere? He modified his wristband to scramble his face for cameras. It will take a couple hours, but we can unencrypt that."

"Let's keep following, I want to see how they get into the house and, more importantly, how they get back out. Let's speed this up, Evan, if we are not going to see his face, we don't need to watch his whole drive," Rusty said.

Evan sped through camera after camera now, taking no notice until the driverless car stopped outside the house in Kensington. Natasha stomped her way to her front door.

"Ciri, bring up her LIFEline stats," Rusty said as Natasha closed her door. As she pulled the stats up, a post appeared. It was the last message of the online presence of Natasha Anderson, and she did not go out on a happy note. Her heart rate was slightly elevated and her locator had her pacing her apartment. The dot stopped moving on the small map on the side of the screen. Rusty could see why - our murderer brazenly crossed the road and knocked at her door.

"Are there any other devices in her location at this moment?" Rusty asked. Ciri paused the feed and touched the bottom left-hand corner of the screen, which was showing Natasha's stats. It enlarged, and she started to type a string of words quickly into a bar.

"Nope," Ciri responded, "it seems anyone who shared her apartment building was out." She hit play, and they saw the outline of the murderer kick forward and then shut the door. Evan reached over Ciri and hit pause.

"Any other cameras in her apartment we can use?" Evan asked. Ciri rubbed her face and looked over the room to where Pender and the ATU were sat.

"We would need approval or wait for the Investigator to get here," Ciri responded.

"Technically, we don't," Evan said, looking to Rusty. "This is still a crime in our jurisdiction, for now. Yes, we need an external investigator to take point on this, but until they show up, it is still with the Area Manager. That's you, Rusty."

"You heard the man. Pull up any cameras you can inside the apartment. This is still our active crime scene until we are told otherwise. I am sure the Investigator would be appreciative of the help."

"We have the camera on her wrist, her phone, and on her glasses, which are located deeper in the apartment. No other ones popping up," Ciri said, as she combed through the page on the computer.

"Pull all three onto this monitor and take it back to before the kick," Evan said, pointing to the largest of the monitors around Ciri. Ciri pulled them up and left the stats on the side of the screen.

The mobile device camera was dark. There were some muffled noises but it seemed to be in her pocket. The glasses revealed a dark bedroom, the door into the living area was open slightly, throwing a light onto the scene. The wrist camera was moving steadily down the stairs showing a glimpse of wall, carpet, and an upside-down Natasha.

"Mute all the other cameras, but leave the video in case we see something," Evan said. Rusty was watching Evan. He had never seen him like this before. There was an air of certainty in everything he did. It was like watching a professional athlete, there was an almost effortless grace to each movement and thought, but under the surface he was aware there were hundreds, if not thousands of hours of practice to hone those skills.

The front door opened, they could see the scrambled face upside down for a split second, and then her hand started to move up. *She is going to take a picture*, Rusty thought. *We have them.*

Then the kick. The murderer kicked the door, which swung forward and hit her. From the angle, it was hard to tell where she was hit, but Rusty would have put cold hard cash that it hit her in the face, because the next images came from the vantage point of the floor.

"They knocked her out," Ciri said with a sigh.

"Probably not on purpose," Evan said, "Did you see the way the hand was moving? She was trying to take a photo and they reacted on the spot." The stats were still strong. "Murderers don't tend to murder the unconscious. They will wake her up."

The locator dot moved in line with the camera. The murderer was dragging Natasha back upstairs. They went through a blue door into a large room. From the glasses in the bedroom, they could see the stalking figure walk around the apartment as if looking for something.

Was it a burglary gone wrong? Rusty thought.

The figure walked into the bedroom, the lights turned on automatically and they proceeded into the room, picked up the glasses, and brought them back into the living room, placing them down so only the ceiling was visible. The same thing was done to the phone in Natasha's pocket and last, but not least, the wristband was removed.

"Are they going to steal the LIFEline?" Evan asked, looking baffled.

"They don't. The devices alerted us to the issue," Rusty said, looking at Ciri.

"Yes, the wristband alerted us to inactivity after a few hours," Ciri responded as, on the screen, the band's feed mirrored that of the other devices.

There were a few minutes of just the ceiling and a collection of different noises. Evan looked at Ciri thoughtfully, his eyebrows coming closer together, "Bring back up the feed from outside, along with those three, and start to forward through until we see something. We can comb the sound files later."

The camera feeds started to jump ahead slowly, but in less than ten minutes, the murderer was back outside.

"Play it," Evan said, but he didn't need to. Ciri had already understood what they were doing and stopped the feed.

The murderer pulled what looked like a large bag from the car and made their way back into the house. Once inside, Ciri started to skip ahead. Twenty minutes passed on the clock, and they could see nothing. Another ten, and Ciri did not need to be told to stop the camera. There was red everywhere on the screen.

There was a silence present with the three figures watching the screens. It was a dark silence, a primal silence that emanates from the days of the cavemen, whose underlying savagery, no matter how many advancements seen in technology and society, seems to hold onto the human psyche.

That silence had power, and the room around them, which at first remained untouched by it, was now being drawn into its ebbing tide. The room fell completely silent. Rusty looked up first, realising the effect they were having and cleared his throat, "Come on team, keep at it."

He tried to keep his voice clear, strong, and with an undertone of authority. In his own ears it sounded flat, but he remembered words of advice he had been given by his first leader in his military days. Major Hawes explained, "There is a moment in battle. The team around you will be in an almost automatic state. Their training will have kicked in and they will be completing their first response, like a well-oiled machine, but no plan survives first contact. Your enemy will be adapting to your response. Now is the time for your Condor Moment - a courageous moment where you will do nothing but think.

"The enemy will act in the heat of that adrenaline-filled filled moment. Your people will act out your orders, so take a step back and try to see the full picture. Think. What is the best course of action?"

Rusty was having his Condor Moment right now, and it was time for his team to see that this was under their control. This murderer was no match for their combined skills, "Keep moving through the feed, Ciri."

The feed continued to move forward until the murderer came out of the door, duffle bag over his shoulder. He went back to the car, dropped the bag in as he jumped back behind the wheel, and started to drive.

"Follow him," Evan said, back to his pose of bent forward, intently looking at the screen and left fist being drummed by his right fingers. They bounced from camera to camera as they followed the car; up past old Hyde Park Barracks, Harrods' lights seen in the background of one camera before moving further up the road, showing the first glimpse of Hyde Park Corner and Wellington Arch. The streets were particularly empty. As the car moved past Buckingham Palace and straight down Birdcage Walk it took a right towards Horse Guards Parade. Where the old Household Cavalry Regiment stood sentinel for hundreds of years before being disbanded, along with the government and monarchy, the car drove through the disused building and...

"Where is it?" Ciri was the first to ask.

"Move backward," Evan asked. Ciri moved the camera angles, but no car could be seen, she rewound the feed and they watched as the car drove into the small tunnel, but never came back out on the other side. There were no cameras in the tunnel and none of the outside ones could get a good view down it. There were no passing drones, no driverless cars in the dark shades of that ancient building.

"Move through the feed. It can't have just disappeared!" Rusty said, looking around the screens and inwardly fuming. It was hard to have 100% coverage of any city, but it was ridiculous, he thought, to think this murderer managed to just find one. Did they know LIFEline? First the facial encryption and now a blind spot. This can't all be a coincidence. The murderer knew things they shouldn't know. *Unless*, he thought, *they are already inside*. No, he pushed the thought away. He trusted the men and women around him.

◆ ◆ ◆

There was a long vibration on her wrist. A feeling of dread seemed to emanate from the place where the tracker touched her skin, all the way around her body, and even paid a visit to the back of her neck, leaving the obligatory hair-raising. A long vibration only meant one thing; bad news. In her life, she could count the amount of times she experienced this buzzing on one hand.

Rachel stood up, placed her bookmark, and closed the book she'd been reading, putting it gently down on the table in the centre of the room. She heard rumours that when books were still easy to purchase people used receipts, string, and even went so far as to bend down the top corner of a page to mark their place. As she walked towards her VR glasses, she resisted the urge to pick her phone out of her pocket. These messages were best seen in VR.

She placed on her glasses and was instantly in a large forest clearing.

There was a stream in the background, which she could hear flowing steadily across a pebbled bank, rustling and splashing, effortlessly soothing. There was a bright sun above the sparse trees whose light was dancing through the swaying branches. A moment passed and her parents were there. Then their friends, some of her close family, and then some of her close friends.

Before Rachel even had a second to register this, connect with her parents or friends, a person they all knew appeared. This last person's entrance was different to everyone else's. For one thing, Rachel would swear that the noise of the flowing river lowered in volume, and the sunlight was being used in a way that would make even the biggest blockbuster movie lighting department jealous.

Emily Walker, a popular chef and food producer, owner of The Walker Restaurants and all associated products, was wearing an old-fashioned blazer over a flowery blouse and a sad look in her eyes.

The look was one trademarked by Grandmothers everywhere, usually kept in reserve for when you skinned your knee as a child. She walked among them, known by all, but she did not know anyone in this crowd. Rachel knew that in hundreds of other VR rooms like this, Emily was being seen and heard in this very same way.

"Sad, sad news, my friends," she started, looking down at the grass that was flattened beneath her pearly shoes. Her voice was soft, kind and its warmth seemed to reflect their surroundings. She did not speak loudly, but it travelled. *No, not travelled,* Rachel thought, *it is just coming from the VR glasses.* She couldn't help but wonder if, like her, Emily was in reality sitting somewhere in her pj's while controlling this conversation in the same way she did as a teacher.

"Sad news," she repeated, "we have had a horrible thing happen in our city. It is extremely important that we come together as a community, that we are there for each other tonight, and over the course of this troubled time. Show those who try to defeat us that our spirits can never be broken. A poor young girl has been murdered."

There was an intake of breath from all around her, and then a silence that was almost deafening before Emily spoke again.

"The finest LIFEline teams from around the world are on the case and are following some firm leads but, for now, we can sleep safely knowing that we have each other, and LIFEline of course. It has never been more important than it is right now to stay updated. To stay connected to those closest to you, so we all know you are safe. All dates have been postponed for the remainder of the week, and we will be outlining a curfew to ensure that every measure is taken to keep London safe," she finished kindly.

As Emily disappeared, everyone started to embrace. Virtual hugs all around, and as Rachel hugged her parents, she was more acutely aware of the distance between them than ever before. They said their goodbyes after a few minutes of catching up, but only after her Dad made her swear to "stay updated, stay online, and don't answer the door to strangers." Her parents did not live in London. Her parents, their friends, and many of those present at this announcement were only here to make the ones in London, their children, feel safe. Like they were a part of a wider community. As she took off her glasses, she wondered if there was a manual at the LIFEline headquarters: "How to break bad news and other fun tips to avert a crisis".

She always felt safe in her little apartment in London. It was the draw of the big city's history, its importance in the English Literature world that piqued her interest as a child. The day she got her first pair of VR glasses she begged her Dad to take her to The Globe. After some persuading, which in hindsight was a lot, he agreed, and they both put their glasses on in the large front garden. Her Dad grew up with LIFEline, but it wasn't as advanced, so he still enjoyed walking in reality as he walked virtually, which was easier to do in wide open spaces, not so easy in the dining room.

The marvellous structure was near enough to the river that you could smell the Thames, which considering the year the Globe was created meant a bad journey for the nose, but the young Rachel did not care. She would run around the outside, trying to see it from every vantage point. Running in between the spectators to get to the stalls to watch the beginning of a play, or to watch the men rehearse for an upcoming play, sometimes with the Bard in attendance. The seed of her love of London was planted there that day, in that moment and flourished, grew, and was nurtured by the greatest writers the world had ever seen. Some of the greatest stories ever told were based in, written in, or thought of in London.

As she looked around her apartment, the darkening city visible outside her window, she was filled with her first sense of apprehension about this place. A chill journeyed from the nape of her neck down to her toes, and she tried to shake it off. She checked her heart rate on her wrist.

Readings were normal. She took out her slim phone, and before she even thought about doing it, she was halfway through a message.

HEY, DON'T KNOW IF
YOU'VE HEARD

She stopped herself. *What do I actually know about Jake?* The thought flashed in the front of her mind, like a notification on her phone, before she even had time to register it. She tried to swat it away. They had been talking for *months* now, staying up until all hours, talking about their dreams and aspirations. He wanted to eventually stop being a personal trainer and become a doctor. He was studying in any free time he had to become a surgeon. She told him everything about her – her difficulty sleeping, her love of books and music - and he did the same.

Rachel deleted the message and started to scroll through the LIFEline feed. There was some information on the murder. After around thirty minutes of reading from different sources, it was pretty clear that the girl lived in London and was murdered after a date. "Why else are they not letting us go on our dates?" - one vlogger exclaimed with a look of satisfaction Rachel felt was a little vulgar given the topic. As she was scrolling following this link, then that one, like Alice going down the rabbit hole, she inadvertently landed on Jake's page.

The page looked the same as it always did. Pictures of Jake, his family, and friends. A reflection of his life, the footprints he was making online were everywhere, his thoughts in blog and image form. She continued her journey past Jake's page and back to following the murder of Natasha Anderson.

Chapter Three

T he L.O.O.P was an underground facility that housed the entire operations team responsible for LIFEline in London. Rusty knew all of the people around him. Knew them better than he knew his own family, even better than he knew his brothers and sisters in the military, and he would have taken a bullet for any of them. Actually, he did take a drone attack and lost a leg for them. He would do more for every person in this room. He knew them – not in the way you know people you just work with –but in a way that was deeper than family. Blood may be thicker than water but there was nothing thicker than the bonds created in this facility.

The doors at the back of the room opened. Rusty looked up, expecting to see a familiar face. This face was not familiar, Rusty stood up and walked forward. *The External Investigator,* Rusty thought, as he took strides forward. There was no other way of describing Rusty's steps. They were deliberate and purposeful, which every soldier learned on day one.

"You move with an aim in mind. A destination. We do not dawdle, we do not hesitate, unless for vigilance and tactical reasons. There are four types of movement," his drill Sergeant shouted at them as they stood rigid on a parade square in the middle of nowhere, "belt buckle crawling towards a suspected explosive, a march like walk filled with purpose, a T.A.B, and running as if your life depends on it. Trust me, every time you run, your life will depend on it. Now, RUN! GO, GO, GO."

The memory flashed in front of his eyes as the external investigator shuffled in. There was no other way of describing his steps. He barely moved his feet, and his eyes roved around the room, as if looking for any sign of danger. A feeling of tightness in Rusty's gut sent a message to his brain. "This guy is supposed to help us?"

He wore round glasses that showed no sign of any tech attachments but made his grey eyes look large and unblinkingly shocked. His hair was grey with flecks of black and stuck up in patches as if it hadn't seen a comb in decades. It may have been a combination of the glasses, the roving unblinking eyes, the shuffling feet, and the dishevelled clothes that made Rusty think this man looked more like an owl than a human being.

As he walked across the space between them, Rusty doing most of the closing of the distance, he noticed Evan entering from one of the side rooms. He obviously saw the investigator enter, too, because he was walking toward him, with a smile on his face. That did more to alleviate Rusty's fears than the appearance of the investigator. Rusty was hoping that smile meant they were sent one of the good ones.

Rusty extended a hand to shake the investigator's, expecting to see a wing or talon come to meet him, and was surprised even further by no proffered hand at all. The investigator looked at the extended hand; his face twitched slightly.

"Don't bother, Rusty. Rae doesn't shake hands," Evan said, catching up with them.

"Germaphobe?" Rusty asked, in what he hoped was a respectful tone. The investigator did make a good first impression, and his second wasn't exactly adding anything new to the equation.

"No, Mr Styles. Detective Levvett is wrong in his assertion. I do shake hands, just not with strangers. The handshake, like many of our deepest traditions and social norms, derives from ancient times, in this instance, I believe Greek. It was to show a sign of peace," the investigator raised his hands away from his shabby clothes, "to show that neither was holding a weapon. I personally do not believe in watering down that sentiment, until I know that I do not mean the person harm."

Rusty stood dumbfounded for a second and noticed that Evan was still smiling. The investigator had a scholarly look, but a voice that sounded like it belonged to a gruff folk singer. The investigator obviously noted the awkwardness, but seemed to not mind it at all, his eyes still roving the room, moving from person to person, his mouth twitching every now and then. No sooner had someone met his eye, than he was onto the next person.

"Rusty, let me introduce Detective Euan Rae. Rae, this is London's Area Manager Russell Styles…"

"I gathered as much," he said. It wasn't an interruption as such, as Evan kept speaking.

"I will remind you that I am no longer a Detective, so you can call me Evan."

"I think you will find, Detective Levvett, that just because you transfer doesn't mean you are no longer a Detective. A doctor, by definition, doesn't stop being a doctor because they stop practising," Rae responded.

The smile did not falter on Evan's face. It was like watching brothers catching up after a long time, Rusty thought, the dynamic seemed to be natural, organic even, and they were striding straight back into it.

Rae looked at Rusty, his eyes no longer moving around the room, "Shall we speak in your office?"

"Of course, this way," Rusty said, leading the way. Rusty took a couple of paces and threw a look over his shoulder to ensure he was being followed. Those shuffling footsteps were eerily quiet, making barely any noise on the hard floor. Rae was behind him, but Evan stayed back. Rusty nodded for him to follow, and as he shook his head to say no with that knowing smile, Rae spotted the exchange.

"Just the two of us will be fine, Mr Styles," he said.

"You can call me Rusty. I thought it would be best to have as much experience on this as we could. Might as well use as much of the team as we can."

Rae kept following Rusty, forcing him to continue leading the way, as Evan stayed where he was. "We will do better from this point onward if we keep things between the two of us."

Rusty sat down at his desk, and Rae perched himself on the opposite chair after he swept the room a couple of times with his eyes.

"Does the lack of your left leg hinder your mobility at all?" Rae asked. He asked it the same way an engineer would ask if you thought you needed more space on your storage device.

"Read my file?" Rusty asked.

"I got a summary report. It didn't mention the loss of a leg, bit of an oversight, but I imagine it was because it does not hinder your mobility. I would rather know now if there will be any problems in the field due to the missing appendage," he responded.

"The field? We have enough tech here to catch this guy without going anywhere near the field," Rusty responded, starting to lose patience with this little man.

"I know it is a trying conversation from your side, Mr Styles, but can you bear with me just for now, until you get the validation you surely seem to need, that I know what I am doing, and I am a fair few steps ahead of you? I will endeavour to get you up to speed as soon as possible, it is in my interest as much as it is in yours for this to be the case. This endeavour will be for nought, if you are not in a position to assist," Detective Rae responded. It took Rusty's brain a few moments to catch up – the words seemed rude, but there was neither malice nor superiority in the gruff voice as it delivered the words. His brain wasn't used to this type of mental gymnastics.

When Rusty didn't respond, Rae spoke again, "You seem to need validation now. Let me tell you two things that should help you make up your mind quickly. We will need to enter the field, as this murderer has intimate knowledge of LIFEline. Knowledge no one outside the organisation should have, which will hopefully help you realise why, the less everyone in this building knows, the better it is for us."

"And my second thing?" Rusty asked.

"You have already made multiple mistakes we will need to try to rectify," Rae responded.

Rusty was getting agitated. He tried to remember his military training, when you had to take orders from superior officers who did not show any sign of being superior to even the lowest of ants, but he still had to smile and take it. It has been some time since he had to utilise those skills, and they were not coming back to the fore without a fight.

"Mistakes?" he asked, not trusting the skills enough yet with more than one word of his vocabulary at a time.

"You have an untrained team on the scene, you have released the news to the public, you have briefed your entire operation on the details, and even enlisted the help of your team to track the murderer. You are rushing into his game, and you don't even realise the game you are playing yet," Detective Rae responded.

"I followed the book, and my team are as…" Rusty started.

"Mr Styles, you followed the wrong book. This is not a petty crime, and I do not doubt your team are excellent in many areas, but this is not one of them. Have you heard of Maslow's hammer? When the only tool you have is a hammer, you start to see nails everywhere. I am paraphrasing, of course, but, as I mentioned, we do not have the time for us to connect enough for you to trust me. Luckily for us, it is not a necessity, this is now my jurisdiction. You will support me, and I mean you alone. Deputise everything else here, this is going to need all of your attention. Tell no one else of the details of our investigation. Our murderer could know someone in that room. Our murderer could be in that very room."

Rusty's head was still spinning when Rae stood up and went to leave, he turned at the door. He had an awkward look as he said, "I know it feels strange when all social niceties are not observed but for me, it feels even stranger when they are without meaning."

He left.

Rusty was staring at the door. It opened and Evan walked in. The smile seemed to have taken up permanent residence on his face. Before Rusty could speak Evan said, "I know, but trust me, Rusty, he is excellent. The best LIFEline has ever seen. Maybe the best investigator the world has ever seen. Strange to see him on a solo case…" Evan finished finally evicting the smile from his face.

"You think he is expecting more than one case?" Rusty asked.

"I have no idea, either that or, well frankly, there already have been more we are unaware of. Rae is an expert at profiling, for that he tends to need more scenes, but we have nothing to worry about," Evan said.

"He doesn't want to use the team at all and thinks we have to go into the field," Rusty informed him.

Evan didn't seem surprised, "Rusty, he's like a savant when it comes to murder. He once caught a killer in less than 3 hours after visiting his crime scenes. Recently, he tended to stick to the North, but I imagine Carter pulled some strings to get the best for London. Trust me here. Follow his advice and it would be like watching Michelangelo work."

"I won't get in the way, but I will not treat our team as the guilty party here. I will still need your help. Something tells me you will need to help me stay up to speed with this guy," Rusty said, thinking over their last interaction.

"Rusty, I don't know," Evan responded. He seemed hesitant. Rusty remembered earlier when he asked not to be involved and again, he wished he could give him that wish.

"Evan, I am sorry, but I need you. You know I wouldn't ask if I didn't think it was necessary. There has been a murder in London. It seems the murderer knows too much about LIFEline to be too far away from our circles. I am going to ask Ciri to take control of the L.O.O.P, and I will feel so much better knowing you are here to watch over my shoulder," Rusty looked at Evan as he spoke. Each word seemed to pain him. Rusty could only imagine the sights he had seen, although it looked like he was going to do more than have to imagine.

"Okay, Rusty, but if it gets too much, I am out," Evan said finally. The look in his eye told Rusty that there was no flexibility there.

Rusty had seen some of the worst of humanity. Even with LIFEline, there has been conflict in their lifetime. Terrorists still popped up, using drones, and other technologies to help spread their fear, but that somehow seemed different. Less personal. Terrorists tended to pick places for shock factor – high-profile events, high-security areas – to show that they still existed.

This murderer picked a person. Stalked them. Entered where they lived, the place they felt the safest, and then took that safety away, along with their life. Rusty physically shook his head in the hope that the thoughts would go away. They didn't. He stood up and walked out with Evan. A thought struck him as he walked.

"Hey, can you tell I only have one leg?" he asked Evan.

The smile returned, "I told you. He is excellent."

◆ ◆ ◆

There are moments in life that change your perspective. Sometimes these moments are small, sometimes, they are large. These moments are varied; a stranger mentions a band you love, and you just connect, a friend's loved one passes away, and you hold their hand as they say their goodbyes. You make no decision to change, but a change has happened. By being there, by being present, by *being* - you change.

As Rachel looked at Jake's profile, she felt that change. She could not stop it, to try to fight it would be as inevitable as trying to not think. Their connection didn't go anywhere – she still looked at his images and felt something there, deep in the pit of her stomach. The late-night introspective conversations still meant the world to her, but she was adding a layer of vigilance. As she looked deeper and deeper into the profile, she justified her behaviour over and over again by telling herself that she was being cautious.

After the announcement, she was scared. It took the unfamiliar feeling to make her realise that it has been a very long time since she felt that way. In some ways, it was the first time she felt that type of terror. She also felt alone in London. Her parents were miles away, even if they did have dinner once a week together, it was virtual. The panic was building as she worried more and more, questioning everything she knew about Jake, LIFEline, and other humans around her.

A knock on her window made her jump. She laughed as she saw the drone that was delivering her dinner. She opened the window, took out the bag of food, and tapped her wrist on the scanner on the top of drone, which dutifully flew away. She almost forgot her dinner with her parents was tonight. She sighed with relief and set herself up on her dining table, slipping on the VR glasses, which plunged her back into her parents' dining room. Even virtually, she found the surroundings comfortable. Her parents beamed at her, but Rachel wasn't fooled, she could tell they have been having a stressful conversation.

She remembered moments when she was growing up, and her parents "discussed" topics that they potentially didn't see eye to eye on. Her mother had a tendency to run her hands through her thick brown hair, which made it look like a harassed cat. The mother that was staring at her right now could have fed her hair catnip. Her father, on the other hand, was harder to faze. He remained calm even in the most trying times – this frustrated Rachel to no end when she was younger. Her friends' parents, especially their fathers, had issues when they started dating, whereas Samuel Fox would invite prospective boyfriends into the house. Allow them to stay over if it got too late. Her mother once commented that, if her father was any more laid back, he would be comatose.

"How are you, sweetheart?" her mother asked, getting up, and hugging her daughter. Dostoevsky said, *"Man is a creature that can get accustomed to anything,"* but, in this moment, Rachel would have liked to challenge that. No matter how many virtual hugs she got off her mother, she never became accustomed to how good they felt. She did not know how LIFEline's technology created the feeling of being hugged from afar, but right now, she felt as if her mother was really hugging her. Her worries and panic started to flow out of her, as if the hug was sucking the poison out of her body. Her father's calm presence, just sitting in his chair with a slight smile that lifted his moustache at the edges, added a level of tranquillity Rachel did not think she would feel so soon after the announcement.

"I am fine now, Mom. I just want to forget all about it," she responded, sitting back down.

"Well, let's not forget all about it," her father said, leaning forward in his seat. He moved very little in the virtual world, even when it was his own dining room. "Don't let it scare you, but do not forget it until it is safe to do so. It has been a long time since we had anything like this, so you will need to not act rashly and be vigilant."

"I am sure they will have all this business sorted soon," her mother interjected, giving her father a look that made him lean back, with his calm smile back in place. "Let's eat." As they ate, the conversations roamed freely, moving from old friends of Rachel's who just got married, "I told you to get onto LIFEline Partnerships early, Rachel. Remember?" her mother said, as the topic came up, for what seemed the hundredth time, "you and Jake could be married already." To her dad's construction business, "It is the intricacies of building a solid building that could be made to look like it is from the past, or the now, or the future. These new technologies are so exciting and great, but they cause more headaches than strictly needed. Who wants a building to keep changing?"

They had just finished their dinner when the conversation inevitably came full circle, but this time it was her mom that inadvertently brought it back up, "How long until your first date with Jake?"

"I don't know anymore," Rachel responded, and, before she could continue, her mother interjected.

"Oh, what's wrong? Did something happen between you two?" she asked.

"No, nothing between us, but we don't exactly know when things will be back to normal with the dating. It seems like they are cancelled for now," Rachel responded.

"That poor girl," her mother said, looking to her father. Something made Rachel think that, whatever they had been talking about before she entered, was about to come up. Her parents loved to think that they were subtle. Rachel didn't have the heart to tell them they were about as subtle as a crowbar.

Her father cleared his throat, "Your mother…" the glance that her mother served her father stopped him mid-sentence, "Your mother and I were just thinking, if you felt up to it, that you could come stay with us for a few days, or a week or so. You can do your job from anywhere, and we would be able to spend some time together."

Rachel smiled, "Honestly, I am fine in London. You both know that I always wanted to live here. I won't let this one thing scare me off."

"It scares me," her mother mumbled.

"Don't worry, Mom. I am as safe as can be. I always have my devices on me, I spend most of my time in classes, or reading, or…"

"Exploring the city," her mother finished with a sad face that would give a puppy dog a run for their money.

"Mom, I promise I will be careful." Her father was nodding.

"Promise to call every night?" her mother asked, pleadingly. Her father rolled his eyes behind her, and followed it up, quickly, with an agreeing nod, when her mother turned her gaze to him for support.

"I will call you every day."

It was very interesting, Rachel reflected as she combed Jake's profile, her parents' concern caused a calming effect on her. Before dinner she was scared, would have probably ended up leaving the apartment to go home tonight, rather than stay here alone; but now, after hearing their concern, she was much more resolved to not allow this thing to beat her.

DO YOU THINK IT'S STRANGE
THAT WE LOVE EACH OTHER
WITHOUT MEETING ONCE?
ROMEO AT LEAST SAW JULIET
FROM ACROSS A ROOM, WALKED
BENEATH HER BALCONY, AND
SAW HER AS THE RADIATING LIGHT
FROM WHERE LOVE COMES.
JAKE

The message popped up on her phone, as she was scrolling through comments and likes of Jake's from some time ago.

HEY YOU, I THOUGHT
YOU HAD WORK TONIGHT?

She also added, respecting the order of the questions:

WELL, MAYBE NOT A GREAT
COMPARISON. BESIDES THE FACT
THAT BALCONIES DID NOT EXIST
IN SHAKESPEARE'S ENGLAND,
ROMEO WAS MORE
STALKER THAN AMOUR. HIS
LOVE MORE OBSESSION THAN
ENDEARMENT.

RACHEL

She pressed send, and continued to write, which was her way:

> **I THINK SHAKESPEARE
> WAS TRYING TO CAPTURE
> LOVE AT FIRST SIGHT TO
> SHOW TO HIS AUDIENCE.
> SO, I GUESS, AND THIS
> DEPENDS ON HOW YOU
> DEFINE "FIRST SIGHT" BUT
> WE HAVE TECHNICALLY SEEN
> EACH OTHER. PHOTOS, VIDEOS,
> MESSAGES.**
> RACHEL

His response lit up her screen.

**CALLED MY CLIENT TO CANCEL
ONCE I SAW THE NEWS. I WAS
ASLEEP SO ONLY JUST SAW IT.
HOPE YOU ARE OK?**
JAKE

Rachel could see he was still typing, so waited for him to continue.

**NOT TO DRAW TOO MUCH
ATTENTION TO ANY SIMILARITIES
BETWEEN MYSELF AND ROMEO BUT**

I MAY BE A BIT GUILTY OF SOME
OBSESSION, OR AT LEAST
OBSESSION-TYPE BEHAVIOUR.
I'VE FOUND MYSELF ON MORE THAN
ONE OCCASION LOOKING THROUGH OLD
PHOTOS OF YOU, COMBING THROUGH
YOUR PROFILE TRYING TO GET TO KNOW
YOU BETTER. SEE WHAT YOU WERE LIKE
BEFORE WE STARTED TO SPEAK.
THIS MAY BE OVERSHARING NOW, SO
PLEASE FEEL FREE TO LOG OFF :D BUT
I HAVE FELT THE STING OF JEALOUSY
AT EVERY GUY THAT HELD YOUR HAND,
AT EVERY LAUGH AND SMILE I MISSED.
SEEING YOU GRADUATE WITH FRIENDS,
VISITING PLACES AND PRETTY MUCH
LIVING A LIFE THAT I AM NOT PART OF.
TOO HONEST?
JAKE

Rachel was shocked at the honesty, although had to admit, especially as she was currently combing his profile, not for the same reasons, but still, that it was also flattering. Jake did tend to share more of his insecurities with her than she did with him, which gave her a feeling of unbalance sometimes, but she was now used to the dynamic. He was more of a sharer. As she thought, her brain went into overdrive. Over-analysing and overthinking everything, taking much longer to respond than she wanted to. *He will see I am not typing too*, she thought.

Ugh, she thought, sighing out loud. *It would be so much simpler if we were born in the 1800 and were pen pals. We couldn't just comb through each other's lives like this then.*

> **YEAH, YOU DO**
> **SOUND A BIT OBSESSED.**
> RACHEL

She hoped he would get the humour. She added a smiling face emoji for good measure. *I wonder, if I was to comb through love letters from the past, would there be some jokes with a scrawled smiley face? Or would the line, "a jest, my love," be commonplace?* Once again, she imagined if they were pen pals, having to wait weeks to see if the joke was taken in the right way, or if it had a negative impact that was festering like an unattended wound.

INTENSITY SCARE YOU?
JAKE

> **A LITTLE, YEAH.**
> RACHEL

They promised honesty when they started to talk, especially as they got to know each other more.

I UNDERSTAND. WHAT'S
FUNNY IS I WROTE THIS
MESSAGE AND DELETED IT,
ONLY TO REWRITE AND SEND IT.
I'D RATHER YOU KNOW, BEFORE

**WE MET JUST HOW MUCH
YOU MEAN TO ME. WE
CONNECT ON SO MANY LEVELS.
YES, YOU'RE BEAUTIFUL BUT THAT'S
NOT JUST IT. YOUR MIND IS
AMAZING. YOUR ABILITY TO JUST
STOP ME IN MY TRACKS WITH YOUR
THOUGHTS ALMOST CAUSES ME
TO HAVE A MINI REBOOT MOMENT!**
JAKE

Rachel laughed out loud at his robotic language. The first few weeks of their texting were tricky, with Jake taking more time to warm up to the conversations than her. He was awkward, clumsy even, in his wording and tone of messaging, but the more they got to know each other, they started to pull back the curtain on each other's lives, the clearer things became. Which was great, because she couldn't just connect with someone on looks alone. Her love for words, books, and stories was something that any prospective LIFEpartner would have to understand and, hopefully, share.

**YOU OPEN UP "HOW
TO APPEAR HUMAN AND WIN
FRIENDS" AGAIN? I THOUGHT
WE FIXED THAT, ROBO?**
RACHEL

**01110100 01101111
00100000 01100010 01100101
00100000 01101111 01110010**

00100000 01101110 01101111
01110100 00100000 01110100
01101111 00100000 01100010
01100101
JAKE

**I'M GOING TO IGNORE THAT!
BUT BACK TO OBSESSION. YOU
ARE NOT THAT BAD EITHER.
ALSO, 50% OF THOSE PLACES
WERE VIRTUAL. NOT EXACTLY
THE SAME THING. I AM SURE
SIR EDMUND HILLARY HAD
MORE OF A STRUGGLE THAN
PUTTING ON VR GLASSES
TO GET TO THE TOP OF EVEREST.
IT'S NOT LIKE HE POPPED UP,
ASKED HIS SHERPA TO TAKE
A SELFIE TOGETHER, AND THEN
WROTE A BLOG POST ON HOW
LIFE-CHANGING IT WAS FROM THE
COMFORT OF HIS LIVING ROOM
5 MINUTES LATER.
THERE IS A DIFFERENCE**

Rachel thought about the first time she travelled to London. She didn't take the modern train, flown, or taken a driverless, high-tech car. She took an old steam engine train, got off on the outskirts of London, and walked in. She still remembered walking along the river, as the sun set. Her thoughts flowed as fluidly and freely as the river on her left. She thought of writers like Virginia Woolf walking these same paths as she was seeking inspiration.

As she walked, besides the obligatory check-ins and posts, she had no other time for the technology around her.

BETWEEN REAL TRAVELLING
AND WHAT WE DO NOW.
JUST THE TRANQUILITY THAT
YOU FEEL, NOT BEING CONNECTED
TO THE VIRTUAL WORLD FOR THAT
MOMENT. BEING CONNECTED TO
THE REAL ONE. THE ONE YOU CAN
HOLD, THE ONE YOU FEEL
UNDER YOUR FEET, AND HEAR IN
THE MOMENT. NOT A RECORDING
OF A MOMENT, NOT A SECONDHAND
MOMENT EXPERIENCED BY SOMEONE
ELSE, BUT BY YOU. YOUR MOMENT
ALONE. DO YOU KNOW WHAT I MEAN?
RACHEL

IN A WAY, I THINK SO.
BUT I HAVEN'T DONE MUCH
TRAVELLING. I HAVE GONE
PLACES, PART OF THE JOB,
BUT THEY ARE CLOSER TO
WORK OR HOLIDAYS – WORK
OR RELAXING – NOT REALLY
THE TRAVELLING YOU ARE

**TALKING ABOUT. I'D LOVE TO
THOUGH. YOU ARE SO PASSIONATE
ABOUT IT, IT MAKES ME WANT
TO PACK MY BAGS AND HIT
THE ROAD.**
JAKE

She smiled at the message and had a flutter in the pit of her stomach. As their first date got closer, the places they talked about kept coming to her mind. She thought she must be boring Jake with her talk of travelling and reading, but he just kept wanting more and more.

**WHERE WOULD YOU WANT
TO GO?**
RACHEL

Jake wasn't typing. She picked up her book and started reading again – giving up her review of Jake's profile.

Rachel checked her phone after twenty minutes. No response or buzz on her wrist, but she still checked. She didn't expect an instant response, she actively detested them. She liked for people to think things through before responding, especially when they were talking big ideas. She was more of a dive in deep to conversations type of person, and moving out and back in, when the mood and energy were there. Jake was more the instant response type of person – almost compulsively. Whereas her parents once accused her, well, mostly her mother, of being extremely deliberate in the way she communicated. Like each word was chosen carefully, almost like they were weighed for impact and suitability, which she thought was a gross over-exaggeration. She just loved words! They deserved thought and the correct usage to convey the right message. Words were powerful, and their meaning even more so. Getting that right was as important in her eyes as any well-constructed building or chemical element.

Her wrist felt the vibration as her phone lit up. She glanced over as she tried not to become too distracted from her book.

THAT WOULD BE TELLING.
JAKE

She finished her chapter, grabbed a drink, updated her post, and then went back to Jake. She was tempted to ask about the delay, but decided against it. I am being oversensitive because of the news, she told herself.

OK. YOU PLAY YOUR GAMES,
ROMEO.
RACHEL

She'd pressed send before even thinking, *so much for all the weight to words, Mom*, she thought, as she reread the message, hoping it didn't seem passive-aggressive. She hoped the joke didn't hit a nerve. After all, he was brave enough to share his little insanity.

AND WHY AM I ROMEO?
WHAT HAPPENED TO
APHRODITE?
JAKE

SORRY, JOKE. BAD TIMING.
RACHEL

Rachel covered her face in embarrassment. Her jokes, which she loved, had a 50/50 chance of finding their mark in most conversations, put her in her fair share of difficult positions. Although truth be told, she had a much better success rate with Jake – who seemed to find her jokes both amusing and insulting in the right measure. She lowered her filter because of that success in their dynamic.

OH, I GET IT.
JAKE

BECAUSE OF MY COMMENT
ABOUT LOVE BEING MORE OF
A FIRST SIGHT THING? I DO
THINK IT IS A VALID QUESTION.
THAT YOU HAVE NOT ANSWERED....
JAKE

TRUE. I HAVEN'T ANSWERED.
I THINK IT'S DIFFERENT. AS IN LOVE
IS DIFFERENT. THE CONNECTIONS
BETWEEN US, NOT YOU AND I US, BUT
RATHER HUMAN BEINGS US, HAS
CHANGED. LIKE THE TRAVELLING THING.
IT HAS EVOLVED, IF YOU WILL. FOR
EXAMPLE, I THINK THAT THESE DAYS WE
AS A SOCIETY ARE GETTING CLOSER
TO THE TIME OF LONG DISTANCE
INTERACTIONS. VERY SIMILAR TO
THE TIME OF PEN PALS

AND LETTER WRITING.
IF YOU THINK OF BRAM STOKER'S DRACULA.
THE STORY IS TOLD THROUGH THOSE
INTERACTIONS, THE LETTERS.
THERE IS ALMOST A FEELING IN THE STORY
THAT YOU MAY NOT BE GETTING THE
WHOLE TRUTH, ONLY THE TRUTH
THAT THEY ARE WILLING TO
SHARE WITH EACH OTHER.
WHEREAS, WHEN YOU READ A BOOK
THAT IS FOLLOWING A CHARACTER
YOU GET TO EXPERIENCE THE WORLD
THROUGH THEIR THOUGHTS, NOT JUST
THEIR WRITING. AS HUMANS OUR THOUGHTS
ARE TRUER THAN THE WORDS THAT
WE USE TO PORTRAY THEM. THAT IS WHY IT
IS SO HARD TO FIND THE RIGHT
WORDS SOMETIMES.
I LIKE HOW TERRY
PRATCHETT PUT IT,
ALTHOUGH HE WAS
TALKING ABOUT FANTASY,
I THINK IT HOLDS MERIT
WHEN YOU EXAMINE IT
AGAINST HOW WE USE
WORDS -
"HUMANS NEED FANTASY TO BE HUMAN.
TO BE THE PLACE WHERE THE FALLING ANGEL

MEETS THE RISING APE."
IF WE PUT WORDS IN PLACE OF FANTASY,
THAT WORKS FOR ME.
RACHEL

OUR (BACK TO YOU AND I NOW :))
DYNAMIC WAS BUILT OVER MESSAGES.
LIKE PEN PALS WRITING TO EACH OTHER,
IN SOME CIRCUMSTANCES CHOOSING
WHAT PARTS TO SHOW EACH OTHER.
AND WHEN WE DON'T HAVE THE
WORDS TO DESCRIBE OUR THOUGHTS,
AN EMOJI OR PICTURE TAKES THAT
PLACE AS WE CAN'T GIVE OTHER
GESTURES. A SIMPLE HUG WHEN
I AM UPSET, A KISS TO SHOW
AFFECTION IS NOT AN OPTION, SO
WE HAVE TO EXPLORE THAT SPACE –
"WHERE THE FALLING ANGEL MEETS THE
RISING APE".
OUR RELATIONSHIP IS IN THAT SPACE,
AND WHEN WE MEET IT MAY BE DIFFERENT.
AWKWARDNESS MAY ENSUE. WE
MAY HAVE TO GET TO KNOW EACH
OTHER ALL OVER AGAIN. WHO KNOWS?
ALL I WILL SAY IS THAT I THINK THIS
IS LIFEline's PLAN. THAT THESE CONNECTIONS
ARE BUILT IN THAT SPACE WHERE LOOKS
ARE NOT THE MAIN MOTIVATION, BUT THOUGHT.

RACHEL

**YOU HAVE GIVEN IT
SOME THOUGHT, HAVEN'T
YOU?**
JAKE

ACTUALLY, NOT UNTIL NOW. I HAVE
THOUGHT THAT ABOUT WORDS
SINCE I READ THAT TERRY BOOK, BUT
HADN'T REALLY CONNECTED IT UNTIL NOW.
JUST THINKING OUT LOUD, AND TRYING TO
CHALLENGE MY OWN THINKING AS I AM DOING
IT. YOU KNOW ME. WHAT DO YOU THINK?
RACHEL

**ANYTHING I SAY WILL
SEEM PRETTY TAME BY
COMPARISON.**
JAKE

IT ISN'T A COMPETITION.
RACHEL

**AND IF IT WAS, YOU WOULD
HAVE WON ALREADY?**
JAKE

OH, FOR SURE.
RACHEL

It was getting very late, so Rachel moved to her bedroom and continued to text Jake for most of the night. His presence calmed her even more than the dinner with her parents, which on reflection, she thought, was probably his plan. Probably the entire reason he cancelled his clients. The unbalance in the relationship, she thought. Even though she was more at ease and hadn't thought about the murder for the last few hours, when it came to rolling over to go to sleep, it still eluded her.

Rachel had a difficult relationship with sleep. The relationship was that sleep made it impossible for her to catch it some nights. A long-suffering veteran in the war with sleep, Rachel prepared herself for battle with it, and, ultimately, her own thoughts.

Chapter Four

N ow the hunter becomes the hunted. This phrase always irked him. He sat in the darkroom; his windows to the outside world were the screens all around him. He had multiple screens, a powerful computer that could have more windows open than a greenhouse, and on those windows, he had his victims. Some of them were maturing, only a matter of weeks to his next kill, and some were at the beginning of their relationships. They all had one thing in common – they were all being hunted. Even himself.

His hunter: the LIFEline teams. They were trying to find him. He had one advantage over his prey, he knew there was always a bigger fish. He typed some messages in response to his prospective LIFEpartners. *Not the partner they are expecting*, he thought, *but their embrace will be just as intimate*. He would be the last thing they would see in this world. He looked at the beauty of some, one had a pianist's hands, the fingers dancing across the keyboard as if they were playing a song just for him. Another had a long neck and limbs with a face so expressive he could read it like a book and skin that seemed almost porcelain.

Hacking into the multiple cameras in people's residences was easy. He could access phones, webcams, passing drones, and smart devices – if it was connected to the network, it was pretty much his eyes and ears. The true beauty was that everything was connected to the network. LIFEline was, usually, under the delusional idea that they were the only ones watching.

LIFEline knew about people because of their decisions, their actions, their likes and dislikes – the decisions they made in the cool light of day while knowing, deep down, that they were being watched by everyone.

He saw their imperfections and saw them as the perfections they were. The data told LIFEline that this one wanted the world to be equal. He has seen her fart and pick her nose at the same time and laugh at the situation. Humans were not just data to be mined for the next big thing or to see what shoes to sell. Humans were a sum of their real experiences. It is easy to be a pacifist while you are standing outside of the ring and the other person isn't trying to knock your teeth into the back of your mouth.

LIFEline seemed to forget what it was seeing was the masks. The masquerade ball of twists and twirls, while he didn't forget. He danced and slipped behind the masks, seeing the beautiful truth beneath. He looked beyond the digital mask that was portrayed. He found the cracks in the façade – the cracks that even they didn't seem to see. They fooled the world with their masks, but lied to themselves in the making, too. When you pull that mask back, usually by force, you expose them. They realise they haven't seen this person, their true selves, never truly lived, and the only thing they now want is outside their grasp: life. They are so comfortable in the mask, acting in a certain way, afraid to be seen by others for what they are: imperfect, that they forget they are wearing one. Acting one way until they feel that is who they are.

"To stay silent is a crime." They speak.

"You can't be sad, look at all you have." They smile.

"But did you take a photo of that place?" They click away. So busy on their devices they forget to live, forget that words need meaning, experiences need to be felt, forgetting you cannot take these devices with you when you go. They lie to themselves until it is too late.

It has been twenty-four hours since he has taken Natasha. He remembered the feeling of guilt, the hint of remorse, and the fear he felt after killing the others. It hasn't come back in full swing this time. He knew it was only a matter of time before he was caught, the same way he knew it was only a matter of time before some of the people on the screen would meet him. Some would, no doubt, make it out alive, probably without ever truly realising how close they were to the brink of death. For now, though, he had detectives tracking him and he had no plan on making this easier for anyone involved.

The most daring spectacle comes with inherent danger. It is what makes the audience hold its breath and want more; we don't watch the tightrope walker to see them reach the other side, we watch for the possibility that they won't. There will be some people reading about Natasha Anderson with horror, some would be reading with sympathy, but others will read with a dark interest, wondering when the next show will be.

◆ ◆ ◆

Detective Euan Rae was waiting for him as he exited his office. It was late and he planned on getting some shuteye.

"Are you all set up with a room, Detective?" Rusty asked, pointedly yawning and stretching out his arms, as he surveyed the room.

"I am all set up but, as I said, I'd like to visit the scene," he responded, looking Rusty directly in the eye.

"You meant tonight? I thought it would be best to wait until morning. Keep the guys on the ground until we get a good night's sleep." Rusty ran his hand through his hair as Rae looked around the room. It seemed that Rae missed social queues, too.

"I am an advocate for sleep. It is essential for the brain to retain information, but the scene is not far from here, and we have some things I would like you to know," Rae responded, before turning and walking away. Rusty swore under his breath, went back to his office to grab his coat, and walked after Rae.

As he passed Ciri, he called over the desk in a low voice that nevertheless travelled well in the heavily screened room, "Take care of the place for me." To anyone else in the room, that would have been a passing remark. They probably would have started cleaning up around the office, but Charlotte Iris knew that she was now in charge. You don't work with someone for as long as they had without being able to say things without saying them.

Detective Rae was standing at the elevator, looking more like an owl than ever as he impatiently shuffled from foot to foot. He wasn't much better as they rode up and came out from under Wellington Arch. He didn't speak in the elevator, and once they were outside, he raised a hand to a driverless car that, on his beckon, drove to meet them where the road met the pedestrian path. The night was clear and there were not many cars out, just the odd driverless car, obviously roaming areas that had more activity from devices.

Detective Rae took the front right seat, leaving Rusty to walk around the car.

As they got in Rae entered a number, more than likely his password or LIFEline badge number, onto the onboard screen and then spoke, "Palace Gate, but please take the scenic route. Give us about an hour."

"An hour?" Rusty asked, as the car moved off right instead of the direct left that would have taken them to the scene. Rusty could walk the distance in half the time.

"I told you, it is in our best interest that we are on the same page, or thereabouts, as quickly as possible, Mr Styles," Detective Rae responded, moving his chair back as far as he could.

As the car drove, Rae turned this way and that as he spoke, making eye contact only when it seemed necessary for him. He pulled a small device out of his pocket that looked like a mobile phone and handed it to Rusty. Rusty flicked through the contents; it was a case file. It had images of scenes – scenes that looked familiar, like red soaked trademarks, some notes and potential evidence. As he shifted through files, he noticed a couple of Rae's comments under images and notes taken from interviews with family members and loved ones.

"You think this is our murderer?" Rusty asked, handing back the device. There were three other victims with similar scenes. It seemed Evan was right; Rae was on hand for a series of killings.

"Yeah, I think this is our perp. He has been building up his confidence, moving from small cities to bigger cities, testing and honing his craft, and now he feels ready for the big stage," Rae responded, watching the flickering distant lights of passing drones in the sky high above the dark trees in the park as they passed.

"You think it is a guy?" Rusty asked, "I specifically tried to stop thinking that way until we have evidence to support the facts."

"Statistically speaking, we do," Rae responded, turning to look at Rusty again, "Four female victims, where his predatory behaviour showed through, starting with him stalking his victims before using brute force. Our killer is most likely a white male, in his early 30s to mid 40s, and is highly organised."

"Organised! He left a bloody mess!" Rusty retorted, "If that wasn't a crime of wanton destruction by a psych…"

Rae interrupted, "He left a scene for us. He is covering his tracks, not in any real obsessive way, just making it less obvious to the untrained eye, but we see straight past that. He is so organised it took us weeks to locate the first victim's body. He stalks his victims for months and then deliberately attacks when he knows they will not be expected to be heard from. He knows how people use LIFEline and is using that against them. He is using that against us."

"What else do you already know?" Rusty asked, his head buzzing trying to keep up.

"Let's start from the beginning, it will be easier that way," he responded, "I was working a case in Scotland, the first image you would have seen on that screen, Melanie Fraser. Her friends called her Mel, lovely girl. I knew her family from when I was younger, I was close friends growing up with one of her cousins, but there has always been a Fraser presence in Inverness. One of her ancestors was once an Earl of Inverness, and the family are very proud, yet a well-liked staple of the area. At first, we thought she was picked for that reason.

Mel moved into a small one-bed apartment, she was training to become a lawyer, and wanted the space to socialise with friends and her intended LIFEpartner. Then in November, on the night of her first date, she went missing. Her friends thought she just hooked up with her partner for the night and forgotten to check in, but LIFEline saw something different. Her equipment was left at home, no check-ins and no activity. I don't know if you have been to any of the smaller cities, where being offline for a few hours is common, but when there was no movement for twenty-four hours the team…"

"Twenty-four hours," Rusty exclaimed.

"I told you, in small cities that isn't rare," Detective Rae didn't let the outburst take him off course. "The team sent two agents over as a courtesy check-in. It isn't illegal for a girl to not use her equipment, and, whereas it would have been strange for Mel to stop using LIFEline, it is around this age that some people do leave LIFEline preferring, ahem, the other way. You have seen the scene that was set for our agents. They were only new members on the team, I doubt Joan will get over the shock of it, but at least she knows that my line of work isn't for her."

"As I live in Inverness, the Country Director asked me to help with the investigation as a personal favour. I don't tend to do things that way, but given that it is my home and my knowledge of this type of crimes, it made sense to say yes. The sooner this person is found the better all around. Inverness does not have even one percent of the coverage of London, but luckily Mel followed the book. Her date was supposed to take place in a very popular restaurant in the middle of town. Witnesses saw her leave after being stood up. They said she looked sad, but wasn't overly emotional. The driverless car dropped her home and he was stalking her the entire way.

"He had on an encryption device that scrambled his face. He drove a normal car with no technology attached at all, which he dumped and burnt out in a secluded field – we found it weeks later. She didn't stand a chance. He knocked at her door, and she barely opened it when he was on top of her. Mel Fraser was no damsel in distress, either. She won gold medals in full contact sports in school and university, but she wasn't expecting that type of savagery on her front doorstep."

Rusty was leaning forward; he was listening so intently. "This is the same guy. He attacked Natasha in the same way. We reviewed the footage earlier today."

"Oh, I know that, Mr Styles," Rae responded, before continuing, not stopping as Rusty made to interrupt again. "Our first suspect, I think you can guess who?" he asked him with a rue smile.

"The date?" Rusty answered.

"We tracked down the date. At first, we couldn't find him, and we started to think he made a run for it, but then, there he was, posting as usual, no mention of Mel on his page or in any of his messages," Rae said, as the driverless car moved further away from the Royal Albert Hall, exactly where they should be going.

"He managed to wipe all the activity? That would take a thorough knowledge of LIFEline," Rusty said, forgetting for a moment his impatience at the distance between them and the crime scene, "I wouldn't even know where to start to do a thing like that."

"I interviewed Colm O'Brien myself. He had the physicality to overpower Mel; he played rugby at university, I remember watching him play as a kid in Glasgow, a lot of talent. Never the sharpest tool in the shed, but I don't think he had it in him for that type of crime. We grilled him for a few hours. I could tell from the first minute this wasn't our guy, but I needed to get to the bottom of how he wiped the activity."

"How did he do it?" Rusty asked.

"He didn't," Rae replied. "We pulled up Mel's account right in front of him. He had no idea who she was, and, given the distance between Inverness and Glasgow, it didn't surprise me. The strangest part was, his account didn't correspond with Mel's at all. Mel was speaking with Colm until past midnight on many occasions and, even though whoever it was talking to Mel did their homework on Colm – mentioning the rugby, family members, his job - there were inconsistencies with the timeline. To be frank, there were also inconsistencies with the content. There were moments in the conversation where you could see that our guy slipped up. He'd start having these deep philosophical conversations, and that just wasn't Colm's profile at all. These were the first indications that this wasn't just going to be a single crime. Our perp had either done this before or was planning to continue, or, even worse, both."

"But the partnerships match?" Rusty asked.

"I questioned that myself and we pulled up the records. Colm was matched with Mel, it was in the system, clear as day. His story is that he received a message saying that he would be matched with someone within the year. No sign of that message either," Rae replied, looking down at the driverless car's clock. "We haven't got long left, and I'd like to get through this as soon as I can. The other sites were the same MO. I had Xander combing through the work for weeks as we searched for the body. I knew from looking at the scene that it was all staged. Someone with a meticulous mind committed this crime, planning each move, and I needed to find the body. See what that could tell us about our perp."

"Xander?" Rusty asked.

"We don't have time for that now, but he is helping us on the case. We found the body in Loch Ness. It is a massive expanse of water, and it took the drones a couple of weeks to scan the depths. Locals kept saying we were looking for the monster, but the monster that committed this crime was not in that Loch. The Loch was the convenient place for him to dump the body – close by and vast. The body was in pieces, wrapped in bags neatly and placed in a duffle bag. It was in the water for long enough that there were no describable traces of DNA that didn't belong to Mel. Just an observation, based on his actions so far, but I think our killer was too good for that anyway. If we found that body the next day, it would be apparent that he washed it in chemicals. We won't catch him through DNA, we will catch him in the act, if at all," Rae said, looking all around. "I didn't know Mel well, but the way he treated her – as if she was a piece of meat to be separated evenly and wrapped up for disposal. I won't forget that soon. It did confirm my suspicions though, this wasn't a brutal, destructive attack. It was just made to look that way."

"I still haven't heard a good reason why this Colm guy isn't a suspect," Rusty said, thinking of his J. Long. Maybe they stumbled onto a group of young men adamant to torture and kill women. A cult against partnerships would fit this crime.

"I'd say take my word, but we both have seen how that has gone so far! It was a clone profile. He mirrored it exactly. Xander says that even the best in LIFEline wouldn't have been able to notice the difference between them. Xander tried to pull up the profile and all he could manage was what it looked like on the night he cloned it. The night he was matched with Mel. It was like looking at Colm's profile twelve months previously. All the activity could not be restored so we had no idea what he did from that point onward," Detective Rae said. "I knew he would kill again and was anticipating a wait of twelve months. Xander was combing LIFEline's records of partners to look for any pattern."

"Pattern?" Rusty asked, finding it impossible to imagine a pattern emerging or a scenario where they caught this guy if he was able to clone profiles that well.

"He is good," Rae responded, almost as if he was reading Rusty's mind, "but as I said, he slipped up. We had all the activity on Mel's profile, so we didn't need to see Colm's cloned profile as badly as we may have wanted to see it. He slipped sometimes. Small slips, but small slips are the breadcrumbs we are looking for. I expect he gets tired of the pretence sometimes, and falls back into his old habits, forgetting he is playing a part."

"We weren't as fast as we should have been. We didn't have twelve months, we had four but this time it wasn't even in Scotland, and he didn't use a clone profile. A perp moving territory so soon and using a new method is very rare. These types of profiles take comfort in their routines. My only thought was we were focused on the wrong side of his routine."

"He moved further south. This time he murdered Jane Stevens in Catterick, a small military town. If we thought we didn't have much footage in Inverness, we found even less waiting for us when we got to Catterick. We had some scenes from the restaurant and the house she lived in from her devices, but we think it was the same MO. Her parents were out when it happened, at her request. It seems she was planning on bringing him home, just for a few drinks, and asked to be left alone until midnight."

"Her Dad knocked on her bedroom door to see if she was home and… Well, when she didn't answer, he saw the scene. The poor man was still shaking as we spoke to him hours later. He thought the blood was hers…"

"How do you mean he thought the blood was hers? It was, wasn't it?" Rusty asked.

Rae seemed to have forgotten that Rusty was there as he became wrapped up in telling his story. "No, I told you. It is all staged. The blood is pig's blood. He splashes it all around the scene, my guess is for dramatic effect, but your guess is as good as mine. Seeing her Dad shake so much tells you how successful that shock factor is."

The driverless car was finally moving towards Palace Gate, but they were only halfway through. Rusty expected Rae to keep him in the vehicle, but when it stopped, they both got out. The night air felt colder, or perhaps Rusty just felt that way because of what was awaiting them. From the way Rae was telling the story, engrossing him so much in the detail, he half expected to step foot in the old military town of Catterick as he left the driverless car. Rae stopped talking as he crossed the road and walked up the path to Natasha's place. Rick Harris was standing at the door, watching both of them intently.

Keep your mouth shut, Rusty thought as he glanced at Harris.

"This the so-called expert here to catch our fucking unicorn?" Rick asked, as Detective Rae reached him. Rae didn't even show the faintest hint of stopping, and Rusty was not surprised to see that he didn't. He walked past Rick as if he hadn't even spoken and started to walk up the stairs.

For a moment Rick Harris, experienced in making others feel uncomfortable and uneasy, swallowed his own medicine as he looked at the retreating back of the Detective.

"He seems like a barrel of laughs," Rick said.

"You don't know half of it," Rusty responded as he followed Rae.

Detective Rae stood at the entranceway. The blue door to Natasha's apartment was opened and it contrasted heavily with the now red room. Rae scanned the room from left to right, taking in all the details, starting low and moving higher with each rove from left to right, like an actor looking out at his admiring audience, wanting to look each member in their eyes as they stood and applauded.

Rusty had been on multiple crime scenes, not only in LIFEline, but also in his military days, but this one shook him instantly. The image on the screen in the safety of the L.O.O.P was horrid, but this was like walking into a living, breathing, nightmare. He composed himself with a breath and didn't disturb Rae. He knew it was best to let the Detective follow his routine undisturbed. He was no expert at this but, get him in a room with a unicorn and he'd break them. Rusty's speciality has always been interrogation. His colleagues said it was his size, but he didn't think so. Once they were in the room, Rusty usually had them dead to rights, and they knew it.

"Same as Inverness, Catterick and Northampton," Rae muttered.

"Northampton?" Rusty exclaimed, "How have I not heard about any of this?"

"Let's not jump ahead, but I will answer your second question – forgive the disregard for the order of your questions – but you haven't heard of any of this because we didn't want the news getting out and going viral. This type of killers tends to crave attention. They usually are the ones reaching out to entice us. I hoped that if we stayed quiet, he would think we haven't pieced the parts together. We wanted to force his hand to gain the recognition he wanted. That reach out would have given us more information. The way he approaches us and from where, and how. Sometimes they try to implant themselves directly into the investigation; sending us tips, being seen as the hero private investigator. Sometimes they enjoy the chase, pitting themselves against us, like Holmes and Moriarty."

"You think he will help us catch him?" Rusty asked, feeling strange still standing in the doorway gazing into the apartment as if scared to enter.

"Not now, we have just broadcasted to all of London, and the world, that he exists. He is probably toasting to his genius. But, to your question, he would never help us catch him on purpose, Mr Styles, but we know he slips up. We need more slip-ups with fewer bodies. What do you see?" Rae said, sweeping his hand across the area.

"Carnage."

"Really?" Rae asked, looking up at the taller man, "Try looking harder."

Rusty looked over the scene. Natasha's devices were placed on the table, her glasses broken but otherwise neatly collected. There was blood everywhere. *Although*, he thought, *supposedly pig's blood*. He looked on the floor where there were gouge marks. *Probably where the knife went straight through Natasha and into the floor*, he thought. *But then*, he reminded himself, if it was all staged and he had neatly… he could hardly even think the thoughts… cut up the body after killing Natasha then maybe they were also to throw them off the scent.

"You mentioned in Catterick that he didn't use a clone profile?" Rusty responded.

Rae looked at him a little longer before allowing his dismissal of the question to pass, "Yes, he didn't use a clone this time. He used a Ghost."

Rusty's stomach dropped at the mention. Ghost profiles were the bane of his existence in the early years of his career in LIFEline. The ATU was plagued with them when he joined. Some of the more politically active of the Dead in London reactivated the profiles of the deceased to sway opinion polls and to commit crimes. They found a few patches and innovative ways to make it near impossible to create Ghosts, but not impossible. Even the best technologies and security protocols can fail.

"This time all we had to go off was the original profile, which was last active the day the young teenage boy, Paul Barnwell, was buried. There didn't seem to be any reason for using this particular account other than Paul would have been about the right age. The slip up here was bigger though. Our perp's conversations with Jane were built around a profile that he fabricated himself, so he was more creative. He was showing a love for literature and the arts. The deep philosophical conversations keep creeping up, even though Jane was not overly keen on them, and on more than one occasion seemed to move away from them altogether. Outside of these slips though, the other 90% of the conversations was matched towards Jane," Rae said.

"His biggest mistake though, even more than in Inverness, where his insights into LIFEline behaviours echoed slightly, was creating that Ghost," Rae said, starting to pace the room as he spoke. "The only people capable of creating Ghosts that good are either working for us or have worked for us.

Seeing as we don't exactly have many people leave us year on year, it seems he is still here. The only question is where is he?"

"You think London." It wasn't a question and Rusty didn't mean it to be one. It was an accusation, and the social queue was translated, read, and understood by Rae.

"I do."

Chapter Five

Rachel was up late talking with Jake, but still set her alarm, even though it was Saturday and she didn't have any work to do today. She was a creature of habit. Saturday mornings she liked to get up at seven am to go for a swim and after, treat herself to breakfast at a local café. Mr and Mrs Horner had her food ready as usual when she entered the café, her black hair still wet and smelling of chlorine. She sat at her usual table and was happy to see that the café was busy.

She took out her book and read as she ate, checking her device sporadically; checking in, taking pictures of the food and tagging Mr and Mrs Horner so more people would see how great this little café was. It pained her at first, when she started to share the posts – she loved to think of this little café as her Saturday morning sanctuary, away from people and most of the technology. There were no cameras in the café, Mr and Mrs Horner preferred for people to have their privacy while here, but Rachel broached the subject one very quiet Saturday morning about the Horner's creating a more online presence, not to take away from their beautiful physically presence, but to enhance it, while ensuring their physical presence remained profitable.

Mrs Horner needed some persuading, but now the business was doing great. They even done well enough to be able to hire some help. Oliver Rudd joined the business months ago and, although he was secretive and shy, he came out of his shell over the last few months with Rachel.

"Top up?" Oliver asked, as he passed with a pot of coffee.

"I shouldn't, Olly" she responded, smiling up, but nodding.

As he filled the mug, he lowered his voice, "Did you hear the news?"

"Of course," Rachel responded, "but how did you manage to?" she asked playfully.

"You are very funny. Just because it doesn't flash right in front of my eyes the second it happens doesn't mean I don't find out," he replied.

"Oh, touchy this morning. Maybe you should have some of your own coffee," Rachel responded, looking him over properly.

Oliver was tall and muscular, with dark hair and a heavy brow. His hands were that of a man who was used to working for a living and, more importantly, they were the hands of a man who did not touch technology. His wrist was free, and there were no mobile devices or VR glasses on him. He looked around at the other patrons, noticed he wasn't needed, and took the seat opposite Rachel, who politely closed her book.

"We have been talking about this for the last few months," Oliver said, again, glancing around, but Rachel got the impression that this time he was looking around to ensure that he wasn't being overheard not for a customer looking for coffee.

"Months?" Rachel asked, leaning in curiously.

Oliver lowered his voice, "We were more surprised to see the news come out the way it did. Our people up in Scotland warned us about something like this months ago. We heard again from our people in the North of England and, recently, very close by in Northampton. We thought LIFEline was trying to keep it hushed up as usual."

Rachel smiled and Oliver rolled his eyes, "What more proof would you need to not trust them? They are hiding crimes. They care more about their safety stats than actual safety."

"Again, we will have to agree to disagree on the subject of LIFEline, Olly. I respect your choice, hell, I admire your dedication. That does not mean I share it," Rachel said, retracing her footsteps over old conversations that most friends have when they possess a difference of belief, but a connection that seems to be able to take on the rocky terrain.

"Well," Oliver said, coming back to the topic, "this isn't the first murder. Just the first one in London. We have known for some time that this was happening."

"Why didn't you say anything?" Rachel asked. Oliver believed in a lot of what she would dub conspiracy theories; LIFEline was genetically coding people through partnerships. LIFEline planted tracers on babies when they were born. Vaccinations were created to control the masses. Mobile phones and the latest generations of internet services were killing the natural world. These conspiracy theories made it extremely difficult at times to believe her friend; not out of mistrust, but out of incorrect information.

Oliver looked down at her device on the table and raised his dark eyebrows.

Rachel sighed, "Well, if you are afraid it is listening why are you telling me now?"

Oliver leaned in, they were almost nose to nose now, anyone looking at them would think they were partners having an early breakfast after a late night. "You are my friend, and I don't want to see anything happen to you. I know your date is soon, but if this murderer isn't caught, please don't go."

"At this moment in time, there is zero chance of me going. All dates have been postponed for now. Did that news not travel through your people?" Rachel responded sourly.

Oliver looked pleased but tried to mask it as she looked at him with an over-exaggerated sad face.

"So, what else do you and the Dead know that we don't?" Rachel asked.

"That is it. We know that he seems to strike in one place and move on," Oliver said.

"You at least know it is a man?" Rachel probed.

"Nope, we are just guessing there, as the people we have heard are dead are all women."

Rachel knew that Oliver wasn't lying to her, and for once felt that maybe the Dead weren't reporting misinformation. The one thing Rachel noticed about the Dead, through her conversations with Oliver, was that when they "knew" something, like the internet service providers destroying the natural world, for example, there was no question they couldn't answer on the subject. The answers would get wilder, more incomprehensible, and they would eventually stop, leaving Oliver with a superior look on his face. The same face she has seen at school as a child on her teachers when she couldn't possibly understand something.

"What are the Dead doing about it?" Rachel asked.

"We are taking care of our own." His response was short and there was a hint of sadness in his eyes as he continued. "The victims are all you. He hasn't touched the Dead. His issue seems to be with you."

"That sounds very much like the Dead," Rachel said before she could stop herself.

"Why should we get involved? We have been telling you all these things for decades," Oliver said, looking at her with an intensity she only ever saw in him when his beliefs were being questioned. Rachel glanced around the room. No one else seemed to have noticed that Oliver's voice was raised, and Mr and Mrs Horner were busy talking to regular customers.

"You know I didn't mean it that way," Rachel said.

"It is fine," Oliver responded, standing, "I don't think it will be long before the townspeople grab their pitchforks and pay us a visit in our underground world."

He walked off and Rachel felt the regret growing already. *Oh yeah, I definitely weigh each word!*

Rachel waved at Mr and Mrs Horner as she left and gave a parting smile to Oliver that she hoped would go some way to mend the bridges. She couldn't just message him later and say sorry, and, even though she lived in London for some time, she was not brave enough to go down to the Dead. Rachel took out her VR glasses from her bag and put them on. There was no change to the world until she touched the side.

She pre-set her glasses to show the world like it was in Shakespeare's day. The sidewalks that, moments before, were mostly bare, with the odd early morning explorer, turned into a still expanding metropolis. Buildings shrank, but the pavements became filled with a tapestry of people and a symphony of voices from all over the world. Rachel loved to walk through the throng and noise of those days, she could barely make out a word, even those that spoke English, and it made her feel content.

This London had the antitheses of the world. Decadent Royal carriages were passing on the streets as beggars, usually missing a limb or two, hands outstretched looking for a morsel of humanity. The clergy proclaimed from corners as prostitutes negotiated in alleyways. Rachel walked through the world, noting the real people amongst her holograms. LIFEline's technology attired everyone in the garb of the times you were in, but they left a glow around real people so you wouldn't foolishly think they were in your world alone. On more than one occasion Rachel stopped and spoken to the holograms to get their stories, which were vivid and real.

She also stopped and spoke to real people too – to see where they were, what she was dressed like in their world, sometimes exchanging images. Sometimes they were just walking down the street to meet friends and seemed to find her approach eccentric. Rachel felt a vibration at her wrist which pulled her from her world.

HOW WAS THE MORNING SWIM?
JAKE

> **OH, VERY NICE. JUST WALKING,**
> **WILL MESSAGE WHEN I GET IN.**
> RACHEL

YOU COULD HAVE JUST
WAITED UNTIL YOU GOT IN TO
SAY THAT :D ENJOY SHAKESPEARE.
JAKE

When she arrived home Rachel took out her phone and responded to Jake's message with a video of her sticking out her tongue. She quickly updated her LIFEline: *Lovely Saturday #swim done and a walk in #Shakespeare's London. We don't know how lucky we are.* The LIFEline feeds that scrolled past her as she looked at her device were all of the same thing: Natasha. The London hashtag was connected to her murder, and everyone was saying how Natasha should be remembered. The murderer should be caught, brought to justice, and forgotten just as quickly.

Olly's words echoed in her mind, *"His issue seems to be with you."*

> **I DID "ENJOY SHAKESPEARE".**

LONDON BACK THEN WAS SO FULL
OF LIFE. IT WAS VIBRANT AND JUST
BRIMMING WITH SOMETHING WE
DON'T REALLY HAVE ANY MORE.

RACHEL

DISEASE? RAMPANT POVERTY? OH,
I KNOW, BEHEADINGS?

JAKE

OH, AREN'T YOU MR FUNNY
ALL OF A SUDDEN. WHAT DID
YOU DO, FINALLY WORK OUT
YOUR FUNNY BONE?

RACHEL

I DO NOT WANT TO GET
INTO A CONVERSATION ABOUT
BAD JOKES WITH YOU. YOU WILL
ONLY WIN. YOU HAVE THE WORST
JOKES!

JAKE

:(

RACHEL

She followed up the message with a video of herself showing an over-exaggeration of sadness.

YOU KNOW I LOVE YOUR JOKES.

JAKE

COURSE CORRECTION?
RACHEL

DID IT WORK?
JAKE

NOPE :P WHAT ARE YOUR PLANS FOR
THE WEEKEND?
RACHEL

BACK ON SHIFT, I HAVE TO MAKE
IT UP TO THE CLIENTS I MISSED
LAST NIGHT.
JAKE

I'M SORRY. I KNOW
YOU DID THAT TO KEEP ME
COMPANY.
RACHEL

NO SORRY NEEDED, NOT EVEN
SLIGHTLY. I WANTED TO KEEP
YOU COMPANY. ONCE I HEARD
ABOUT IT BEING SO CLOSE TO
WHERE YOU ARE I COULDN'T
NOT CANCEL THEM. IF I DIDN'T
I WOULD HAVE SPENT THE ENTIRE

NIGHT WORRYING ABOUT YOU.
YOU ARE NOT TALKING TO ANY
STRANGERS ON LIFEline ARE YOU?
JAKE

NONE STRANGER THAN YOU : P
BUT NO. JUST YOU AND MY FRIENDS
AND FAMILY AS USUAL.
RACHEL

THAT IS GOOD, OR AT LEAST MAKES
ME FEEL BETTER.
JAKE

WHAT PLANS DO YOU HAVE FOR TODAY?
JAKE

SOME PLANNING, WRITING, READING
AND A WALK WITH SOME FRIENDS. IN
VR BUT BETTER THAN NOTHING.
RACHEL

Rachel thought about sharing the news with him about the other potential crimes, the ones Oliver thought LIFEline were covering up, but hesitated. Jake was great in many ways, a great match in all areas, but he had a tendency to come across as jealous. When she started talking to Oliver in the café, he asked a lot of questions about him, and anytime she complimented Oliver, Jake went silent or short for a few messages until the topic changed. When she mentioned it to friends, they said they would be more annoyed if he wasn't a little jealous. She decided that it best to mention it.

I THINK I UPSET OLIVER THIS
MORNING.
RACHEL

She hoped she wasn't imagining the response taking longer. The chat showed Jake typing a response. Rachel scanned her LIFEline to see if there were any updates she might find interesting. Some of her class were out enjoying the sunshine in areas all around the globe, although the majority of them were localised in the EMEA region, mostly for the time zone sake.

OH, HOW COME? DID YOU DISAGREE
ON THE DEAD VERSUS LIFEline AGAIN?
JAKE

NO, IT WASN'T THAT THIS TIME.
HE MENTIONED THAT THERE
SEEMS TO HAVE BEEN OTHER
MURDERS, THE DEAD KNOW
ALL ABOUT THEM. THEY HAVE
BEEN FURTHER NORTH AND
THIS IS THE FIRST ONE IN LONDON.
RACHEL

THAT IS INTERESTING. YOU DIDN'T
BELIEVE HIM?
JAKE

NO, I DO BELIEVE HIM. THIS
DIDN'T SEEM LIKE THE OTHER
TIMES. THOSE TIMES MADE
ME FEEL LIKE HE WAS TRYING
TO MAKE ME BELIEVE WHAT
HE WAS SAYING. LIKE I WAS
SOMEONE TO BE SAVED.
TODAY IT SEEMED LIKE HE WAS
AS UNSURE ABOUT WHAT IS
HAPPENING AS WE ARE.
RACHEL

OK, IF YOU BELIEVE HIM,
WHY DO YOU THINK HE IS UPSET
WITH YOU? SORRY JUST MISSING
THE ISSUE :D
JAKE

I THINK I IMPLIED THAT THE
DEAD DON'T CARE ABOUT US.
RACHEL

THE LIVING? :D
JAKE

NOT FUNNY. I THINK I
HURT HIS FEELINGS.
RACHEL

SORRY, BADLY TIMED JOKE.
I AM SURE HE KNOWS YOU
DIDN'T MEAN ANYTHING
BAD BY ANYTHING YOU SAID.
YOU ARE USUALLY GOOD AT
SAYING WHAT YOU MEAN, SO
MAYBE YOU MEANT WHAT YOU
SAID? IF IT HURT HIS FEELINGS
THAT SUCKS, BUT IT DOES HAPPEN,
EVEN TO THE BEST OF US.
JAKE

YES, I SUPPOSE. HE SAID
SOMETHING I FOUND
INTERESTING THOUGH. HE
SAID IT WOULD BE JUST
A MATTER OF TIME BEFORE
WE HAD PITCH FORKS AND
WERE CONFRONTING THE DEAD.
RACHEL

WHY IS THAT INTERESTING?
JAKE

IT MADE ME THINK, AND I COULD
BE OVERTHINKING THIS, THAT HE
THINKS THIS IS SOMETHING
TO DO WITH THE DEAD. HE EVEN
SAID THE DEAD WILL CONTINUE

TO TAKE CARE OF THEIR OWN AND
SEEMED PRETTY SAD ABOUT THAT.
RACHEL

FULL DISCLOSURE, I HAD TO READ
THAT SENTENCE LIKE 6 TIMES
BEFORE IT MADE ANY SENSE TO ME.
I ALSO WOULDN'T BE SURPRISED IF
PEOPLE STARTED TO THINK THE DEAD
HAD SOMETHING TO DO WITH THIS,
ESPECIALLY IF THERE ARE MORE SPREAD
OUT ACROSS THE COUNTRY.
THE TWO COMMUNITIES LIVE SO
DIFFERENTLY. WE ARE ALL ONLINE,
LIFEline KNOWS WHO WE ARE AND IS
ABLE TO NOTICE IF WE ARE ACTING
STRANGE. THEY CAN STEP IN AND
INTERVENE BEFORE IT IS TOO LATE.
I THINK LIFEline MADE A MISTAKE NOT
MAKING THE WEARING OF DEVICES
MANDATORY. IF THIS PERSON HAS DONE
THIS BEFORE IT
WOULD MAKE SENSE THAT LIFEline
CAN'T TRACK THEM AND ONLY
THE DEAD ARE OFFLINE.
JAKE

I DON'T THINK IT WAS A MISTAKE
MAKING DEVICES OPTIONAL. PEOPLE

**ARE DIFFERENT AND WHEN YOU START
TO TAKE AWAY OUR OPTIONS THEN I
THINK WE MOVE AWAY FROM WHAT
MAKES US HUMAN.**
RACHEL

**EVEN IF THAT OPTION CAN SAVE
PEOPLE'S LIVES?**
JAKE

**WE HAVE HAD THIS DISCUSSION BEFORE,
AND I WOULD LIKE TO REMIND YOU
THAT DURING THAT CONVERSATION YOU
WERE ALL FOR LIFEline EASING SOME
OF ITS RESTRICTIONS. :D**
RACHEL

**TRUE. IT WASN'T LIFE OR DEATH THEN
THOUGH AND NOW IT COULD BE.**
JAKE.

◆ ◆ ◆

Rusty's head was still reeling from the night-time excursions with Detective Rae when he woke up. He checked the time.

"Perfect," he muttered, as he swung one leg out of the bed, trying to locate the other. He quickly attached his athletic prosthetic and rummaged until he found the kit he would need. The shorts were tighter than he remembered them being the last time he donned them, and the t-shirt did more bunching around his gut than he felt was necessary. He didn't think he let himself get out of shape by much, but the mirror and time were less kind than his thoughts.

He entered the gym less than twenty minutes later and saw exactly what he hoped the second the doors opened. Ever since his illness, Evan exercised almost religiously. He once said to Rusty that it was his good health that helped him bounce back so quickly from his cancer. Rusty secretly thought that it was the doctors, technology, and trillions of pounds that were poured into the health system by LIFEline, but that was not something you said to people who overcame life-changing injuries or conditions.

Evan was on the treadmill, a light sweat was visible even from this distance, but Rusty imagined if he was running as fast for as long his light sweat would be more akin to a monsoon. Evan gave him a slight nod as he ran and Rusty jumped on a treadmill close by, but not too close. He remembered that Evan was like him in some respects, his training was personal, so he gave him space and started to work close by, more to show Evan he wanted to talk than interrupt.

After thirty minutes of hard work on the treadmill and some weights, a stitch, a downpour of sweat all over his body, aches and pains all joined the mirror and time in refuting his thoughts – he really was out of shape! *I got to start getting back in here more often,* he thought, as he watched Evan meticulously clean down the weights he was using, before returning them to the racks. There were VR headsets, treadmills and machines that enabled you to run a route up to the Eiffel Tower, Mount Rushmore, The Great Wall of China, train in the snow in Russia, and run up the iconic steps in Philadelphia, but Evan and Rusty favoured a low-tech work out.

Evan walked over to Rusty as he was stretching out his back.

"Just up for some morning exercise?" he asked.

"You know I am not," Rusty responded, starting to stand.

"If Rae's presence gets you in this gym more often, we will have to see if he will stick around after he catches the unicorn," Evan said, taking a shallow sip of water from his bottle.

"You mean once he catches his perp?" Rusty said, grimacing, and not only because of the aches in his body and ego.

Evan laughed, "This is really bringing it all back. Rae still insists on not using common terminology? I can't say I am surprised. What did he say?"

Rusty recalled last night, "I mentioned unicorn, not out of any intention to annoy him, but you'd swear I purposely knew he disliked it. He started banging on about mythology, and unicorns being the rarest and purest of mythological creatures, as if that had anything to do with it. I tried to tell him where it came from…"

Evan just laughed as Rusty continued, "…but he was having none of it. Said that he would suggest I call our perp a perp or an unsub or even person of interest (POI for short) so that we don't underestimate him."

"Him?" Evan asked, raising an eyebrow.

"Yes, let me tell you all about it," Rusty started. Evan started to move towards the door and Rusty hesitated, "let's just stay here."

"Why?" Evan asked.

"Rae seems adamant that this guy works for LIFEline," Rusty responded, and was disappointed to see no look of shock on Evan's face.

"I was thinking the very same. Either he works for LIFEline, has connections here, or is a member of the Dead who has done their homework. It's the only reason I could think of to explain away his sudden disappearance in the footage," Evan replied, still walking to the door. "Trust me though, we don't want to stay here. Rae will be in here in a couple of minutes. Let me go shower and I will meet you in your room. I would protest and suggest following Rae's advice, but seeing as you just did a half an hour workout just to talk, you must be desperate."

Evan entered his room without knocking forty-five minutes later, clean and ready for a day of work. Rusty's red hair was still wet from the shower, and he didn't have his prosthesis back on yet, but started to update Evan as soon as he entered the room.

"Interesting," Evan responded, once Rusty relayed all the information he received yesterday.

"Very," Rusty replied, "but I am playing catch up here Evan, help me out. We have four victims and our unicorn using two separate ways to connect with them; clone, to ghost, back to clone, and back to ghost profile again. He is staging the scene to throw us off the scent, but not enough to stop us from realising, and Rae is convinced that Inverness, Catterick, and Northampton were all warm-ups for London. Why?"

"Well, and I haven't seen any of the evidence here, so still juggling a bit in the dark, but it could be to do with the behavioural differences in London. Our unicorn did seem to know the city very well – you can't figure that stuff out about London on just a map or satellite. Inverness, Catterick, and Northampton are very small – the right amount of recon could get a unicorn pretty comfortable with his surroundings for one night of debauchery. I expect the first big city he went to would be where he wanted to be. I imagine Rae was thinking the same. Is Rae set on it being a man?"

"Yes," Rusty said, "one of the first things I asked him. He said because the victims are all women, and the very nature of the murder seems predatory, makes it highly likely it is a man."

"That does make a lot of sense. The book says don't jump to that kind of conclusion until evidence is irrefutable, but Rae is extremely good at rewriting the book on the go. So, correct me when I am wrong here Rusty, but Mel was talking to a clone profile, Jane a ghost, Matilda a clone, and Natasha a ghost profile. They have no connection to each other, and no similarities at all in appearance, demeanour and any other area?" Evan asked.

"That is what Rae said," Rusty responded.

"Okay, because that doesn't make much sense. Most serial killers will have a pattern, a territory, or even a type of victim, something that draws him to them. Think of it as an alluring element for him. Something he can't stay away from, even if he tried, but this seems almost random," Evan said, scratching his head.

"Well, Rae seems to think he is home in his territory now," Rusty said.

"I hope so," Evan said.

Rusty looked at him, shocked.

"Rusty, it is much easier to start piecing this together when you know what pieces fit where. Right now, all we know is that this guy has killed four people, with no connections at all, and no similarities. We know he likes to throw pig's blood around, but no real reason why, that we know of yet. Is it ritualistic? If it is, why are there no other ritualistic elements? If he stops moving, we can start closing the net, and set a trap for our friend," Evan said, a light coming into his eyes Rusty wasn't sure he has ever seen before.

"Why did you ever get out of this work? You seem to like it," Rusty asked curiously.

"The chase was always exciting, but then you remember that every time you miss the catch, someone else pays the price. That on my mind and a well-timed illness gave me time to reflect on what I want to do. I would rather be bringing people together than putting people away," Evan responded.

"These are my thoughts on it so far, with that limited information," Evan continued, "it is either a LIFEline member: Rusty, I mean a LIFEline London member. The insight we saw on that camera yesterday is not easily received without some serious connection to the inner workings of our specific system. I doubt the unicorn had that much knowledge of his other locations.

"It could be a member of the Dead: the Dead know our system as well as we do, they have spent decades staying off our radar. We have seen past unicorns who were members of the Dead using both clones and ghosts, so we know that it is feasible. They have no problem using the technology for some things, they just don't want it "using them". Of course, it could be a mix of both, two people working in tandem. Rare in these types of crimes, but not unlikely. If it is two people, there will be a dominant and submissive profile. Maybe the submissive is doing the sweet talking for twelve months, that would explain the shift in pattern in the chat history, one minute the mirroring personality and the next one philosophical."

Rusty rubbed his head, "Two unicorns? You think that is likely?"

"I am not Rae, Rusty. I do not rule anything out, no matter how unlikely. Until I have my perp in cuffs, and enough evidence to put him away, everything is up for debate," Evan said, walking to the door. He was due at his morning meet up and Rusty was due with Rae in ten minutes.

"Thanks, Evan. Same time, same place tomorrow?" he asked, with a grin.

"Of course, boss," Evan replied.

"Cut that out, you know I am not asking as a boss, I am…" Evan cut him off.

"It makes me feel better thinking I am ordered to help, boss. Then I don't feel so bad for helping you break Rae's code. If he finds out, tell him you made me, right? Took me ages to get a handshake!"

Rusty groaned as he entered the main L.O.O.P room. Director Carter was in the middle of the room talking to Detective Rae, who seemed to be looking anywhere but at the animated Director and Dan, who was too polite to go back to his computer.

Director James Carter was a man of many words, most lacked the substance to fill a balloon. Rusty recalled Rick Harris once saying that he was full of hot air, which he felt was unfair. Hot air could be quite useful in its own way. It could warm up a room and help with balloon travel. The only time Carter was useful was by sheer chance. "If you said enough words some of them would make sense to someone eventually" seemed to be his life motto. It reminded Rusty of the old adage about monkeys and typewriters.

Carter lucked himself into a position of authority in LIFEline in London, one of the top cities in the world, and the only one who believed Carter was the right man for the job was the man himself. When Rusty became Manager of London his first duty, a responsibility he took onto his own shoulders, happily, and the one duty he believed got him a great deal of respect from the entire room instantly, was directing their Director out of the building.

Luckily for the team, the Director's visits were few and far between. Director Carter did not work up the ranks in LIFEline's innermost workings, which put him in an awkward position in more ways than one. He had a family in the system, he was in the system, so even though he was cleared to review all the data necessary to do his role, he was, at the same time, restricted from reviewing that data. Rusty, not so secretly, thought this was a blessing as Carter sometimes struggled with the elevator, so he couldn't imagine him navigating the complex system he was supposed to be in charge of, if buttons were such a struggle.

Another blessing was that any decision that had to be made about the operational elements of LIFEline for London, which should be Carter's job, was a conflict of interest. He would recuse himself and give the say to Rusty and his team. This gave Rusty one of the most active management roles in LIFEline, in one of the top cities, which did not go unnoticed by LIFEline leadership, nor by Carter, who liked to show up unannounced, like right now. Rusty waved at the Director as he entered the room, and with a simple look at Ciri made it clear that all the screens should be turned off.

"Carter," Rusty said, shaking his hand, as the screens around him blinked off, "shall we go to my office?"

Carter was about to respond until Rae cut across him, "I am sorry, we have already exchanged pleasantries, there should be no reason for Director Carter to join us."

Carter seemed taken aback, "Detective, I assure you that I am essential to…"

Rae interrupted him, "You seem to misunderstand me. I am not in any way questioning your validity in this room, that is not my role here. I am questioning your validity in my investigation. I will have no outside help of any kind." Rusty felt guilty as he sought out Evan, who he just realised never entered the main room with him, but waved his team in from the shadows and taken a room. He probably foresaw this. "Mr Styles, I will await you under the archway, but please do not linger. We have a lot to do and only a short time to do it."

Rae shuffled off and Carter looked after him.

"Is he..." Carter pointed at his head, "alright?"

"Evan says he is the best," Rusty responded.

"Well, who am I to question greatness? I was just watching a documentary the other day about this remarkable woman, Helen Keller. Have you heard of her? Anyway, she wrote all these books, was a scholar, a deep thinker, and some think a true genius, *and* she was deaf and blind." Director Carter's face took on the look of a man that has just discovered the truth of the universe and is happily sharing this knowledge with lesser mortals. "How are we in LIFEline making it easier for the Helen Keller's of this world to thrive? We must do more, Rusty."

Rusty looked at him blankly before saying, "Sorry Carter, I have to go. Kid," Rusty turned to Dan, "can you show the Director out?"

Director Carter looked pleased that he shared his knowledge. "I will get D to book some time for us to connect on this when you are less busy. I think we can change the world."

As he watched his retreating back, Rusty thought, *only that man could work for a business that was actually changing the world every single day and not understand its importance.*

Chapter Six

Detective Rae already had a driverless car ready, but the contrast between the night before could not have been more pronounced. Where last night was dark and empty, with driverless cars roving the streets like stray dogs looking for a way to be helpful, the day was vibrant and full of life. There were people jogging through the archway with VR glasses on, in one of the best cities in the world, and yet probably virtually somewhere else. Driverless cars were picking up and dropping off at a conveyer belt-like pace. The sun was shining, and it was hard to believe that there has been a murder in this city.

Rusty entered the driverless car as Rae entered his pin and said, "Waterloo please, oh, and take the scenic route, thirty minutes should do it."

Rusty said nothing, but his silence seemed to speak volumes.

"Do you know why I entered my code?" Rae asked.

"Of course. I had the need for privacy in my time too," Rusty responded.

"I have made it very clear," Rae said, looking Rusty in the eye for an uncharacteristically long time, "that I think the profile I am considering points me in the direction of LIFEline. I think the probability of them being in the L.O.O.P is around seventy five percent."

Rusty made a disgruntled noise and rolled his eyes.

"Something I said was annoying?" Rae asked.

"Nothing gets past you," Rusty responded before he could stop himself.

"Care to elaborate, Mr Styles, or is this unpleasant back and forth a type of bonding exercise you do?" Rae asked. Rusty looked at him to see if this was a joke. His face might as well have been written in Latin for all the good it would do Rusty to decipher the meaning.

"No bonding here, you will be happy to know. Just a phrase comes to mind when someone pulls a number out of mid-air like that," Rusty replied.

"I would like to hear it. I am fond of phrases, adages, and general quotes. There is a lot of wisdom in words, if you know how to look at them in the right way," Rae said.

"There is a wrong way to look at words?" Rusty asked, feeling he would regret it.

"How about you tell me the phrase and I will tell you my thoughts on words? A fair trade of ideas to start our day will help the mind get in the flow for what is in store," Rae said, looking for the first time like he was enjoying himself.

"Well, it's no phrase you have probably ever heard, it was one we used all the time during my military days. Give a coward a number and they will find a way to hide behind it," Rusty said, feeling slightly uncomfortable saying it. Rae seemed to be weighing the merit of the sentence, like a prospector seeing what parts were gold and what parts just dirt that would flake off at the touch.

"I assume the intent is to assume I am a coward hiding behind the seventy five percent chance that they are in the L.O.O.P?" Rae said.

Rusty didn't say anything as the car continued to move through the London streets.

"In this logic, does it make me brave if I am pursuing the other twenty five percent instead?" Rae asked.

"It was just something we used to say. When people said a mission had a ninety percent chance of success you would see how people would jump up to be part of the team. When the odds were much lower those same hands did not go up. A lot of people are willing to be the hero, not a lot of people are willing to be a member of the numerous nameless dead," Rusty responded, purposely not looking at Rae.

"So, to play the numbers was seen as the coward's game? I can see how that would play a part in some settings, and I am sure, given your experience, that you have come to understand that to want to live is not a cowardly move. Sometimes the bravest thing we can do is protect ourselves, even if others think poorly of us for not putting up our hands. Thank you for sharing, I like that… 'Give a coward a number and they will find a way to hide behind it.

"And to the "wrong way" to look at words: words can be elusive and devious if given the chance to be. We prescribe meaning to words, but can have no say over the way those words are interpreted. How they change shape in their respective realities. What is a simple pleasantry to you is too familiar to me. A word you love has grown to offend me. If I wrote a book tomorrow on peace there would be those who line up behind it to start a war," Rae finished.

"So, do you mean that people are the problem when it comes to words?" Rusty asked.

"Yes and no. People find the beauty in words and also the horror, but I don't like to let words away with the role they play in that. If we say words inspire us, it is also good to remember that some inspiration is bad. Take our murderer. He is inspired to commit murder. He will feel a release from it and may feel little to no remorse for his victims. People may prefer we didn't call it inspiration as the word is pure, yet using words to suit your view of the world and not the meaning of the word is just trying to make everyone see things your way. Words do have that power," Rae responded.

"Like calling him a unicorn," Rusty muttered under his breath. "Well, maybe," Rae said, and Rusty was surprised to see a smile cross his face, "but calling him a unicorn is simply inaccurate. Just because people start to use a word to describe something doesn't make it true. If I called the sky green and it became popular should that mean we shouldn't challenge that? Or, even more extreme, should we change the definition of green to fit the reality I am trying to create? Language is alive and words are the atoms that make it spin this way and that. I believe we cease to be human when we stop questioning what builds the world around us. More so for us, those who work in LIFEline who are in the world creation business."

Rusty couldn't help but notice that Rae seemed to be enjoying himself, but was making an effort to pull himself away from the conversation.

"So, why are we going to Waterloo?" Rusty asked.

"To chase the other twenty five percent down. There is only one other group that knows London as well as we do. The Dead. They have an understanding of our system and a little bit of a vendetta against LIFEline," Rae responded.

"But they are only twenty five percent as likely to have done this, but my team is seventy percent?" Rusty asked.

"No, sorry, I should have clarified, it is a seventy five percent probability that it is a LIFEline team member in the L.O.O.P, seventeen percent that it is a member of the Dead, and an eight percent chance of a close family member of one of the LIFEline team. Xander has run the numbers and they are clear. He is looking into family connections to every LIFEline member today and will have any flags for us by the time we finish," Rae responded.

"Do you think it could be more than one person?" Rusty asked, voicing Evan's idea.

"Very unlikely, although I can see why you would think that given the change in the pattern of conversation, but it comes back to our words, Mr Styles. You use certain words; you probably do it without thinking. You misspell certain words, say a certain phrase or use a certain cadence in your punctuation. Your words can be as revealing as your DNA, more so as they can show not only who you are, but how you think when you wrote those words. Xander has run the conversations and we are pretty sure that we are dealing with one perp." Rae said.

"Pretty sure?" Rusty asked.

"Well, I didn't want to hide behind the numbers."

Rusty just looked at Rae blankly and he smiled, "I am joking."

"Good one," Rusty said, with a straight face, "Will I get to meet this Xander?"

"Yes, we will do a full debrief today when we get back. He will need to be updated on our progress too," Rae said.

"I thought we didn't want outside help on this," Rusty said.

"Xander is not outside help. He is my eyes and ears in places I can't be," Rae said seriously, "but back to more pressing matters. The Dead. I can't see any reason for them to do this."

"Are you blind?" Rusty asked incredulously. "They think we are pushing them to the outskirts of humanity, they think we are genetically engineering the human race, they think we are killing people with technology, and hiding all these stories from them. Should I go on or do you have enough?"

"None of that is new. The Dead live in their own world, outside our system. Yes, we see the vocal ones who are keen to open our eyes to the error of our ways, but that is nothing new. If you have done any extensive reading on religions of the past, converting heathens, and pointing out how right you are, is practically a ticket to entry. If you think our perp may be seeing the world through a lens of righteousness, rekindling some of the violence of religions of the past, it is an interesting concept, but not one I feel we have much reason to pursue at the given time," Rae said.

"Well, I was going to say it would be just like them to kill LIFEline users to make their point. They see it as them and us. Forgetting the supplies and support we give them to survive. They still seem to think they managed to master their own faculties," Rusty said. He was part of the team that ensured that the Dead had enough to live comfortably, and it wasn't an easy task. They wouldn't accept charity from outsiders, so jobs had to be created where none were needed. Trades done at a substantial loss, giving the Dead an over-exaggerated opinion of their work and their craftsmanship.

Worst of all, in Rusty's opinion, was the way people actually bought their goods at inflated prices because it was "vintage". It was vintage all right; it was dumped there by the very people buying it back.

"Yes, well, obvious personal feelings aside here, Mr Styles, these people decide to live their lives in the same way as we do. We do not plug into LIFEline and we decided to join the company to help manage that world. One slightly different decision at a different time in our past and who knows? We could be living down there, enjoying a different type of freedom," Rae responded, as the driverless car drove down the river Thames.

"What is that?" Rusty asked, whipping his neck around quickly at a passing blur in the air.

"I assume you mean what are they?" Rae asked, pointing out more drones. Some were flying high above the water, scanning its surface from a height, others were right at the water's edge, surveying the walls and any nook along the river.

"Yes, what the hell are they doing? We can't just start sending drones all over London, people will panic. We have to control how this news gets out, and frame it in the right way at the right time. There is an art form to this type of communication, trust me, people have been telling me for years!" Rusty said, watching members of the public who were glancing up at the drones, and then as if they were no more than a flock of birds, going back to their day-to-day activities.

"I assure you, Mr Styles, people will not care. They will assume we are making a new VR tour or movie for their enjoyment. The astute ones who put the pieces together will not be surprised to see us scanning the river after a murder. All three other bodies were found in a body of water close by. For us, that leaves the river, the canal, and a few dotted estuaries around London, but I bet we will find Miss Anderson in the Thames. Given the location of our perp's last stop on camera, it is obvious he was going to the river," Rae said, taking no more notice of the drones.

"So why are we taking the scenic route today? Do you have more to tell me?" Rusty said, more to get off the topic. This was the first time in years that something happened in London without his supervision. He trusted his team to do anything in his absence. They were fully trained, and a lot of them were better than he was in so many areas that he felt foolish rubber-stamping their requests. This was different. Someone outside of his team had their hands on the reins, and he didn't much like the feeling.

"Yesterday we got you caught up on what has happened so far. What has physically happened, I should say. There are three main elements in my mind when it comes to this type of crimes. Forensic evidence, the victimology, and what behaviour we can see from the perp. Let me tell you what I am thinking of our perp's profile so far," Rae said.

"Yes, you said, it is either one of my team, their friends, or the Dead," Rusty interrupted.

"That does remain the case. I can see you are obviously irritated at the idea of a team member being the perp..."

"I am not irritated at the idea of a team member being a perp," Rusty said, with a sting in his voice, "I am annoyed at you thinking it is one of my people. The long shot sometimes wins you know."

"If it was only a feeling then I would understand your irritation with me, but all the signs point that way. By all means, if it makes it easier for you to continue this investigation thinking I am wrong, then go right ahead. You are right, sometimes the long shot wins – although I am not a fan of the wording. But as I said, I do not have the time, and given our interactions so far, I don't think I even have the patience to make you trust me. The proof will be in the pudding," Rae said.

Rusty sat quietly, looking darkly at the smaller man.

"Back to my original point though, let me tell you what I am thinking about our perp. Not where they may be, but who they may be. Something happened almost two years ago that made our perp contemplate killing. I am not sure what that was yet, although I have my theories, but it is clear that our guy was not in a good place, so he started to reach out to connect with others. His intent? To murder them. There is no place for doubt there. He created fake profiles, if he only wanted to talk to them and the murder happened in the heat of the moment, that first time there would be no reason to have those clone and ghost profiles.

"So, he was always planning to kill. He has a kill bag, a getaway car, and is very meticulous about his planning. He hooks them for twelve months, speaking to them, getting to know them and, sometimes, even letting them get to know him. He leaves nothing at the crime scene and even takes the body, which would lead us to think he had remorse until we saw what was in the bag. Remorseful killers do not tend to chop up their victims. The desire and urge to kill will continue to build up. Like an addict, he won't be sated, ever. The more he kills, the less he will feel, driving him on more and more, chasing down that hit."

"You think that maniac is in the L.O.O.P?" Rusty asked.

"He wouldn't act like a maniac. He would barely seem different to most except for the absences needed to commit the crimes. Seeing as all those crimes were in places where the trips could be done in slightly less than a full day, it wouldn't throw up any flags. His meticulous planning, stalking of our victims, and then subsequent attacks with very little gratuitous violence, makes me think our perp comes across as careful, calming, and maybe even a bit regimented," Rae said, as the car stopped at the old Waterloo Station.

Rusty and Rae exited the car, with the large building in the middle of the roundabout to their backs, the steps leading into the old building were directly in front of them. The statues of War and Peace looked down at them as Rae led them left, through a tunnel that went under railway tracks, and then to the right. Twice Rusty tried to engage Rae in conversation, but to no avail. On his third attempt, Rae just said, "We can talk about anything else but the case. If they wished, your team could hear us here."

They were at one of the old entrances of the underground station. Rusty looked over his shoulder to an old military club he had fond memories of. It has been too long since his last day off and the refreshing conversations with some of his old friends in there. Rae didn't even pause for a beat as he walked into the old building, past some members of the public, and to the disused escalator.

"I guess we don't give the Dead the joy of power to run these?" Rae asked, looking at Rusty with an owlish grin.

Rusty leaned forward, felt a slight twinge in his lower back from the gym this morning, *I really got to start exercising more*, he thought again, and pressed a button. There was a moment's silence, a whining noise followed by some creaking, like an old wheel in need of oil, and then slowly, gradually, the escalator started to inch forward in a shuddering motion. As Rusty and Rae stepped on, it continued its shuddering descent into the darkness below.

"Are you experiencing an injury, Mr Styles?" Rae asked seriously.

"No, just overdone it in the gym this morning," Rusty responded.

"I can show you some stretches that should help, if you wish. Later, of course," Rae added, like a man that thought if he didn't clarify he would be expected to perform the task now.

"I will be fine. Just been some time since I was in the gym. The body isn't what it used to be," Rusty responded.

The Dead liked the darkness, well, in truth, the Dead liked the idea of darkness. The underground, which had long ago become the home for the Dead in London, was filled with old-style lanterns and skylights that gave them the only natural light down in the underbelly of the city. The Dead lived underground, but they did not stay at home all day and night. They came up to work, socialise, protest, and show off their skills in everything from music and the arts to pick-pocketing and small crimes.

"In a hole in the ground there lived a people. Not a nasty, dirty, wet hole but one of comfort," Rae said, into the thinning darkness.

"What?" Rusty asked.

"Just paraphrasing Mr Tolkien. The Dead always remind me of a people that would fit into one of his kingdoms of Middle Earth. They sit on the outskirts, sometimes not bothering anyone, and wanting to be left alone, and at other times taking the spotlight as they try to change the world. Very Hobbit-type people, although I am glad they wear shoes, I am not the biggest fan of barefooted people," Rae said.

Rusty was acutely aware of how much that gruff voice was travelling in the tunnel as they neared the end of the escalator and prepared to step off. He has been in the 'land of the Dead" a couple of times, but he never felt like this before. *Maybe it was because it is just us two with no weapons or way to call for back-up,* he thought. *Or,* another part of him thought, *maybe it is scarier when you are hunting a monster in the darkness.*

As Rusty looked into the dark tunnel, he scoffed. He had been in truly dark places, caves in the middle of the desert where when you lifted your hand to your face you couldn't see it, not even when you hit yourself in the eye. This darkness had a nice glow that illuminated their way. *Any knight coming to slay a dragon in here would have to work hard to get lost,* he thought.

The long corridor, once filled with the coming and going of passengers, was now a small part of a large underground network that connected a civilization. Members of the Dead could enter at Waterloo and come up in any area of the city. Waterloo had alcoves built into the walls, some there since the original building, some added as rooms. The rooms' intent was varied and plenty – Rusty saw normal-looking sitting rooms, old-fashioned libraries, kitchens and schools but has also seen the darker side of the Dead's community with drug production and criminal activity hidden amongst these seemingly peaceful settings.

As they walked further in their footsteps echoed – Rusty's purposeful walk clapping more than the soft shuffling of Rae – but the difference was not respected by the echo that liked to mix the two sounds into a duet that travelled that bit further. The duet called the Dead out of some of the rooms at hand. At first, they looked Rusty and Rae up and down, mostly out of curiosity - *Obviously looking to see if we have wristbands,* Rusty thought –but even the absence of wristbands did not stop the gazes moving from curiosity to distrust at the two outsiders.

"Who should we be looking to speak to, Mr Styles?" Rae asked.

Rusty looked at Rae, "I thought you would know!" he whispered back as quietly as he could, but the echo picked up the hiss and gave it room to travel further than Rusty thought was possible.

"Your city, Mr Styles. If you were chasing a lead to the Dead, who would you ask for?" Rae asked, as if they were deciding on a menu in a restaurant. There was not even the merest trace of a whisper in his voice, which was attracting the attention of some of the larger-looking gentlemen.

One such "gentleman" extracted himself from a room, calling over his shoulder, "I have no idea where she is, but someone has to stop them just traipsing in!" He turned to face them, and, despite his words and size, he asked pleasantly, "What can I do for you, sirs?"

Rusty stepped forward, the man was roughly his size, but didn't stay out of the gym in the last few years, "We are looking to speak to Gideon. Is he around?"

"Who can I say is asking?" he asked, looking at both Rae and Rusty's wrists and scowling slightly.

"Tell him it is Russell Styles. He will no doubt remember me," Rusty responded.

"And your friend?" the man asked, looking at Rae, who was looking like he was going to walk around him.

Rusty extended his arm, as if to introduce, but also to block Rae from moving. This was not his first dealings with the Dead, who did not like to have their authority questioned by outsiders.

"Detective Euan Rae, and you are?" Rae responded, looking at Rusty's arm, but thankfully did not push the subject, or the arm, as Rusty lowered it.

"Detective?" the man asked.

"It is not very polite to keep guests standing at your door and not tell them your name," Rae observed.

Rusty tensed and started to number the people around him and Rae – especially between them and the escalator - as he expected a confrontation. The big man just grinned, "The name is Mohammad. Most call me Mo, Detective." The man nodded at a skinny woman close to the back of the long tunnel. She left in the blink of an eye, swallowed by the darkness, as Mo nodded for them to follow him to a side room. The side room was small, and it was clear that it was set to the side as a holding area. It had a couple of chairs, a table and not much else in the way of décor.

"Best for you to be in here," Mo said, "a couple of LIFEliners walking out there isn't a great idea."

"LIFEline's jurisdiction does cover the Dead too," Rae responded, "and we are here to ask questions about the recent murder."

"You mean murders?" Mo asked.

Rae and Rusty said nothing.

"Listen, Detectives," Mo continued, "take some advice, when Gideon gets here, don't think we don't know what is happening in the world. News travelled just as far and as fast when people weren't online. In those days it had a tendency to be very accurate too. A stranger online wants to scare you, but the word of mouth works on well-travelled roads built on trust. The source and direction trusted over generations, but closed as soon as it is unreliable or unsafe. We know there is someone doing things they shouldn't be…" as Mo spoke a man entered the room quietly, "…and we know he is not on our side. Talk of jurisdiction all you want detectives, but your technology and your pieces of paper won't hold up down here."

"Mo, that is enough. Gentlemen, can we offer you a drink?" Gideon asked, walking forward, hand outstretched to Rusty.

Rusty shook the hand and introduced Rae. Gideon did not proffer his hand. *How does he already know?* Rusty thought. Gideon was a skinny man with long dreadlocked hair that had flecks of grey, like falling snow in the dark hair, and a close-trimmed beard. His eyes were the colour of an oak tree and seemed to hold the age and wisdom too.

"A cup of tea wouldn't go amiss, Gideon," Rusty responded, as Rae nodded his assent. Mo left the room. The Dead didn't have leaders. Their whole setup was built on the disdain the Dead held for authority – they felt that authority and the corresponding power that came with it corrupted absolutely. Of all the leaders they didn't have, Gideon was the most respected, by both sides. He cooperated with LIFEline on criminals in his city, once saying to Rusty, "We choose a different life than that of the online one chosen by our brothers and sisters, but we still hold the values of a true society. If we have wolves among us, then we would also like to see them revealed, but be warned, if you use our values against us to insert an online presence or try to take our people without cause, it will be you that we treat as a wolf."

Rusty respected the unofficial leader and could see why the Dead flocked to him for guidance and counsel during difficult times and why, when there was a tough decision made by him, he was not questioned.

"I assume you know why we are here?" Rae said.

"Yes," Gideon responded. His face shifted, and a look of weariness and sadness lingered in his eyes, "those poor girls murdered across the country. Are we any closer to apprehending him?"

The usage of "we" heartened Rusty somewhat, as Mo entered the room and deposited three cups and a large pot of tea along with the necessaries to complete the drinks. Gideon stood and poured, asking in turn for their preference in the taking, as Rae answered him.

"We have some ideas and are ruling out some of the less likely," Rae said simply.

"I assume we are the former "less likely"," Gideon remarked, before moving on, "Do we think he will keep moving? Will London also just be a stop off on his dark tour?"

"We don't believe so," Rusty said, picking up his tea and taking a sip. "We think he is going to continue to strike in London. He has worked on his M.O. in other locations, honing it to a level that would stand up under the scrutiny of the London LIFEline team," Rae said.

"Why London?" Gideon asked.

Rusty half expected Rae to tell him that he suspected one of his team's involvement, but Rae just responded, "The challenge. The difference between a big fish in a small pond and a big fish in the ocean. We believe our killer wants to face off against the best while committing his crimes. It shows his arrogance, maybe his youth, and definitely his confidence."

"I assume you are not informing everyone this way?" Gideon asked, looking at Rusty.

"We need information and Mr Styles thinks you are the one that could help us," Rae responded.

Gideon took a moment, taking a sip of tea, and, Rusty thought, buying himself some time, "I can of course help, but do not expect the sympathy of the Dead as a whole. They see this as a LIFEline problem. Many of them are not happy with you hiding the information from the public…"

Rae went to interrupt but Gideon just raised a hand.

"Detective, you must understand that we are talking about a people who do not trust you. Every move you make is under scrutiny and even if it makes sense to one of the world's best Detectives, that doesn't automatically mean they will agree with what you are doing. We value truth above comfort. This murderer is not killing the Dead and I think you know that they are not one of our people. If you thought they were a member of the Dead you would have shown up with more than just two. So, we are happy to help where we can, but we will not jeopardise who we are to save you." Gideon looked sad as he finished.

"Jeopardise who you are?" Rae asked.

"We have no technology here and that will not change," Gideon said.

"You mean you have no new technology," Rae said.

"Are we really going to be pedantic about the word technology? You do know what I mean, Detective," Gideon responded looking disappointedly at Rae.

"You mistake my meaning, Gideon. You have just stumbled upon our reason for being here and I thought it best we explore the subject," Rae said.

"I thought you were here for my help?" Gideon asked, raising an eyebrow as he looked the small Detective over.

"We are," Rusty said, "Rae has some specific questions he thinks you may be able to help with."

"As you seem to know already, our perp left each city after committing his murder. In London, he simply disappeared. One minute we had him the next he was gone and…" Rae said.

"And the only way to disappear in London is to go underground," Gideon finished. "Alas, the first thing I can't help you with. We will not setup any surveillance at our points of entry and if we see any external ones, we will block their views."

"No surveillance needed, Gideon," Rusty said, leaning forward before Rae could speak. He had a good feeling that Rae was going to tell Gideon that any illegal activity, like blocking camera views of London, would result in prosecution. "Have you or any other members of the Dead seen any outsiders using your tunnels…"

"Home." Gideon interjected simply.

"Any outsiders using your home to navigate the city off our grid? It is in both our interests to stop this. He has only attacked LIFEliners so far, but if he walks into one of your rooms and is confronted, he may react," Rusty finished. Gideon didn't look like he needed the added persuasion, but Rusty thought it best to give it both barrels.

"The Dead's lands cover vast areas, in some places going deeper than you would imagine. If you give me an idea of the locations, then we can see what we can find out for you," Gideon responded.

"Thanks, Gideon," Rusty said.

"No thanks needed yet. It could be for nothing if we do not find what we need." Gideon stood up and left the room, returning shortly with a pen and notebook. There were scrawlings visible as he flipped from page to page. He stopped on a page and wrote something, looked up and asked, "What areas should I enquire about?"

"Horse Guards Parade, Westminster, Green Park, St James' Park, Victoria, Knightsbridge, Sloane Square, South Kensington and Hyde Park Corner to start with," Rae said.

Rusty tensed as the last station was mentioned and Gideon caught his eye with a puzzled look.

"We don't occupy the old Hyde Park Corner stations and undergrounds, but I would imagine you know that given the fact you would have slept there last night," Gideon said, circling the last area in his notebook.

"I believe you have access to the surrounding locations? The last underground maps I looked at showed a multitude of walkways directly under and around the L.O.O.P," Rae responded.

Rusty could feel the anger bubbling up. He once heard that anger was a choice you made. You allowed yourself to feel annoyed by something, which made you angry. As the blood seemed to boil in his body, rushing towards his ears, and no doubt making his face red, he never felt so sure that the statement was full of it. He remembered his military training and tried to compartmentalise as Gideon continued to stare at him.

"The location of the L.O.O.P makes it easy to navigate around, but I think you now misunderstand me. Why would you need information on the surroundings of your own office?" Gideon asked. "Most of the Dead stay clear of that area. Way too close to the big brother."

"My point exactly," Rae responded, "our perp will be aware of this point and may take advantage of such a location."

Rusty would hand the keys of the entire operation of LIFEline over to Director Carter in the morning if Gideon fell for that cover. If Gideon had issues with it he obviously felt now was not the time to discuss these.

"This will take a couple of days at the earliest. When you don't spy on your people twenty-four hours a day it can be hard to track down who was where in the last few days," Gideon said with a small smile.

"There is just one more thing, back to your technology. If I wanted to buy a fully working car in London – low tech, literally an old school vehicle, no trackers, GPS, cameras, or self-drive capabilities, who would I talk to?" Rae asked.

"You have asked two questions there. The second one should have been phrased who would talk to you? The answer to that one, unfortunately, is no one for free. The Dead believe in a fair trade and that extends to information, and before you say it, no, they do not want a bribe. They just won't give you something for nothing. The first question, same thing, if you wanted to buy one, I would assume it is legitimate. If a killer wanted to buy some, I don't think they would want the paperwork?" Gideon responded.

Rae looked impressed for a moment and then just said, "Yes, if you could answer your questions instead that would be for the best."

"Well, luckily, it is an easy answer. The Fry family. You will find them at Vauxhall Station. To get the right answers from them you might want to leave the hard questions at the door and take a bag of cash with you – or something valuable. They don't tend to answer questions for free," Gideon said with a smile.

"They have never been asked questions by me," Rusty said, returning the smile.

Gideon frowned, "Just remember, Mr Styles," Rusty took note of the use of his second name, like a child being reprimanded by a teacher, "a delicate hand can do more masterful work than a fist."

"Nicely said," Rae said automatically.

"Gentlemen, if you have nothing else, I would like to get back to my morning. There are some bonsai trees in need of assistance, and I am feeling the urge to sit behind a piano and stretch my fingers," Gideon said, standing up when Rusty and Rae showed no sign of more questions.

Gideon walked them to the escalator, turned off the still moving one they came down on and turned on the up one. Rae stepped on, but Gideon held Rusty by the shoulder, leaving the Detective alone on his ascent. Once the darkness swallowed Rae, Gideon said, "Do you think he is right? Is the wolf among you?"

Chapter Seven

I t was dark when Rachel got back from her VR walk with her friends. They found the story of Natasha's death interesting. The worry she has seen in her parents and Oliver wasn't reflected here. Her friends lived in different cities, and different countries, some were married, and some in long-term relationships. They were not concerned for Rachel either, "Oh, Jake is besotted with you," her friend, Claire, said, "even look at last night. He took time out of work to spend with you, because he knew you would be scared. I agree with Oliver and Jake though, don't talk to any new people until this lunatic is caught."

The word jumped out at her, not through any inflection of Claire's voice, but through its inaccuracy. As a young teenager, she loved to watch crime shows and was especially prone to those involving murder. When she first started to pick up books, she started her journey in an almost backward fashion, picking up the classics that delved deeper into the darker elements of the human mind and existence, then travelled from that darker pathway towards the lighter and brighter children's stories.

It was easy to believe and hope that the people who committed such atrocities were inhuman. That they were monsters incapable of feeling emotions, that they were bottled chaos, only managing to seem coherent on the surface, while hiding a deep and disturbed inner turmoil. The problem was that the cruelty and ferocity attributed to animals were closer to home with humans. Humans alone enslaved their own people, used their own people as sport in games with caged animals, and explored the furthest horizons, with conquering at the forefront of their minds.

Rachel opened her mobile device, and put on her VR glasses, pulling up a virtual room where she could start her research. A keyboard and monitor appeared in mid-air and there were blank walls all around her. She used this space to write essays in school, and plan lessons as a teacher, but now she was here for a different reason. So far, her thoughts were based on feelings, on the reading of those books that long ago delved into the dark places of the human mind. Right now, she wanted to do the delving herself. She wanted to see if she could help find who was doing this.

Just like yesterday, she started with Natasha's page, which was receiving a high volume of posts, well wishes, and charitable donations to LIFEline on her behalf. It was almost impossible to wade through the current of people posting as the page refreshed and refreshed, but she clicked on an image of Natasha and saved it – she grabbed it with her hand, threw it up against the virtual wall to her left, and wrote the word, "Victims" above it. She clicked the image and Natasha's details appeared to the left of the image, along with the date the picture was taken. She removed the date, but left the details.

Well, she thought, *that is the easy one done.*

Ollie mentioned other victims, potentially three more. She moved back to her workstation and her fingers hesitated for a moment.

Will an alarm go off somewhere if I type this in? she wondered.

She typed the letters in, slower than usual, as if each stroke being deliberate would make a difference: Murders UK. The screen flickered. Rachel found herself looking at the red hair and pale face of Natasha Anderson again. She scrolled down with her hand and found other stories, but none from any time in the last few weeks or months. There were flashes of the

Yorkshire Ripper, Jack the Ripper, and some of their kindred spirits from the past. She scrolled to the next page. The first line of a post caught her attention.

"Just questioned by LIFEline. Weird questions about some girl I never even heard of @Matilda Hawes #confusingday." The guy, Raj, posted it publicly and it barely gathered any attention. In one of the comments, someone wrote the words, "probably murdered", which, due to her search, were bolded. When Rachel clicked on Mathilda Hawes' tagged name, it brought her to a profile. She did not need to look far to know that this girl was no longer alive. The first post said it all: "One month gone baby girl! We will find the person that did this! Sleep well #angel." Rachel felt a rush; *that was a lot easier than I expected,* she thought.

An hour later she had four profiles on the wall of her research room, the word "Victims" seemed to stand out a lot more prominently now that the smiling images of these women were below it. She placed them in chronological order, furthest left was Melanie Fraser, next to her was Jane Stevens, then Matilda Hawes, and finally Natasha Anderson. Besides the smiling faces, she could see no obvious similarities. Books she read in her teenage years about murderers and serial killers spoke of Victimology. So, if it wasn't appearance, then there were only two things she could see that they all had in common. They were women and they were going on their first dates. *If that is all they are targeting, then I fit the bill,* she thought darkly.

I need more information, Rachel thought, as she looked at the images. The books she read, movies and shows she watched, were all chasing their way around her mind. The detectives always had access to all this information. Crime scenes, full details of the crimes, autopsy, witnesses, and interviews with family and friends to build up their case and get an idea of the character of their murderer. They looked at it all for even the most subtle of clues. Rachel took off her VR glasses, walked to the window, and rubbed the bridge of her nose as she tried to think.

As she stood at the window, her wrist vibrated, and she looked down to see a message from Jake on her mobile device.

HEY, HOW WAS YOUR WALK?
JAKE.

She was about to reply, and then it hit her. She went to her bookshelf and started to rummage around. She always thought that the way someone stored their books could tell you a lot about them. Her books were categorised and alphabetised, but they lay flat, stood up at angles, and in any way that would make them fit. She found the old black hardback book under a large graphic novel, pulled it out, and went back to her desk.

The book was a gift from her mother. After an argument one day, her mother walked into her room, placed the book down gently on her side table, and left. Since that day, Rachel must have read it a dozen times, cover to cover. *The Criminal Mind: A Glimpse Behind the Curtain by M.R. Braize* had real-life case studies, interviews with different types of criminals, but mainly killers and, most importantly, a thorough breakdown of what to look for in those types of crimes. Rachel opened it and got a feeling of excitement that can only be attributed to revisiting a favourite book, rediscovering the love and memories that lay within its pages. As the reason for opening the book came back to her though, that excitement retreated into shame.

There was a section called *Victimology*; she flipped to it, glancing over the pages, more to remember than read, when a quote jumped out:

"the way the victim is chosen is important and gives an insight into how the offender thinks, which subsequently affects how the perpetrator acts."

I don't know enough about the victims to figure this out, Rachel thought. She went back to the contents to review other aspects that killers and investigators said were important to them. She was very aware, having read this book so often, that each killer is different, some take trophies, some leave signatures, some plan to the very last detail, while, for others, it is an uncontrollable fury. The contents listed *Geographical Profile,* which wouldn't help her unless the killer stayed in London. Right now, they seemed like a nomadic killer.

"Moving from place to place, this type of killer can move almost compulsively, killing as they go, and harder to find due to jurisdictional worries."

Next was *Modus Operandi,* which she knew would need a lot more information on to be able to explore this. As she reviewed the contents, and thought of different, ingenious ways to try to get the information, she put her VR glasses back on, and looked at the images of the four victims, again.

She felt the sadness for each of the women creep again, before she added new headings to keep her mind busy: *Geographical Profile,* under which she placed a map of the UK, pinning each crime scene location as best she could. She added the letters *M.O.,* but left the heading alone, adding nothing here yet. She followed with *Motive,* and then, on consulting the book, she added the word *Profile.* Contacting family and friends was an obvious way to start to build her knowledge, but that was a line she was just unwilling to cross. Reaching out to people in their grief, playing her own Sherlock Holmes, was not something she was willing to do. LIFEline would never give her the access she would need, after all, she was just a schoolteacher!

"How am I going to do this?!" she said out loud, getting frustrated at the number of obstacles starting to creep up on her. Her parents always said she could have had a quieter life if she learnt to let go of certain things, but she already knew this was not one of them. With her VR glasses on, she could look around the room and still see her book in her hand.

"Ollie," she said out loud, before continuing the thought, *he knows more than he is saying. If the Dead know that there have been more murders, then I bet he can find out more information.* The plan was starting to formulate, as she sat and thought more. Tomorrow was Sunday. She would go for her swim early, make another stop off at the café, and ask Ollie. She would get as much information as she could out of him.

In the meantime, she refreshed herself on more of *The Criminal Mind* book, stopping now and again to write things on the wall that she thought would come in useful. As Rachel worked, the message from Jake went unanswered - she knew he would understand. They spoke a lot, but they spoke when they felt like properly talking to each other. They settled that very early on in their connection – neither of them was a fan of talking to others who were half-listening, as they went about their day-to-day. She would message him back later, when she could focus on him; right now, her undivided attention was busy.

◆ ◆ ◆

Rae and Rusty spent more time navigating London than Rusty had in years. They walked along the river at places, seeing the drones scanning every inch of it, through Green, Hyde, and Regents Parks. Rusty felt like a patrolman. Both feet hit the ground, but only his right could feel the surface of the pavement underneath. Even after all these years, that pavement still felt familiar. He knew it was his mind romanticising, but he felt that if he closed his eyes, those feet could take him anywhere in this city. Euan Rae was shuffling along, his feet making a noise more associated with slippers than the shoes he wore, as if he was a cartographer doing his best to map the entire city in a day.

On multiple occasions, Rusty asked what the plan was and Rae's only response was; "To get a feel for the city."

Rusty hasn't been out this long in some time, but he didn't think it was just his imagination telling him the city did not look as busy as it usually did, especially on a Saturday. That was the day they expected the most footfall around the city. People still loved to experience the "hustle and bustle" of London and see the iconic sites that stood the test of time - 221B Baker Street, The Palace, Fleet Street, The Globe, St Paul's, Harrods - but today, all these sites had a severe reduction in their audience.

Rae insisted on walking all over the city, like a sightseer, crossing at one bridge, then back on another. Finally, as the sun went down, and they found themselves at Greenwich, Rae hailed a driverless car and inserted his code.

"Did you find out what you needed to in the miles of walking today?" Rusty asked, flopping down in the chair. This was the most exercise his body has seen in years, an early morning gym attendance and an expedition around London. He would have to reward it with something big and calorie dense when he got back to the office.

"I found out a good deal, yes," Rae responded.

"Any of those highlights going to make it into the conversation for the ride back to the L.O.O.P?" Rusty asked, sarcastically.

"Some will yes, but I think I would prefer if you could tell me anything you may have found out today. After all, this is your city. I haven't worked a case here in years and the city has changed a lot," Rae responded, looking out the window as the driverless car effortlessly navigated the roads.

"I didn't think this was going to be a test," Rusty responded, shortly.

"No test, just humour my curiosity if you will, Mr Styles. I do believe you will add real value to my own observations. If I didn't, I would have just left you in the office and proceeded alone," Rae responded, and again Rusty was surprised by his straightforwardness.

"Well, the first thing I noticed was the serious miles I put this prosthetic through…" Rusty started.

"Yes, I noticed that too. I was impressed to see the manoeuvrability and stability of the piece. I was wondering if it would hinder you, but I think we have more to worry about with your other leg," Rae interrupted.

Rusty decided to ignore the jab. He still wasn't sure Rae understood or cared how his words were being perceived, "I also noticed that London was not as busy as I would expect on a Saturday in July. With a clear day like that in London, we would expect some queueing in the more popular locations."

"Ah, I am glad that this was not just me. I thought, with the increase in LIFEline accessibility and engagement that has been reported in the last few years, that London has seen a massive decrease in attendance," Rae replied.

It is like he is talking about a concert, Rusty thought, but only responded with, "Yes, we did see a decrease in overall footfall, but not to the low numbers we saw today. I know we have suggested vigilance in our message to the public and a kind of curfew at night, but we wouldn't have expected this drastic of a decrease in one day."

"People fear the unknown. Correction, the majority of people fear the unknown. In a world where you can talk to everyone you love from the comfort of your home, you may be inclined to use that service, but on a nice day, you will venture out to connect with others. Now add an unknown element, you may leave and never come back. There is a perp on the loose that may end your life. Are you going outside?" Rae asked.

"Me? You are damned right I am. Somebody thinks they can scare me by rushing at women, killing them when and where they feel safest. They will find it a lot harder to scare me," Rusty responded.

"That was rhetorical," Rae said, not turning back from looking out the window.

"Even a rhetorical question can be answered," Rusty shot back.

"Evidently so. Anything else?" Rae asked.

Rusty tried to think. Nothing came to mind, so he just shook his head.

"Thank you for sharing. The decrease in footfall is very telling," Rae started, "People do not feel safe in the city, our perp will love that. He is meticulous in his planning and in his crimes. The staging was meant to go reported, I think the fact that we have not reported on his crimes until now may have frustrated him. As we did not make it known to the public about his other crimes and his other victims, he will be keen to correct that. Our perp will more than likely be reviewing the impact his work is having as we speak. Probably through the camera systems in the L.O.O.P, but it was worth us exploring the city to see if we spotted anything out of the ordinary."

"You probably didn't notice, but most people we have seen were travelling in pairs or were talking on their devices. I would put good money on the fact that those using the VR glasses were not alone either. Did you observe anything else?"

"Yes, the last two times we were near the river, around Tower Bridge and the Old Royal Naval College, there was no sign of drones anywhere. Very odd, it would be typical to see a few scattered around, reporting, and sending back information," Rusty responded, as the car took a turn, and the Shard stood tall in the backdrop of the window behind Rae, who was smiling.

"Oh, well done. That was a good spot. We accessed and commandeered the drones for our search. Now, most may believe that the lack of presence would be due to them already having scanned the area. What do you think?" Rae replied.

"I think we found what we were looking for. Ever since those drones disappeared, your walking became a little more hurried, I almost heard a footstep at one point," Rusty responded.

"Even better observation than I thought, Mr Styles," Rae said, "I do think there is hope for you after all. I would like to get back to Alexander as soon as possible, it is very unlikely that our perp has left anything else for us, but we must prioritise this." The car drove on. It also hasn't slipped Rusty's attention that Rae wanted to be back in the L.O.O.P as it got dark and that they were not taking any detours. The scenic route that he was used to was not being traversed on the speed back to the office. *He really thinks someone is slipping out at night to murder people*, Rusty thought.

"There has been a time delay in the murders," Rusty said, trying to assuage his own fears and give himself some time to work all this through in his mind, "so we are not racing against the clock."

Rae looked him in the eye, and Rusty wished that he would just continue his constant roving. When he was looking at him, Rusty felt that he may be getting a taste of what it was like for a mouse when they were spotted by an owl.

"If I am right, and I do think I am, the murderer is now in his home ground. He will have the home-field advantage, and for him, that means renewed confidence, and potentially less of a cooling-off period. The last cooling-off period was a month. We may see less. He may be stalking his next victim as we speak," Rae replied.

As the driverless car pulled into Hyde Park Corner, Rae was out of the car, and they were both down the elevator as quickly as their legs would allow. The car journey wasn't long, but Rusty's leg muscles were aching for a break at every step. In his mind he satisfied them with thoughts of the rest that was down in the L.O.O.P, a trick he used on endurance runs as a youth.

Once down in the main control room, Rusty looked around, as if he expected to see the body of Natasha Anderson lying by one of the monitors. Rae walked towards Rusty's office and entered without hesitation, which, although it annoyed Rusty, also made his legs happy.

There better not be a dead body in my office, he thought, as he walked in and looked around the room.

Rae was already sitting down and taking out some cases from his inside jacket pocket. He lifted out a pair of VR glasses and a small set of earbuds no larger than the tip of Rusty's index finger. The earbuds were black, and the letter A was on the flat side of them. Rae didn't speak as he put the glasses and earbuds on, motioning to Rusty to follow his lead, as he sat down, which he did with trepidation.

Rusty has not been "in" LIFEline for a very, very long time, but Rae was already starting to talk to whoever they were meeting, so he didn't have time to think about it as he dove into the system.

He was in what looked like a hospital room and on a table in the centre of the room were the remains of Natasha Anderson. When he was blown up, Rusty didn't lose consciousness straight away, but went into a type of catatonic shock. In that state, he looked down at his leg, which was further away from his body than anatomically possible. He found it, in his state, comical. Until the weeks and months of nightmares started.

As he looked down at the body of Natasha, there was that same anatomical impossibility about it. The killer chopped the body into pieces. The edges were not, as he had seen with his own body, frayed and jagged in a mess of skin, but clean and straight, as if cut by a butcher. *No, not a butcher,* Rusty thought, *like a surgeon.* The head was cut away from the torso halfway up the neck, the torso was cut just above the hips, with the arms removed from it, and the legs from the hips. Both sets of limbs were cut in two at the elbow and knee joints, respectively. They were placed in a way that made Natasha look taller.

"The duffle bag kept the majority of the river wildlife away, and the plastic coverings around each limb kept the body in better condition than we would have hoped otherwise," a tall man with pitch black hair said from the side of the room.

The body and the memories occupied Rusty, but now he noticed the man that must be…

"Alexander Cho, but everyone calls me Xander," the man said as if reading his mind, steeping forward with an outstretched hand.

"Russell Styles," Rusty said, shaking the proffered hand.

"As I was saying," Xander continued, "the body is in good condition. Modus Operandi fits here, too. Clean cuts and very little bruising on the body, except for the first attack. No sign that there was any post-mortem violation of the victims. It almost seems like he is reverential in his treatment of the body. Are you sure it is not a sign of remorse, Euan?"

Rusty felt it was a strange thing to call a body that was chopped into pieces in "good condition".

"No, I don't think we are dealing with a remorseful perp here. He is doing his best to make it impossible to track him down. The staging of the murder, obvious to the trained professional, enough to throw off local officials, taking this much time to dispose of the body, it is not quick or clean work to do this, but he takes the time. This is part of his compulsion. He stays in control, meticulously to the very last moment, as he gets rid of the body," Rae responded.

"Where was the body found?" Rusty asked Xander.

"At Westminster Bridge," he replied promptly. "We checked the surveillance and user cameras that were in that area at the proximate time; we spotted our perp walking to the side of the bridge. His face still scrambled, but he took his time, dropped in the bag, then walked straight across the bridge, and went underground at Waterloo."

"Waterloo!" Rusty exclaimed.

"A coincidence," Rae said.

Rusty looked at him incredulously, "You have fewer arrows pointing to my team. How do you know this is a coincidence?"

"Mr Styles, please keep your voice down," Xander said, "members of your team can overhear some of this conversation. It is a bit muffled, but still. If our perp is on that floor right now, we need to be vigilant."

Rusty glowered at Xander, but Rae replied, "Well, maybe not a coincidence, but a false set of breadcrumbs. Our perp wants us to go down that particular rabbit hole. That will go in our favour after today if they have been watching us. They will think we went down to chase their lead and not our own."

"Any update on the car?" Rusty asked.

Xander looked confusedly at Rae, who just grinned sheepishly, "I didn't tell him. We have had a lot to catch up on."

"The vehicle was exactly where he left it, at Horse Guards Parade, in the tunnel, in a blind spot. He used an old sentry door to enter the building and seems to have disappeared, but all the searching through the old London archives shows that there are many underground passages leading from that location to the river, the Palace, and other locations. It was of strategic importance during revolutions, wars, and for the odd Royal love affair," Xander updated Rusty.

The information was all adding up, Rusty tried to keep calm as he asked, "Anything in the vehicle?"

"Clean," Xander replied.

"Everything," Rusty said, keeping his voice, and, he hoped, the anger he felt in each word, down, "fits this being a member of The Dead. No technology used, intimate knowledge of the underground system, and travelling all over the country unchecked. My team are not exactly spending their spare time cave diving in the London Underground!"

"Agreed, Mr Styles," Rae responded, still examining the body of Natasha, seemingly unperturbed by Rusty's line of questioning, "our murderer knows exactly how to point the investigation towards an unsuspecting community of The Dead. I think one of the questions we need to ask is: why?"

"Does the answer 'because he is one of them' seem too easy?" Rusty replied feeling the anger raise its head. He didn't know if the anger was solely because his team was being accused, or because the man doing the accusing hasn't looked at him in the last five minutes and was doggedly refusing to see other scenarios.

"Exactly, Mr Styles. Our perp so far has not missed a step. As he stalks, we can't see who he is. He uses vehicles we have been unable to track because they are old, and even when we find one unburnt it is untraceable, no DNA, no hint at all. He knows our blind spots, he kills quickly, but takes his time with his method, because he knows how much time he has. He disposes of the body knowing he is safe out in the open. A very high risk, unless you know that you are not at risk, because you know the system inside and out," Rae put an emphasis on the word inside as he moved around the body of Natasha, his face showing some signs of sympathy to his victim as he spoke.

"You think he did all this planning and thinking, preparation, and then just walked straight home? Leading us to his front door? Use some of those observation skills from today, Mr Styles. What are they telling you now?"

Xander was just standing in the background as Rusty continued to think.

"Anything different at all with Natasha?" Rae asked Xander, changing the subject.

"Besides less decomposition because of the time, no. It seems a single wound to knock unconscious, then strangulation," Xander replied, but his words were fading out to Rusty who was thinking of his team. They were a room away, although, as he was in this VR world, they seemed further.

Could one of the team be responsible for this? he thought as he looked at the hewn body of Natasha Anderson.

◆ ◆ ◆

He sat in the van as the darkening London streets started to quieten. The curfew that LIFEline imposed was keeping the majority of people off the streets, but not all. LIFEline had a softer approach to these types of restrictions, even when there was a predator on their streets. He watched as his prey walked around the corner right in front of the old theatre at Tottenham Court Road.

At this point, he would usually start to feel the build-up as he watched, but nothing happened at first glance. *Maybe you shouldn't have changed your plan,* he thought. *Or maybe it is because it is your first time with a man.*

Derek looked around through his glasses. If shyness was ever personified, Derek would have a running shot of being it. As he looked around the dark street, he kept dipping his head like someone expecting a solar eclipse. He watched as Derek pulled out his device, checked the time, and put it back in his pocket. He was still early – early for a date that shouldn't be happening. Naughty Derek!

He thought he would have to coax one of his prospective dates out, but shy, meek Derek just couldn't wait for next weekend's disco or whatever event the LIFEline team alluded to. Derek spotted the street piano on the path and smiled, his baggy dark clothes hung and bounced in unison with his hair as he made his way to it. He sat down at the little bench as his stalker moved the van slowly up the road, closer to the piano, parking as close as he could.

Hoping he looked just look like a lost manual worker he jumped out of the van near the piano and looked around. Derek looked up. Their eyes met for the briefest of moments and both were met with disappointment.

Derek thought it was Andreas, they said they would meet by the piano. Andreas didn't know yet, but Derek wrote a song for him. He arrived early to try to get some practice in. He ignored the other man, who was now looking around as if lost and started to press the keys, moving around the piano with a fluidity that always surprised him. His fingers deftly manoeuvred this way and that, as he found each note and chord, his confidence building as the music echoed around him. He started to hum the song before adding the words.

What is going on? he wondered as he looked around. The street was pretty bare, some stragglers were walking, heads down and fast-paced.

Usually at this time he would feel the excitement. He would know that he was going to be able to satisfy his need, but as he looked down at Derek, when he expected to feel that rush of adrenaline nothing happened. The music that started, slow and light at first was building. The melody carried around the little crossroads area, and then Derek's voice joined in and interlaced with the keys.

"It was cold, but you were not far behind,
The light was strong but you,
You said that you would never mind,
Mind if I tell you the truth or told you
The lies that they all fell in love with
The love lies that fell into your eyes
Lies, that with love do benefit"

Derek's shy demeanour evaporated as he played the piano. As his voice danced from note to note on his final song, he listened. Derek's voice was beautiful and what a swan song to have. It was like Derek was singing just for him. As the London night closed in, he removed the small metal pipe from his pocket and flicked it out. The song was beautiful, the audience was indifferent.

"Your eyes that hide the truth

Your eyes that light the fire in my soul
That bares the sweetest of fruit,
The fruit that helps us control
Your eyes are the truth,
But your eyes hide the truth
The truth is that true love lies
True, love lies,"

Derek's fingers missed the keys, but his blood did not. A sprinkling of red hit the white and black keys as his eyes unfocused and everything went black. The song's last notes echoed down the long street as he pulled Derek into the back of the van that was ready for his night's work. He managed to set the van up quickly earlier that night. The whole time wondering if he was going to make a mistake. He was rushing, he didn't like that. The chances of making a mistake were so much higher when people acted rashly, he has seen that himself. As he lay Derek's body down and flicked on the torch, he felt the old familiar feeling.

There you are! he thought, trying to chase it, but afraid it may depart like a startled deer.

As he stood beside Derek outside, he felt nothing as his song echoed around the high buildings. He hit him harder than any of his other partners because of the lack of connection. Now, in the safety of the van, he could see that he cracked his skull from the caved-in section on his head.

So, I can get this feeling with men, but not from stalking them. That is interesting, he thought to himself. *Best stick to the ladies going forward, but this will go some way to mess up their investigation.*

He removed the LIFEline devices and stored them in the glove compartment of the van while he worked. He wrapped parts of the body carefully so that he would be able to cut without too much mess. He pulled an apron, head torch and visor from his bag, admiring them like old friends. He went to the bag and removed his bone saw from its case. It shone in the torchlight heroically, like Excalibur. It was so sharp it melted through Derek's flesh as he pressed it on the neck, removing the head first. He felt the release of tension in his own body, like knotted muscles being massaged. A total release, like he managed to remove his own concerns and worries with the release of the head.

He went from top to bottom, ridding his body of tension, feeling release that he imagined was only possible while washing away sins. When he was done he felt like a renewed man and Derek was now totally unplugged from this world. He placed him carefully in the prepared duffel bag. Just like the women, Derek would be known as one of his victims. Derek would hold a special place for him. He taught him something after all. Not all victims are created equally.

He cleared up the inside of the van, put everything back into his kill bag, and placed it on his back. He removed the duffle bag and placed it beside the piano, before going back to the van to tidy up. When he did a full wipe-down, he pulled out the pig's blood and sprayed it all over the inside. He retrieved the LIFEline devices from the glove compartment. He placed Derek's VR glasses, wrist strap, and mobile devices in the centre of the mess, feeling a sereneness wash over him as he closed the door. He picked up the duffle bag and threw it over his shoulder, where, as usual, its strap lay comfortably over the strap of his kill bag. The weight felt comforting as he walked away from the van.

I have enough time to drop Derek off at his new place before my next move, he thought.

Chapter Eight

I
t was late. He didn't need windows to know that it was past midnight. He also didn't need the slight cough that Euan Rae made to tell him he wasn't alone in his room.

"Mr Styles?" the gruff Scottish voice called.

In the darkness, with no clues to the dimensions, that gruff Scottish voice could have belonged to a giant with a penchant for snapping backs over his knee.

"Hmmph," Rusty responded into the darkness, his brain still fogged with sleep making finding words impossible.

"We have a caller, Mr Styles," Rae said.

"What do you mean?" Rusty asked, swinging up in the bed, gesturing to the light to turn on, which it did obediently.

"Our perp has decided to make contact," Rae responded. Rusty grabbed his leg, shoved it on in a rush, and started to look for yesterday's clothes, which seemed to have gone to the wash.

Rae watched him become agitated and interjected, "There is no rush. We do not want to be running after this man. The longer he mus wait the less power he will have. As time ticks by I am sure he is becoming more and more incensed. We can use that to our advantage."

"What are you talking about? We can get his location!" Rusty responded, throwing on a fresh pair of trousers and a t-shirt.

"He is not that incompetent, Mr Styles. If he wanted us to know his location it should be the last place we go. No, I think our perp is getting anxious about how close we are getting and is trying to find out exactly what we know. He must know we have connected the dots on the cars and the Dead," Rae responded shuffling around, his eyes roving the untidy room.

"Or he was down in the Underground when we were there. Some of those Dead did not look pleased to see us talking to Gideon, did they?" Rusty asked, walking to the door.

Rae followed, frowning slightly, "There are a hundred reasons why the Dead would be unhappy to see strangers going Underground. Also, if they were a member of the Dead, they would already know what we were told. I don't think Gideon would hide our questions from the other members of the Dead."

"You are adamant it is one of my team," Rusty said, with exhaustion that had nothing to do with the lateness of the hour, "What do you know that you haven't told me?!"

As they entered the L.O.O.P's main room Rae just said, "It is not what I know, but what I can prove that is important," but refused to elaborate as the room around them was not empty.

It was late, "2 AM" according to the monitors around him, but this room was never empty.

"What are you doing up, Ciri? You can't burn the candle at both ends, I need you running this place not holding it on your shoulders!" Rusty reprimanded.

"Rusty, I was asleep. They woke me when the message came in and I tried to verify it, but it is impossible. It is bouncing all over the place, but it keeps repeating the same message over and over," Ciri responded, pointing at a screen in front of her. "I pulled it onto this device and off the wider system, but I think if they wanted to, they could open it public again. This person has some serious skills."

The message was simple, but rung out like a bell, a bell waiting to be answered:

GOD IS DEAD. GOD REMAINS DEAD. AND I HAVE KILLED HIM
ANDREAS

"He is going for the shock and awe approach, Mr Styles. I am neither shocked nor full of awe. He is dangling a thread, if we pull it correctly, subtly enough, who knows where it will lead?" Rae said.

"That sounds familiar. "God is dead"? Ciri, did we run a check on the terminology?" Rusty asked.

"No need," responded Ciri, "a popular philosophical statement, although altered, from German philosopher Nietzsche."

Rae glanced momentarily at Ciri with a look of admiration, before his attention moved back to the screen.

"What should we respond?" Rusty asked, watching the newest message come in. The message seemed to be coming in every ten minutes, pinging in, incessantly, trying to gain the attention of the team.

"Oh, nothing here. Miss Iris, can this device be moved?" Rae asked.

"Yes, I purposely moved it to this device so you can use as needed," Ciri responded, removing the tablet away from the dock and handing it to Rae, who shuffled towards Rusty's office. Rae turned at the door, as if reminded of his manners at the very last moment, "Thank you, Miss Iris. Can you have someone tell Evan that we require his assistance?" He entered the office without a backward glance at Rusty who didn't move.

"I will go get him. You go get some sleep. That is an order!" Rusty said, rushing to the rooms.

Rusty knocked on the door with what he felt was enough force to tell the occupant that there wouldn't be a second knock. When there was no answer he reached for the handle, opened the door, and entered the room. Evan looked groggily at the light streaming into the room. His face betraying a moment of fear before he came to his sense, "Rusty, what is it?"

"We need you in my office, Evan. As soon as possible, the perp has reached out," Rusty said.

Evan jumped up, smiling, "Excellent," he muttered, although, Rusty suspected, more to himself than to him.

"I will be right there," he said, doing the universally known one-legged dance as he pulled his trousers on.

Rusty returned to his office, Rae was still gazing at the screen, but with one difference, he had the earbuds on that they used earlier as they worked with Xander. Rusty looked questioningly at Euan, who just threw him the earbuds again, this time saying, "Keep them until we are done. Xander is an extremely useful person to have as a contact."

"You woke him too?" he said, following Rae's lead and just putting one earbud in while storing the other in his pocket.

"Well, I don't sleep much anymore, Mr Styles, so don't be too concerned," the voice of Xander responded to him.

"Call me Rusty," Rusty said, looking at Rae who was swiping, pinching, and touching the tablet in front of him as if trying to break a code.

"Ok, Rusty," Xander said, "Rae was bringing me up to speed on where we are in your absence. Seems our perp is bouncing the signal and location of this profile, one Andreas Ortega, all over the world. The last ping I have places him in Moscow, but no surveillance camera shows him there."

"You are looking at surveillance in Moscow?" Rusty asked, his head spinning just thinking how quickly Xander was able to chase these leads.

"Investigators would be pretty useless if we weren't given full jurisdiction while investigating, Mr Styl... Rusty," Xander corrected himself. "Bad news," he continued, "is that this Andreas is connected to a Derek Conway who is no longer updating his profile and seems offline. I hope not permanently, but I am less than optimistic on that front given this message and what we know so far."

"He is escalating, and a lot quicker than I thought possible," Rae responded. "His first murders were months apart, albeit getting closer with each one, but to go to two in less than a week this fast is more than I expected."

"Maybe you were right earlier," Rusty said, "Maybe those other murders were practice for London. This is the first time he would have killed two in one city. What are you two talking about?" Rusty finished, walking over to the chair, and looking over the detective's shoulder.

"Oh, nothing yet," Rae responded. He stood up and pulled a chair behind Rusty's desk so they could both see the screen. As Rusty watched the new message come in, Rae stopped flicking around the system and looked at the map of London that Rusty had on the wall of his office.

Rusty has seen people playing online games, like poker and chess. The partners didn't show much on their faces, or with their actions, and Rae was impossible to read as he said, "Okay," swiped the keyboard up and wrote a message back.

IF YOU ARE REFERRING TO THE BIBLICAL GOD, THEN I THINK YOU ARE MISTAKEN. YOU HAVE NO POWER TO KILL THE IDEALS OF GENERATIONS. IF YOU MEAN THE NEED FOR HUMANITY TO FIND MEANING IN THEIR EXISTENCE, TO FIND THEIR PURPOSE, I AM AFRAID YOU HAVE LESS POWER HERE THAN AN OLD-FASHIONED BOOK BURNER.

"Em," Rusty started, "what are you doing?"

"The common thread we have seen so far in our perp is his attraction to discussing big ideas. He seems to crave conversations about that which we do not know. He is drawn toward the unknown. This man of meticulous planning shows off his power, but he is like a moth drawn to the flame of the knowledge he cannot hope to possess. Let's see how he reacts to a bit of powerlessness while we work."

"While we work on?" Rusty asked, but Rae just nodded for silence as Evan entered the room.

Evan stopped off at the canteen and grabbed hot drinks for all. He handed Rusty a coffee, "Ah, thanks, Evan. You are a lifesaver," Rusty said, as he took the first hot sip, feeling the drink warm him and uncloud his mind.

"I assume you are still more of a tea man, Rae?" Evan said, handing him the cup.

Rae just nodded politely as Evan placed the cup on the table.

"He is responding," Rusty said, seeing the three dots that were an indicator to show someone typing.

"What is happening, Rae?" Evan asked, his voice slightly concerned. "I really don't want to be pulled in on this." Rusty could hear that tone, the same one from the meeting a few days before. It clearly said, I have seen things, but not happy to see them again!

Rae ignored him for a moment, Rusty thought he was going to just ignore him as he watched the dots pulse, but then he looked up, "Evan, you are better at the geographical profile and victimology than I. I just want to sense check some things with you, live. If our perp is indeed on the other end of these messages, we may be getting some very subtle messages."

"Geographical profile? Has he killed again?" Evan asked, looking from Rusty to Rae.

"I surmise as much," Rae responded.

AH, DETECTIVES. NICE TO MEET YOU, BUT YOU DISAPPOINT ME. THE GOD I REFER TO IS NOT IN THE PAGES OF OLD BOOKS OR THE EXISTENTIAL CRISIS OF HUMANKIND. THE GOD I HAVE KILLED IS ONLINE. IT IS YOU, AS YOU USE THE LIFEline NAME, YOU SHARE ITS FAITH.

ANDREAS

SPEAKING OF SHARING A NAME AND FAITH, SOME GOD SLAYER YOU ARE, HIDING BEHIND YOUR CLONES AND GHOSTS. IT IS YOU THAT DISAPPOINT. IF YOU HAVE NO MORE TO SAY THAN THE RAVINGS OF A MADMAN THEN WE WILL LEAVE THE CONVERSATION HERE AND TREAT YOU AS SUCH.

LIFEline

Rusty looked from Rae to Evan, concerned that Rae went too far and then Xander, making Rusty jump, just said, "This is not Rae's first time dealing with megalomaniacs, Rusty. This perp's desire for power, or to be in control, will make him respond. He cannot leave this conversation without impressing upon us that he is a superior being to us."

Rusty opened his mouth to respond, but Rae shot him a look and Xander said, "Best if we keep our conversations private for now. Evan was a great detective in his day, but he is not aware of my existence, and it seems just plain rude for us to chat in his presence."

Rusty could tell there was more to it than that. Rae's distrust of his team was obviously shared by Xander. *At least Evan is cleared,* Rusty thought, as they watched the pulsing messages come in. Evan was not paying too much attention to the screen. He looked at Rae with the look of a pupil watching a master artisan carve a sculpture from a plain block of marble.

IN A WORLD WHERE WHEN YOU DO NOT CONFORM, YOU ARE SEEN AS NOT EXISTING, THE ONLY WAY TO LEVEL THE PLAYING FIELD IS THROUGH REVOLUTION. AS THEY SEE THEIR GOD BLEED, THEY WILL CAST IT ASIDE FOR THE FALSE IDOL IT IS AND FIND THE REAL MEANING OF LIFE.
ANDREAS

AND THIS NEW MEANING? I ASSUME HAS YOU AS ITS NEW GOD.
LIFEline

AH, YOU CONTINUE TO DISAPPOINT, I AM AFRAID, DETECTIVE RAE. THERE IS NO GOD AMONG MEN, ANY MORE THAN THERE IS A GOD AMONG SHEEP. THERE IS DIVINITY IN LIFE THOUGH. IN LIVING YOUR LIFE, SEEING THE STARS, BEING IN EACH MOMENT, AND CHERISHING IT. I WILL NOT BE THEIR GOD, BUT THEIR MARTYR. A SAINT THAT BROUGHT BACK MEANING IN THE REAL, PHYSICAL WORLD.
ANDREAS

YOU ARE BRINGING MEANING TO LIFE BY ENDING IT? A LOVE FOR THE PHYSICAL WORLD BY INCITING FEAR THAT KEEPS PEOPLE INDOORS AFRAID OF THEIR NEIGHBOURS?
LIFEline

Rae looked almost bored, but Rusty's heart leapt at the mention of Rae's name in the message. As if that increase in heart rate was expected or heard, in his ear Xander just said, "A usual tactic. The perp is trying to get under his skin by showing he knows exactly who he is talking with. A rookie move, really. Rae and I expected better from a meticulous planner than this," Xander said, thoughtfully.

A REVOLUTION NEEDS A SPARK. LIFEline HAD A SPARK OF TECHNOLOGY, A SPARK OF PANDEMICS, AND DISTRUST, TO FUEL ITS ADOPTION. I HAVE SHOWN THE WORLD THAT THIS GOD CAN BLEED. I WILL CONTINUE TO SHOW THEM THAT NOT ONLY ARE

YOU A POWERLESS GOD, BUT AN INADEQUATE ONE. I HAVE ALREADY DISCONNECTED ANOTHER, THIS VERY NIGHT, IN THE HEART OF YOUR CITY. HE FELT SAFE. HE FELT PROTECTED BY HIS WATCHERS. HE WAS WRONG.
ANDREAS

A ONE-MAN REVOLUTION. ONE MAN AGAINST INSURMOUNTABLE ODDS. IN ANOTHER STORY YOU COULD HAVE BEEN THE HERO, BUT UNFORTUNATELY, YOU HAVE BEEN CAST AS LESS THAN A VILLAIN. CATCHING YOU WILL BRING ME NO MORE JOY THAN A DOCTOR CURING A TEENAGER OF ACNE. YOU ARE A BLIGHT ON SOCIETY AND I AM JUST THE ONE WHOSE JOB IT IS TO BEAT YOU. TO BRING YOU IN TO RECEIVE THE TREATMENT YOU NEED. YOU WRAP YOURSELF IN THE ILLUSION THAT THERE ARE OTHERS WHO CARE ABOUT WHAT YOU ARE DOING. THAT THEY WILL WHISPER YOUR NAME IN

SECRET. THAT THEY WILL TOAST TO YOUR MEMORY. THEY WILL NEVER EVEN KNOW YOU EXISTED.

LIFEline

Rusty felt that Rae went too far, and Evan's face was also one of incredulity. He looked as if he wanted to interject, but kept his silence. Rusty could see it straining him. After all, like Rusty, each life lost in London was their responsibility and this lunatic seemed to want to start a war.

Xander's voice came back into his ear, "Rusty, I know it is hard to believe, but Rae is in total control here. The perp has a very high opinion of himself and a self-righteous goal. He will react. Just watch."

THOSE WHO DO NOT WANT TO BE A PART OF A NEW WORLD WILL REMEMBER THE FEAR THEY FELT. THOSE WHO REALISE WHAT I AM DOING IS FOR THEM WILL JOIN ME IN UNPLUGGING THEMSELVES AND THOSE WHO HAVE ALREADY BEEN UNPLUGGED HAVE MY FACE BURNED INTO THEIR MEMORIES AS THEY MOVE ON.

ANDREAS

"Rae," Xander said, "Derek is not at home. The last ping was at Tottenham Court Road. I have reviewed the surveillance of the last ping. He was there. He was attacked and it does seem he was killed in a van and moved Underground. He didn't bother to even move the vehicle this time or stalk his victim home. Some other things do not fit his usual M.O. He didn't strangle him, but hit him viciously from behind."

WE ARE TO BELIEVE YOU UNPLUGGED SOMEONE ELSE TONIGHT? DID YOU LOOK INTO HIS EYES AS DEREK MOVED

ON?

LIFEline

Evan looked at Rusty with a look of confusion, but Rusty just gave him a reassuring nod.

AH, FINALLY SHOWING UP TO THE CONVERSATION, DETECTIVE RAE, YES, DEREK LOOKED INTO MY EYES AS HE LEFT THIS WORLD. THE VAN, WHICH I AM SURE YOU HAVE ALREADY FOUND, I LEFT FOR YOU AS A LITTLE GIFT.
ANDREAS

"Evan" Rae said, taking a break from the screen, "plot Tottenham Court Road, Palace Gate in Kensington and Westminster Bridge on that map behind you of London, and tell me what it tells you."

Rae probably, deep down, meant it as a question, but the words that travelled from that deep place to his mouth came out as a direction and Evan stirred. For a moment Rusty thought that the usually quiet, calm, but confident Evan was going to lose his temper, but the moment was gone quicker than it appeared. It was like watching someone shake off a fly that was annoying them as Evan grabbed some markers from the desk drawer and started to work on the map. As he worked, Rae moved to a different screen and typed a message. Rusty was waiting for him to press send before realising that he had written it to show him.

HE IS A SPECIALIST IN GEOGRAPHICAL PROFILING AND VICTIMOLOGY. IF HE DOES NOT SHOW US THAT THIS PERSON

MUST BE USING THE UNDERGROUND AND THAT THEY ARE
BASED CENTRALLY THEN WE HAVE A WORRY.

Rusty bustled and turned to Rae, but Xander just said, "Every single person in this building is under suspicion, Rusty. Except yourself. We have run the dates into the system to see who was not present when the murders were committed, who has the knowledge of the system to be able to work like this and is male. That list is not extensive. It is our role now to review each in turn. Evan stands out more than most, if not all, with his knowledge of London LIFEline, partnerships, and the workings of an investigation."

Rusty wanted to ask how they still suspected Evan when he was in the room with them, and the murderer was typing a message to them then he realised something. Rae was responding to the perp while watching Evan's hands work on the board. It was like he was expecting Evan to do something.

AND WHY DO WE DESERVE SUCH A GIFT?

LIFEline

The dots pulsed; the perp was responding. Rusty looked up at Evan too. If he was somehow typing and drawing his outlines on the map at the same time Rusty could not see how. Rae seemed to come to the same conclusion, although he looked less pleased than Rusty about it.

DETECTIVE, TO BE HONEST WITH YOU, THE GIFT WAS MORE
FOR ME THAN YOU. YOU SEE, I FEEL LIKE I HAVE BEEN
PLAYING A GAME OF CHESS WITH AN UNWILLING PARTNER
WHO HAS NOT HAD FAIR WARNING. NOT AS CHALLENGING.
NOW WE ARE BOTH ON THE SAME PAGE, I CAN TEST MY

KNOWLEDGE AGAINST LIFEline's BEST AND BRIGHTEST. OH, AND MR STYLES.

ANDREAS

Rusty blushed fiercely.

"Don't react, Rusty." This time Rae said it. Evan turned, surprised, but on seeing them looking at the screen went back to work as if there were no interruption. The presence of the voice in the room and not just in his ear brought him to the realisation of how weird it must be for Evan in this room. To him, besides the typing, there was no sound. Rusty had the constant update and commentary, if not guidance of Xander, as they worked.

AGAIN, YOU SPEAK AS IF YOU ARE SOME HERO AT THE GATES OF A CASTLE WHICH HOLDS A SLEEPING DRAGON. YOU WANT TO AWAKEN THE SLEEPING DRAGON. TO HAVE THE FIGHT OF EPIC PROPORTIONS. YOUR DO HAVE A FLAIR FOR THE DRAMATICS IN YOUR SELF INDULGENCE –

Rae looked up at Evan again, who was still filling the map in, back turned to them. He looked at Rusty and nodded.

Rusty walked from behind the desk to the map. Evan turned and they could both hear Rae's fingers tap the screen. The noise was muffled, but as there were no other sounds, it travelled in the room, "Teacher set you to task, too?" he said with a slight smile.

"I think he is just tired of me reading over his shoulder," Rusty responded in a whisper.

"You know I can hear you, right?" Rae said, not looking up from the screen.

"What are you"… "Rusty," it was Xander... "doing here?" Rusty asked Evan, feeling it would have been weird to stop talking as Xander interrupted.

Rusty found it hard to concentrate on both people speaking at the same time.

"Good, get close to Evan. Rae is about to send a message…"

"Well, you see," Evan said, pointing to the three areas he mapped out on the map, "there is a prevailing theory that murderers like our unicorns…"

"You know I hate that word," Rae said.

"…if Evan is somehow getting these messages, I do not think he will be able to mask his reaction. Especially given the fact that he is doing something…"

Evan ignored the interruption of Rae, "are planned in the comfort zones of those same unicorns. They either travel out of areas that they live in or work within those comfort zones."

"… it is a lot harder to mask our emotions when our focus is elsewhere. It is like getting caught blindsided," Xander finished.

Tell me about it, Rusty thought, as the conversations all overlapped. "That is what this is," Rusty said, pointing at the different colour circles.

"Yes, you see these three green circles are Kensington, Tottenham Court, and Westminster Bridge, the ones Rae wants…"

"Rae has just pressed send, see if you notice any differences at all. The clenching of a jaw, widening eyes, making a fist, anything that would make you think he is unduly annoyed," Xander interrupted.

"..as you can see, they are close to each other, so there is a lot of overlap. The three red circles are extended out further. This would be to see where the unicorn could live. He may travel in to commit the crimes. Remember, he was driving a car that disappeared in the last crime."

"No longer the last crime and no longer lost. We have the vehicle," Rae said, standing and moving to the map, leaving the tablet on the desk, face down.

Evan turned, "So he has killed again?"

"It would seem so. We have footage of Tottenham Court Road…" "He showed no signs of annoyance or anger. Rusty did a good job of keeping him distracted," Xander said. Rusty felt annoyed at the use of the word "distracted". He did not suspected Evan and was just curious about what he was doing.

"…but he went straight back underground. I have a few things to ask you, Evan. I just want to get your help one last time, then you no longer need concern yourself over these crimes."

"Thanks, Rae. I got out of this business for a reason. I have seen enough monsters to last a lifetime. Trust me, it is better bringing people together than it is shackling them," Evan responded, looking up at his handiwork on the map, "Although, this did bring back some good memories. Plotting out a map and closing in on a unicorn that had no clue they were about to be caught. Some very good times, old friend."

"Yes, indeed," Rae responded, reaching up to touch the spots on the map, "Kensington," he tapped the map, "our first crime scene in London. Westminster Bridge," again he tapped the map, "our first dump site. Tottenham Court Road," the last tap, "our second crime scene, being closed down by the A.T.U as we speak. What do you think?"

"I think we are looking for someone central. Someone who has been using the Underground to get around. I have been thinking about it, having nightmares is probably a more adequate description, since assisting Rusty at the first scene. The way he disappeared, the way he seems to be aware of the technology we are using. He isn't only central. I think he may be in this very building," Evan said, looking at Rusty with sadness etched on every line of his face.

Rusty couldn't believe his ears. Even Evan seemed to think someone in the team was capable of this.

"Whoever it is though," Evan continued, "is adept at hiding it. I have no idea who would be in a position to want to do this and say what they were saying on that tablet."

"What if I told you that I was doubting it was a man?" Rae said, still scanning the map. His face showing nothing, Rusty was reminded again of those that played online poker. Pushing the stakes, and the chips, with no show of emotion.

"All the victims have been female so it points towards a male, but I would agree, from the footage we have seen so far, even with how physical the attacks are, that I would not rule a female out. A lot of the London demographic have taken physically demanding combat training and come out the other end," Evan responded.

"It is not just that. Our latest victim was a man," Rae said, looking sidelong at Evan.

Evan looked confused, but then said, "I don't want to get pulled into this any deeper than needed to help here, but I wouldn't let that change your mind on the gender. Remember there are a lot of unicorns in the past where their victims were just victims of circumstance or opportunity. They may not even play a role in the choosing of the victim."

"Thanks for the help, Evan. I will have a review of the map, but your thoughts on the subject are extremely helpful and confirm some of my suspicions," Rae finished, looking dejected.

Evan walked to the door, hesitated, looked back at Rae, went to speak, thought better of it, and opened the door. He left and the door almost closed;

then, as if he steeled himself on the other side, he stepped back in and closed the door behind him.

"Did you think I had something to do with this?" Evan asked, looking from Rae to Rusty.

"No, of course…" Rusty began.

"Yes," Rae responded, looking up at Evan with no hint of apology. For a moment Evan seemed flustered, "So all of this was like some sick test for you to prove that I was the unicorn?"

"You do know how much I dislike that word," Rae said, looking annoyed, which given the accusations against him from a colleague Rusty thought was pretty brazen.

"Oh, sorry I hurt your feelings using the word. It is just the part where you think I am a homicidal maniac that is becoming a sticking point for me!" Evan responded.

"It is not my feelings. It is the inaccur…" Rae started, but was interrupted by Xander.

"He is being sarcastic," Xander said, sounding resigned.

Evan turned to leave, turned again and asked, "I assume I have pleased your lordship!"

Rae perked up a little, "For now, yes."

Evan left the room, closing the door a little harder than he had when he entered. Rusty looked down on the table. The dregs of his cold coffee and Rae's teacup were still sitting there.

There is just no way a *man that brings you a cup of coffee at 2 AM is a bad guy,* he thought.

Chapter Nine

Rachel was sitting at her regular table in the café, hours later than she would usually be on a Saturday, and she was also missing her book. She felt like she was leaving the apartment without an essential item, like a friend, or those dreams where you leave the house only to find that you do not have your clothes on. At least for her, it was a conscious decision. She felt that it would only get in the way of the conversation with Oliver.

Oliver was navigating his way around tables, cleaning up after the lunchtime customers, who seemed much fewer than the Saturday breakfast crowd. When he spotted her sitting at the table, he looked slightly taken aback before moving over to her.

"Hey, sorry, didn't see you come in. The usual?" he asked. Oliver's voice had a forced calmness and a slight cheeriness that she was not used to hearing, and she knew, *he is still thinking about our argument yesterday.*

"Yes, please," she responded, in what she hoped was her normal tone, but felt herself questioning even that.

As Oliver went for the coffee, she steeled herself. He brought back a cup and a small selection of biscuits and went back to the till before she could say anything. Her gaze travelled around the room that had only two other customers, who were now paying up with Oliver.

"A lot quieter on a Sunday. Is that normal?" Rachel asked, as Oliver walked back over with a cloth in hand.

"Oh yeah, much quieter on a Sunday. I think that Mrs and Mr Horner don't like the idea of the place being open without them, too. We have never even tried to increase business on Sundays. I open for the regulars and close around midday. How come you popped in?" he finished, looking at the clock on the far wall, moving away slowly to a table close by to clean. His voice still had the peculiar tone and Rachel had the distinct impression that he was trying to stay away from the topic of yesterday.

"I just wanted to talk to you," Rachel said, taking a breath before trying to continue, but Oliver interrupted before she managed to get a word in.

"Listen, I am sorry about yesterday," he started, making her feel worse, "I was just concerned."

She felt a rush of gratitude, which was followed quickly, and unapologetically, by a feeling of annoyance. *He was not supposed to apologise for her outburst.*

"No apology needed," she responded, "if friends can't have an open conversation on important topics they disagree on, then they are not going to be friends long." She smiled as she finished, hoping that he knew it was mostly a joke comment and not meant to say they shouldn't be friends.

He returned the smile, but Rachel noticed he didn't exactly look pleased. She knew that they would need to address whatever problem arose from yesterday, but she felt a wave of impatience wash over her. She was tapping her leg under the table, which had nothing to do with the amount of caffeine in her system.

The impatience swelled again and this time she executed a deft move, like a veteran surfer gliding along the wave, "If you finish soon I would love to talk to you about the current," she couldn't find it in herself to say murders so lamely aimed lower and landed on "crimes?"

Oliver looked up at her from his work and, as an avid reader, she could only describe his brow as furrowed.

"What do you think I know?" he asked, the hint of defensiveness apparent in his tone.

"I think you know more than I do, Ollie. I was doing some research last night and there is not a lot I could find out," she finished.

"Of course not. LIFEline aren't just going to broadcast these murders. Why are you researching them though?" he asked.

She practiced a response to this already in her mind. Some people liked to practice responses in mirrors, Rachel preferred to practice in her mind. It stopped her from having to look at herself, which she found off-putting. Her approach meant she could think about what the other person's reactions would be, whereas she already knew what she looked like. "I want to know as much as I can so I can make sure I am staying safe. If LIFEline are deciding what the majority of people need to know that is fine, for them, but I am deciding I want to know more."

Oliver looked slightly impressed, but then responded, "I still don't know what you think I would know."

"I have a feeling you can get more information than I can, or at least your people will know the answers, or where I can find them," she responded, taking another sip of her hot coffee, hoping he would want to help her.

"My *people*?" he responded, and she was happy to hear his sarcastic voice return as he rolled his eyes at her.

"You know exactly what I mean, so don't pretend to be offended. We had enough of that yesterday," she finished. She felt it may be too soon to mock yesterday's altercation, but found that path an easier one to traverse than the one involving multiple apologies and inner reflection. Right now, Rachel's energy was being channelled towards getting as much information on real-life problems.

He looked at the clock again and responded, "Give me ten minutes to close up and I will meet you outside." He did not seem annoyed at her bringing up yesterday, and she was almost positive she saw a ghost of a smile play around his lips as she joked about it. He deposited her coffee into a takeaway cup, and she picked up her bag and left, feeling both rushed and satisfied. Oliver obviously didn't want to linger over yesterday's issues either.

As Oliver closed up the café, Rachel realised that she never spent time with him outside of work. There were a few things that, ultimately, jumped to her attention; non-apron-wearing Oliver wore a brown leather jacket, he looked very handsome in the normal light of day, and, most obviously, he had no technology. Rachel had just liked and shared a couple of posts on LIFEline, and was about to don her VR headset, when she realised, while looking at Oliver approach her, that this would not be a polite thing to do.

She stowed the VR glasses in her bag, slung it over her back, and started to walk, unaware of where she was going. Oliver started to take side roads, talking to her about LIFEline the entire time. She felt the absence of her devices more vividly than she thought she would. Her fingers even moved, unconsciously, towards her equipment from time to time, and she had to exert a conscious effort to stop herself. Oliver's voice was washing over her as they walked.

"Many people don't realise that when you are above ground like this there are hundreds of cameras tracking you," he pointed to a couple that were on the top of buildings, passing drones, signs and lamp posts.

"Most are used for VR and AR to triangulate people's whereabouts and help with the rendering of the different worlds people can walk through," Rachel responded, automatically.

Oliver just looked at her curiously.

"My dad works in that department. Infrastructure. You would be surprised by the technology and thought that has to go into buildings," she said. "I will invite you to dinner one day and he will no doubt bore you to tears about projectors and signal masts."

"Well, that is not all they are doing, trust me," Ollie said, looking left and right as they came out of a side road, and he started to cross towards a large, red-bricked building.

As Rachel looked around, she could not help noticing that the people they were passing with their VR headsets did not seem to notice the cameras or, and she knew this because she was usually one of these people, the number of strange-shaped graffiti on the walls.

Following Oliver, she asked, "Are there usually this many graffiti on the walls?"

Oliver looked in the same direction and just let out a small laugh, "That is not graffiti, they are markings, like a secret language. So, for example," he said, leading her over to the red brick wall and pointing at one that was shaped like a circle with arrows all along its exterior, "this one means transport available. This one," he moved to one that was just a lot of wavy lines rising up, "means hot meals are available. Your VR will cover up anything it deems unpleasant, even if you have them on to walk in just the," he used air quotes, "'real' world."

Rachel took a step back and looked across the walls, "Isn't this Paddington Station though?" She remembered it from one of the VR tours she did of London. It was once a bustling station for the metropolis. People from all over the country coming and going through its magnificent structure.

"Paddington Station to you," Oliver responded, "I just call it home." Oliver walked through a large archway that opened up into a large concourse. Rachel was surprised that more people weren't looking in, but the area was quite abandoned looking. Oliver noticed her looking back over her shoulder and just said, "If you want to know what we know you can only find out down here. No member of the Dead will speak to you up here with all these watching." At that moment the fluttering sound of passing drones distracted her as she looked up. It seemed to be going around the building, as if determined to not engage the area.

If she expected Oliver to give her a moment to adjust, to work up the courage for the moment of crossing that invisible threshold, she was sorely mistaken. Like the leader of an expedition in a grand fairy-tale, Oliver continued to walk into the building. Rachel was disappointed that he wasn't swallowed by any darkness, she felt that would be more fitting for dramatic purposes, but the midday sun, and the fact that the roof of the building seemed to be open, stopped any dramatics in their tracks.

Rachel followed him in. In the concourse, there was just a smattering of people talking and doing what looked like household chores. There was a woman following a toddler around, the toddler was making full use of all the space, running in and out of the shafts of light that poured down from above, while jumping from tile to tile. Some of the strangers greeted Oliver with a nod and a slight frown towards Rachel, but he just nodded back and said nothing. He led her to a side set of stairs and looked down at her feet.

"Good choice of footwear," he said, as he made his way down the stairs. She favoured a pair of black trainers that morning as she thought they would probably be walking a good deal. They went down into the bowels of the station, taking stairs and corridors, and even jumping onto the tracks at certain points to pass families. The Dead were not at all what she expected.

Ever since she was a young girl she heard of the mysterious Dead. The people that lived outside of LIFEline. She imagined them to be living in some state of squalor. Reduced to the edges of a civilisation they did not agree with, but what she found was just people.

Side rooms where people were cooking and sharing food. Families out on platforms swapping stories with laughter coming easy and what looked like a lot of games being played with younger children. At one point, she was even sure they passed a classroom. There was food stocked in places with a lookout handing parcels out. As they passed this area, Rachel heard the lookout say to a child that was eyeing what looked like a store of chocolate biscuits, "Now, Lee, your Mother picked up enough biscuits to keep you happy for a month just two days ago!"

Oliver seemed to be a popular member of the Dead; many members called greetings as he passed their rooms, some even calling after him, but he just kept walking, smiling politely, and nodding at others.

"Mr Popular. I didn't know that you were Royalty," Rachel mocked, as a group of young teenage girls called after them.

Oliver blushed slightly, but responded, "The Dead don't have Royalty. We are not big on being told what to do by anyone."

"Then why are you blushing, your highness," Rachel asked, "or would it be your lowness down here?"

"If you must know, my parents used to be, like, unofficial leaders of London when I was growing up," Oliver called over his shoulder, as they continued to walk down.

"Used to be?" Rachel asked.

"Yup," Oliver said, and the tone was enough to stop her mocking, but her curiosity stored it in the use for fun later pile, ideally when not in a deep dark place.

Oliver stopped and she bumped into him.

"Sorry," she responded, rubbing her nose, which bounced off the back of his shoulder blade.

They were in an Underground tunnel, and ahead of them was an old Tube train. The doors and windows she could see were full of dancing light.

"Listen," Oliver started, seriously, "do not, for any reason whatsoever, no matter what happens, use any of your devices in here. Keep your wrist strap hidden under your sleeve, that device in your pocket stands out a mile in those jeans, so throw it in your bag. It shouldn't have any signal down here, but still. Mistrust is inherited down here."

"What? Why?" Rachel asked, stubbornly, while she still did as requested.

"Well, Lewis hates technology," Oliver jumped up to the tube, "more than even most down here." He opened the door and reached back to help Rachel. Rachel did not take the offered hand.

"Sorry, your lowness, but this damsel can open doors for herself," she mocked, as Oliver rolled his eyes and entered the carriage. At first, Rachel thought they entered a ransacked room, but then her eyes adjusted to the light, and she realised that they seemed to be in some sort of aviary, although she did wonder if it was called an aviary when the only birds present were pigeons.

"Lewis." Oliver's voice carried down the carriage and the pigeons looked at him curiously, before going back to staring into the abyss with a look reserved for the dim-witted. The door at the back of the carriage opened and a voice, which must have been Lewis', called back, "Down here."

When you hear a voice you get an image of a person, and the voice of Lewis should be arrested for slander. The voice should have belonged to a muscle-bound action star, the actual owner of the voice was overweight, with wavy blonde hair that fell over a bespectacled face in curtains, as if to hide the mass. Lewis was in a much cleaner room, with one pigeon in his hand, taking a piece of paper from the leg of the held pigeon. Every surface, including the shelves on the walls, was filled with books that looked like they had been compiled by someone who only had a vague idea of how books were supposed to look.

"Who is she?" he asked, eyeing Rachel over Oliver's shoulder.

"A friend," Oliver said simply, before continuing, "we need information, Lewis."

"It is the only reason to come to me," Lewis said, with a look of pride.

"It is about the current murders happening across the country," Oliver said.

Lewis looked up.

"Have you heard about the latest attack?" Then he shook his head and continued, "Of course you haven't, I only found out myself this morning." Rachel noticed he was sitting in a chair that had wheels, like an old-fashioned office chair. He spun in it and pushed himself, gliding along the cluttered carriage with more grace than she thought possible for a man of his size. He pulled up a book that he was obviously still working on.

"What do you want to know?" he asked.

Oliver looked at Rachel, signifying that she could go ahead and ask her questions.

"Well, everything?" she responded.

Lewis looked at her impressed, then the look changed to one slightly darker, "I don't think you realise what you are asking."

"Oh, I do," Rachel responded, stubbornly. "I imagine there is some vicious things in that file. For example, it would be very rare for a man to attack that many women without a sexual motive, so I imagine there has been some rape, maybe even post-mortem."

Lewis looked at her shocked, "Your imagination seems to be darker than this! So, I guess I will start there, they weren't sexually assaulted, pre or post-mortem, as far as any of the medical experts know."

"How were they killed?" Rachel asked, she instinctually went to take out her device from her bag, but caught herself even before Oliver gave her the look that could kill. She took out a notebook and pen, "Can I take notes?"

"Of course," Lewis said happily, "the pursuit of knowledge is the noblest of pursuits."

"So," Rachel repeated, "how were they killed?"

"Strangulation, mostly. Although it seems the latest was bludgeoned to death, there has been no examination of the body yet. That bludgeoning could have been an overzealous attempt to incapacitate before strangulation," Lewis responded. Rachel paused to see if Lewis would continue; when he didn't, she prompted.

"Anything else about the murders, the scene, for example, that seems to stand out?" Rachel asked.

"This latest one stands out the most," Lewis said, "if we weren't already certain it was the same person, we could be forgiven for thinking there are two murderers on the loose."

"Why is that?" Rachel asked.

"Well, besides changing from the nomad pattern we have seen up until this point, the latest victim was killed outside. Well mostly outside. On all other crime scenes," and at this Lewis flipped back a couple of pages, then some more, "our victims were killed at home. They were stalked home, then attacked in a place that they felt safe, almost like a message to LIFEline."

"He is escalating," Rachel muttered, more to herself than anyone else.

"What is that?" Oliver asked.

Rachel looked at Oliver, who sat down on what looked like a box of books, "Escalating? When a suspect starts to increase the number of crimes and break away from their regular patterns. They tend to unravel, become more unstable and unpredictable before the end."

"More unstable and unpredictable than being a murderer?" Oliver asked, raising his eyebrows, but Rachel just ignored him.

Lewis interrupted, "It is what I thought at first. That the murderer was becoming sloppy, that maybe our most recent victim was in the wrong place at the wrong time, rather than the meticulous planning I have seen so far on this case, but then the more information that is coming in, the more I am sure that is not the case at all. It seems, similar to the last victims, the murderer was talking to them as their prospective partner."

Oliver's shock was written all over his face, as he said, "They are talking to this guy for a year before he kills them?"

"Yes, and the worse thing is that it seems impossible for LIFEline to track who he is. He is using what are called ghost and clone profiles," at the questioning look on Rachel's face, Lewis continued, "Ghost profiles are those of people who have died and been reactivated. Clone profiles are indistinguishable from the real thing. You could be talking to a clone, and everything would look absolutely fine. All activity and links would go to the normal profile and you, as the person being scammed, would see the activity they wanted you to. It was members of the Dead that, unfortunately, created these techniques. Another reason to stay away from technology! It brings out even the worst in us!"

Rachel felt scared for a moment, thinking of Jake, and even some of her students. Any of them could be a ghost or a clone. She always thought Oliver and the Dead were full of crazy theories but, while she was in this enclosed space far underneath the ground, she could not help but feel apart from the world above. She reminded herself why she was here.

"You called him he. Have they narrowed it down to a man?" Rachel asked, thinking that she thought that same thing, based on the victimology, but now that a man was killed, it made her question her assumptions.

"Yes, they are pretty sure that it is a white male. The planned and meticulous nature of the murders has the lead investigators thinking that it's a man in his early thirties to mid-forties. More than likely someone in a well-paying and respected role," Lewis replied.

"Where did you get all this information?" Rachel couldn't help but ask.

For the first time Lewis did not look comfortable answering her question and then Oliver said, from his perch on the box of books, "Listen Rachel, Lewis has his ways of getting information from around the city and beyond. Old ways that humans have known for a very long time, predating LIFEline, and we are happy to share as much information as you need to know to be on alert, but that is one piece of information you will never know unless you want to quit the system."

Oliver stopped abruptly. There was a moment of silence. Then the swift noise of creaking as a heavy man stood up on an ancient floor, relieving his chair for a moment.

Rachel noticed that Lewis was also a lot taller than she would have guessed from his seated position. His face that looked slightly concerned a moment ago, was now contorted in what could only be described as fury as he towered over them.

"You brought one of them here!" Lewis bellowed.

In the opposite carriage Rachel could hear the pigeons shuffling around and, no doubt, some taking flight, from the sound of wings that reached her, as she took a step backwards. If there was anything to fear, Oliver did not show it on his face. He stopped dead in his tracks while speaking, but did not stand up when Lewis did. He was looking up at the larger man, unabashed, and just said, "Lewis, she is a friend. I want to help her. What happened to the pursuit of information?"

Lewis was still glowering, "Little Miss Information will no doubt share all this information, changing it to match her theories, as if the truth can be moved around to suit her whims!"

"I won't!" Rachel exclaimed, annoyed at this shift in attitude towards her, as if she was less than human.

"I am just supposed to trust a LIFEliner?" Lewis said, slumping back in his chair, but closing the book, as if she made a move for the information.

"You are supposed to trust my friends," Oliver said, and this time there was a tone in his voice that made Lewis look away from him.

"I don't care if you trust me or not," Rachel started, "but you are both beyond moronic if you thought LIFEline would allow that information to stay on the site while they are searching for this murderer." It was the only card she thought she could play under the circumstance. She needed more information and playing into their inherent distrust of LIFEline would hopefully help her get it.

"What other information do you need?" Lewis asked, coldly.

"You said there was a new case in London. Where was it?" Rachel asked, taking her notes once more.

"Tottenham Court Road, right by the old underground station," Lewis responded.

Rachel felt better that she was getting more information, but much worse that the geographical profile would be getting closer and closer to the murderer being in London.

"You said he killed this guy outside?" she continued.

"It seems he wanted to show LIFEline just how much better he is than them. He killed him in the open and then pulled him into a van to cut up the pieces before discarding the body," Lewis responded.

Rachel remembered some odd things she has seen yesterday on her walk. "Is he discarding the bodies in the river?"

Lewis looked up and could not hide his look of admiration. "How did you know that?" She also noticed Oliver looking at her from the corner of her eye. What was she to say? I was obsessed with criminal shows as a child, and read hundreds of books on how they acted, and how they were apprehended, which gives me a bit of an edge for spotting strange things?

She settled for, "I noticed a higher number of drones around the river area yesterday. There was some chatter online that it was for a new immersive movie experience, but that was a lot of immersion for one river."

Before either of them could interject more, she had a couple more things she wanted to ask, "You mentioned a van? Did they use vehicles in the past and, if so, how come LIFEline have not been able to track them?"

"Excellent question," Lewis replied, seeming to warm to her again, "you see, it seems our murderer is keen to try to have the investigation pointing in our direction. He has used old vehicles, purchased from the Fry family down near Vauxhall, and picked them up months ago. Gideon was here yesterday asking about it. He was speaking to the investigators yesterday and wanted to double-check the information."

Oliver interrupted before Rachel could ask her other question, "Why is Gideon involved?" Oliver sounded annoyed, and his face moved beyond annoyed, as Lewis replied.

"As I said, the investigators dropped in to see him and get information."

"He probably treated them like cherished guests," Oliver said, bitterly.

"Oh, yeah," Lewis said, in a sarcastic voice, "because we would never catch the Rudd family fraternising with the enemy."

Oliver looked at him darkly, but before either could say anything else, Rachel jumped into the silence. The silence was probably meant to be making a point, but she thought they could have their dramatic political conversations when she had the information she needed, "How many vehicles did he buy?"

"No idea," Lewis said, "we don't track every single move our people make. The Frys said it can't have been more than ten vehicles."

"Ten vehicles! Where would he be hiding so many vehicles without being spotted?" Rachel asked.

Oliver just looked at her with pity and said, "Anywhere. London is not exactly packed full of people. There is an abundance of space underground, in car parks, in high-rise car parks, all no longer in use, thanks to your self-driving utopia."

Rachel looked at her notebook. She had the cause of death, how he was connecting with his victims, means of transportation, the newest location to map, and the way of disposing of bodies, but one thing was still bothering her: "How is he getting around?"

She asked it more to herself than the occupants of the room, but Oliver answered, "The vehicles."

"I didn't mean that," she said, "when he was killing one-off, in smaller areas, he was driving in, killing, getting away, with little to no issues, as those places do not have as many cameras as London. You said it yourself, Ollie, as we walked here, there are a lot of eyes around London. These cameras are specifically designed to have picked him up and never let him out of sight until he left London. So, how did he manage to kill twice in London?"

"Best question you have asked all day," Lewis said, with a hint of a smile, "you see, the other way that this murderer is trying to point the finger squarely at the Dead. He is using our underground system, our scrambling technology, again, known to have been created by one of our communities, and our stressed relationship with LIFEline."

"I thought the Dead don't like technology? For a people who don't like it you seem to be developing a taste for it," Rachel said, tentatively, remembering the outburst from the seemingly bookish Lewis.

"Oh, we don't, but there are many communities of the Dead. There is a group based in Finland, they call themselves the Wizarding Dead. They like to tinker with different technology, mainly to hinder the technologies of LIFEline tracking them. Not all countries and areas are lucky enough to have the underground systems and infrastructure we have here in London to stay off the radar, so they have to be a bit more," he paused, before saying, "creative."

Rachel's brain felt full to capacity as they said their goodbyes to Lewis, but before he would permit her to leave his pigeon-filled carriage, and follow Oliver back onto the tracks, he made her make one promise and gave her one piece of advice, which felt more like a lecture.

The promise was easy – although maybe not logistically easy.

"The information in that notebook should stay offline," he looked at the retreating Oliver's back, as he continued, "You are not looking just to stay safe, you are looking to find this guy, and more power to you, but this guy knows too much about LIFEline, so if they find out you are getting closer, so will he. Promise me to keep it all offline."

"I promise,' she said.

Oliver stopped at the end of the tunnel and looked back, surprised to see her so far behind, "You coming?"

"Just a moment," she replied.

"Don't trust all the information online either," Lewis said, "there was a moment, a very long time ago. It is mentioned in one of the books in my carriage, when we moved our knowledge, our information, from the page to online. Making information accessible to all. An amazing idea that was poorly executed. There was no online moderator, no credible sources, no source of truth, and history started to be rewritten, first by those who found it funny to annoy the masses, then by those that had a lot to gain from that misinformation. If all can access and all can edit then there is no truth. If truth is what has happened, what you can see and feel around you, what you read and know, then those who have the power to influence those feelings have a monopoly on truth."

The words echoed around her mind, as she followed Oliver back up the stairs, passing more and more people. Oliver was in silence, too, until they got close to surface level.

"So, still thinking of dating online, now you know that it could be life or death? Surely someone like you can find a man the old-fashioned way," he said.

He probably didn't mean it to be a jab, for it to sting as much as it did, but the words landed and made her stomach drop. She retaliated before she even thought about why she felt that way, "You know, for someone with so much infinite wisdom, it is amazing that you are only a follower of this cult, and not its Supreme Leader." She stalked out of the concourse, not looking back to see if he was following, or to see his face.

Chapter Ten

The room was lit half-heartedly by the screens all around him. The darkness was in every corner, lurking as if in wait for the opportunity to immerse the entire room. The screens were in a constant flow of movement, as conversation after conversation was taking place with his future victims. After the announcement of another murder in London, his victims were sharing their concerns, their thoughts, and their deepest fears. He could feel that fear spreading now, like a web, with him at its centre.

After his chat with Detective Rae and Mr Styles, their announcement to LIFEline this evening was very different to the last one. There was no more pristine LIFEline approach; no more old ladies trying to keep the masses happy and calm. Charlotte Iris was wearing a fine pant-suit, her short blonde hair was brushed back behind her ears, and her tone was one of vigilance as she reported the details. *Or at least the details Rae was willing to share,* he thought. She barely finished her last words when his devices started to light up.

He could still feel the rush from yesterday. It was less than twenty-four hours ago, but the adrenaline felt like it was coursing through his veins. He remembered watching Derek's body, wrapped in its bag, be swallowed up by the running waters of the Thames. The back and forth with Rae as he goaded the Detective to come play. He knew that Detective Rae would not waste any time in discovering the body, diligently examining every aspect of the corpse, after that goading. Rae would be back following his old lines of investigation, but he still felt he was a few moves ahead of the prestigious Detective. The chat with the Detective has been quite insightful.

For one, Rae had the inept Mr Russell Styles to contend with, having his every move questioned in London, no doubt. Whereas he was conducting his solo masterpiece. Every move accounted for, every tune played expected, within time, and with the grace expected at this level of performance. Each move set to harmonize with the last, to confuse the Detectives, to strike terror into the people of LIFEline, and to, spectacularly, make them see the error of their ways. It was said that Technology was the how but Art was the why. Art could move people to greatness and his art was being created now. To move the masses.

Speaking of every move accounted for, he thought, as he turned to one of the screens. There was an issue with one of his players in this symphony and the wrong note was struck. The note wouldn't be noticed by an amateur ear, but even the slightest mistake could disturb the melody– or worse, give them away. He logged into the faulty account and started to review the code, digging deep into the algorithms.

Just as I suspected, he thought, *it is perfect. So how did it go wrong?* He reviewed the log and the transcripts of the conversation, it seemed the account took the night off work. He started a conversation with the whole premise of keeping his target company. To let her know that he was there for her.

That is not in the programming, he thought. Thinking it through, he played out the scenarios and logic, using his own uniquely built system to test this specific algorithm and its evolution. Each program he set up followed the same basic rules. They had a life to live – give or take the pre-programmed; the absences from work for sick days, family emergencies, and other human-ish behaviours. Big game on the VR that ran into overtime? A certain percentage of the accounts would be "feeling under the weather" to mimic that actual under-the-bottle feeling.

Being connected to the LIFEline systems meant the accounts could also monitor any other activity live – if one of the accounts lived in Central London, and there was a power outage, an unscheduled demonstration by the Dead or any other noteworthy event, then they would be one of the first to mention it. He made the systems up in a rank and file logic – if it was a P1 issue the account would go silent, or more active depending on the occasion, for a few hours, maybe even a day – a P1 was a family death, a loss of job, a severe weather warning - all the way down to a P5, drink spill on device, visiting relatives, etc.

Two days ago, an account should have acted as if it was business as usual, but instead, it took a P1. He disrupted it at one point, but decided it was better to let the program continue to not cause more of an alert. The account talked well into the night. The accounts were built to continually design and evolve, intelligently. They would run possible responses to conversations through millions of options in nanoseconds, responding in the most likely way to engage positively. Their life was to keep their targets happy until D-Day. The breach was a small hiccup, but could be enough to be fatal. As the tests were being run and coming back clean, line after line being cleared, he wondered if it was just a logical evolution for the account.

He did not expressly enter that the accounts should not engage in any new or suspicious ways around any news of murder. As he was thinking this through; *Should I add that programming or leave it up for the accounts?* Thinking that, after all, he built them to react, to be the perfect accompanists for him, when the screen he was running tests on lit up.

I AM SO SORRY FOR THE

**RADIO SILENCE, ESPECIALLY
AFTER YOU TOOK TIME OFF
TO KEEP ME COMPANY.
FEELING LIKE A SHITTY PERSON.**
RACHEL

Speak of the Devil and they shall appear, he thought, as he started to type a response.

◆ ◆ ◆

Rachel calmed since returning from her trek in the underground with Oliver. She listened to Lewis, and as soon as she returned home dismantled the virtual investigation room, while setting her bedroom as her new HQ. It felt weird printing the photos, writing notes on sticky paper, and adding them to the walls.

Being a teacher comes as an advantage, she thought, as she realised that she had everything she needed to set up. After she recreated the room, adding in all the information she received today, she looked at the details until her brain hurt. It joined the pain she felt, if she was honest with herself, on her ego. Not from Oliver's slight, but from her response. She took out her device and put up a status, liked some photos – mainly to make up for the silence she had this morning while underground, which didn't go unnoticed by her friends or her parents.

"Someone else has been killed!" her mother positively screeched when they spoke, "for all we knew they got you, too!"

Her absence seemed to have gone unnoticed by one person though. Jake didn't message at all today, and, as she remembered this, she felt her stomach lurch again, as she realised she didn't respond to him since they last spoken.

Feeling slightly guilty about having spent the morning with the obnoxious Oliver when she could have been talking to Jake, she picked up her device and wrote:

I AM SO SORRY FOR THE
RADIO SILENCE, ESPECIALLY
AFTER YOU TOOK TIME OFF
TO KEEP ME COMPANY.
FELLING LIKE A SHITTY PERSON.
RACHEL

She thought that he may give her the silent treatment. He was not usually the type, and they reiterated to each other on many, many occasions that they never wanted to be those people who just messaged about the mundane and boring day-to-day. They didn't hold each other to a clock on responses, but this was the longest they had gone without talking and it happened straight after a full night of talking. She let out a sigh and smiled to herself, as she saw the dots denoting Jake responding.

HEY STRANGER ;) GLAD
TO SEE YOU REMEMBER
ME!
JAKE

❖ ❖ ❖

I AM SO SORRY FOR THE
RADIO SILENCE, ESPECIALLY
AFTER YOU TOOK TIME OFF

TO KEEP ME COMPANY.
FELLING LIKE A SHITTY PERSON.
RACHEL

> HEY STRANGER ;) GLAD
> TO SEE YOU REMEMBER
> ME!
> JAKE

He paused, looking at his response, pulling up the account and the statistics of their match. The response seemed good to him, but no typing yet. The statistics highlighted that both Jake and Rachel enjoyed making fun of each other, but he thought it just didn't look right so he added:

> HONESTLY, ALL FINE THOUGH.
>
> I HAD TO MAKE THOSE HOURS
> BACK FROM THE OTHER NIGHT.
> JAKE

OH I AM SO SORRY ABOUT
THAT! I SAID I FEEL SHITTY,
WHAT MORE DO YOU WANT
FROM ME!?!
RACHEL

He sat there in silence. What did he do to illicit such a response? He moved the chat to a separate window as the systems continued to run diagnostics on the account. He gave the account data a full wide screen and typed into a search bar the phrase "What more do you want from me!?!" There were hundreds of instances and he breathed out with relief. It seemed to be an inside joke.

◆ ◆ ◆

YOU SCARED ME THERE FOR A MOMENT! I ACTUALLY THOUGHT YOU FELT SORRY AND A SHITTY PERSON.
JAKE

The response took longer than she would have thought and was not at all what she was expecting in response. Usually, when she, or he, said that the other knew that they were joking, but were sorry. It was a great find by her, if she did say so herself, that they both adopted.

YOU REALLY AREN'T HELPING WITH YOUR RESPONSES TODAY! THAT TIME OF THE MONTH?
RACHEL

◆ ◆ ◆

What do these two talk about? he thought, as he now searched the data again for more of an insight into how they talked. *It is a really bad time for the A.I. account to be down.* Okay, period jokes, fine. Also, in the top ten humour sections were toilet humour, some common VR shows, and movie and book quotes. He felt impressed with his creation, albeit a little out of his depth for this conversation.

He remembered speaking to Rachel a little, as he looked at a camera that showed her in her room with what looked like posters all over her walls. They spoke about life, about how technology was great, but couldn't hold a candle to real art. It was going to be hard to navigate her towards these shores, where he would feel comfortable, without rousing suspicion. He continued to read other mentions of period jokes and hoped copying and pasting one would seem like a call back more so than a botched response.

◆ ◆ ◆

I THOUGHT WE WERE SYNCRONIZED?
SO YOU ALREADY KNOW IT IS!
JAKE

> **OH, SORRY TO HEAR, I GUESS**
> **WE ARE FLOWING APART.**
> RACHEL

She laughed at her joke, and because Jake seemed to be in a slower humour today, she mercifully added:

> **FLOWING INSTEAD OF**
> **DRIFTING. GET IT?**
> **HUH? HUH? :)**
> RACHEL

OH, I DO GET IT. THE JOKE,
NOT THE PERIOD. HOW WAS

YOUR DAY?
JAKE

She thought about the question and hesitated in her response. She wanted to tell him everything, but felt it wasn't the time. It wasn't that she didn't trust him, just what Lewis said still echoed in her mind. She knew LIFEline was monitored. Hell, she had been in trouble in the past thanks to that monitoring, but what if someone else was seeing these messages? The someone who she was trying to find. Also, in the back of her mind a voice said insistently, *he is not the biggest fan of Oliver and if he finds out that you ignored him while spending time with him, he could get even weirder than he is being now.* She settled for the truth, but just a part of it.

◆ ◆ ◆

MY DAY WAS FINE. FEEL REALLY BAD ABOUT THAT POOR GUY WHO WAS MURDERED. IT SEEMS, FROM ALL THE MESSAGES ONLINE, THAT HE WAS A GREAT PERSON.
RACHEL

Before he could stop himself, he responded with how he felt about this. After he pressed send, he cursed himself. He scrolled through Jake's profile and found that this was not something the personal training saint would say. He passed his hand over his eyes and hoped that Rachel would not take it too seriously, but her response prompted him to continue the conversation.

THAT IS BECAUSE BAD PEOPLE
NEVER DIE. HAVE YOU NEVER
NOTICED?
JAKE

HOW DO YOU MEAN "BAD
PEOPLE NEVER DIE"?
RACHEL

HAVE YOU EVER READ AN
HONEST OBITUARY? YOU
COULD BE THE MOST HORRIBLE
PERSON IN THE WORLD BUT WHEN
YOU DIE PEOPLE ARE QUEUING
UP TO TELL EVERYONE THAT
YOU WOULD NEVER HURT
A FLY. THAT YOU GAVE TO THE POOR
AND THE NEEDY, AS IF GOD IS LISTENING
BEFORE YOU GET JUDGED.
JAKE

I CAN'T SAY I HAVE READ MANY
OBITUARIES. A HIDDEN PASTIME
OF YOURS?
RACHEL

NO, NOT HIDDEN. I JUST
REMEMBER WHEN I WAS YOUNGER
THIS OLD LADY ON MY ROAD

**DIED, AND EVERYONE WAS REALLY
SAD AND SAYING LOVELY THINGS.
SHE USED TO STEAL FROM HER
NEIGHBOURS, SMASH PEOPLE'S
WINDOWS, AND CUT THEIR CAR
TYRES, BUT THE MOMENT SHE DIES?
PROMOTED TO ANGEL!**
JAKE

**DON'T WORRY. IF YOU DIE
I WILL BE SURE TO TELL
EVERYONE HOW HORRIBLE
YOU TRULY WERE.**
RACHEL

THAT IS ALL I ASK.
JAKE

He felt that he turned that around very successfully. *Maybe I should close the A.I. account and take this one personally,* he thought, as he watched Rachel on the camera. Her facial features were set, and he could not even guess what she was thinking, but she had striking dark eyes that he couldn't stop gazing at. He checked the timeline on the profile and was happy to see that she wasn't far away from meeting him.

❖ ❖ ❖

He must be having a bad day. Probably tired and moody, Rachel thought. She recalled other times when he got like this. Jake was usually optimistic, maybe even annoyingly so, and a bit romantic about certain things.

Every now and then, though, he seemed to suffer small sharp bouts of depression. They never lasted long, and he bounced back so quickly she didn't like to ask much about it. If they stayed together, she planned to address it and be there for him, but, at this particular moment in time, she was waiting to be invited into that darkness with him.

She looked out the window and resolved to wish Jake a nice night and go to Tottenham Court Road to see the crime scene for herself.

◆ ◆ ◆

The morning after the incident with Rae and Evan, Rusty went to the gym early to try to catch up with Evan, but found it empty. He exercised, half because he was in the room and dressed for the occasion and half because he wondered if Evan was just late. As he finished up and made to leave, Rae entered.

"Ah, good morning, Mr Styles. Gideon confirmed the leads on the vehicles he mentioned, it seems it is the business in Vauxhall, which is run by a family of the Dead. I also think it would be a good idea to visit the crime scene later today," Rae said, as they passed each other.

"Great," Rusty responded, annoyed at not catching Evan and from the sweat rolling into his eyes, stinging them.

"Don't forget to take Xander with you. We obviously can't use him underground, but we can at the scene. He has already successfully located the remains and the family of Mr Conway," Rae said, continuing to the closest treadmill.

Rusty deviated on his way back to his room, following the smooth corridor walls, going deeper into the maze that was the L.O.O.P, to where the rest of the team slept, once again locating Evan's room. He knocked a little lighter than last night. Evan opened the door, half smiling, muttering, "I thought you wouldn't want to catch up now I am a suspect."

"I am sorry about last night," Rusty started, but Evan just interrupted.

"No, I am sorry. I should have realised when Rae called me into the room that he suspected my involvement. In his shoes, I would think the same. I have a unique knowledge," he continued, sitting down and gesturing for the sweaty Rusty to do the same, "and the insight into both the partnerships and LIFEline systems is too much to overlook. If I thought about it objectively, I would have come to that conclusion myself, but I was too busy trying to help."

Rusty just nodded. He didn't know what to say, now that both Rae and Evan pointed it out, it was very easy to see why the roads lead to Evan.

"Well, Rae may suspect you, but not me. There is just no way you could be involved in this," Rusty responded.

"I think the problem is that in a lot of ways, I could have been involved," Evan responded.

"Yeah, but after last night even Rae can't suspect you," Rusty replied, smiling, "there is no way you can be in two places at once."

Evan looked sceptical, "Again, the problem is that there are many ways a person can be in a room while still talking through LIFEline, Rusty. You know that."

Rusty thought this through last night after Evan's departure and even discussed it with Rae. It was one of the reasons he visited Evan's room. He stood by his team, trusted them with his life, and Evan more than any other, well, except Ciri.

"To have used the advanced technologies needed to pull off last night you would need an entire room of computers," Rusty said, looking around the bare room. "You barely have a plant in this room. A wall full of monitors might stick out a bit."

"Hey, you are preaching to the converted here, but I am thinking from Rae's perspective. Something I used to do extremely well, putting myself in the shoes of others to figure out their next steps. For all he knows I have a secret room in the wardrobe that leads to my diabolical plan," Evan said, shrugging.

"What will be his next steps?" Rusty asked.

"Well, I am pencilled off the suspect list for now, but he will be keeping an eye on me as he continues to strike others off that list," Evan said. "That list probably consists of myself, one, if not both, of the Harris twins. Pender, he is too high up in the A.T.U not to be a suspect here. Couple of members of his team too – more than likely Anderson and Singh and, oh yeah, the kid."

"You have given this some thought," Rusty said, "but if the kid is guilty, I will eat my good leg."

"I checked some of the absences around the times of the crimes, the backgrounds of some of our colleagues, and those are the likely suspects. They could be working with outside help too, but I think not," Evan said.

Rusty was silent as a theory he was working on floated to the surface again and he voiced it with Evan, more to bounce the idea around than anything else.

"We are assuming that this is a member of our team, someone inside the L.O.O.P, trying to make it look like it is one of the Dead. I can't get passed the idea that it may be a member of the Dead trying to make it look that way. We are going to Vauxhall today to speak to some of the Dead and this time I will get some questions in. Try to get them to start playing ball."

Evan looked thoughtful, before saying, "Of course, it is possible but if Rae thinks…"

"Rae is not some infallible being," Rusty said.

"He is pretty close," Evan said, smiling.

The comment followed Rusty as he met the Detective in the L.O.O.P sometime later and on their journey to Vauxhall, which was a direct route this morning. Rae had his earbud in, and Rusty followed suit once in the vehicle. Xander was running through the details of yesterday's crime.

"Some big deviations away from his usual pattern here. He caved the skull in with a blunt object, in what was most likely a fit of rage, but he had the van ready for his usual disposal method. Targeting a male victim this time goes against his victimology though. Very rare for a serial killer to change between genders in his victims once a pattern is established. This type of fluidity in gender is much more common in female serial killers," Xander was saying.

"Rare, yes. Unique, no. I am still certain it is a male suspect we are looking for. My theory is that he chose some male victims to throw us off the scent, but he was unaware of the effect it would have on him. We have seen the other tapes, he likes to stalk his victims, unknowingly, just on the edge of their awareness, and then strike in a place of intimacy, their homes. He was ready because he didn't want to be intimate with this man in any way. He jumped out of the van right by him, probably expecting the thrill to kick in, and when it didn't, he lashed out. This, I think, was the only part of last night that went to plan for him," Rae looked at Rusty as he spoke, "I think it is safe to say that his next attack will be soon, and it will be a female victim. Have Ciri speak to the people of London."

It was like Xander was reading Rusty's question before he even thought it, "I will connect you through."

Rusty passed on the information to Ciri as quickly as he could. He knew he did not need to belabour the point; Ciri knew what she was doing.

"We still think it is a member of my team?" Rusty asked.

A look of annoyance shot across Rae's face, but was quickly replaced. It happened so quickly that Rusty was sure that if he hadn't been watching so intently, he would have missed it, as Rae shuffled around and looked out the window.

"It is still our best theory, yes, Mr Styles, and I can help us continually question this by promising that the second we are no longer pursuing this line of enquiry you shall be the second to know."

"It can't be Evan though. I think we proved that last night," Rusty said, stubbornly.

"We did not prove anything last night, other than the fact that if it is Evan he is more aware of this investigation than I'd like," Rae responded.

Rusty thought that there may be a hint of accusation in the tone, and was on the verge of responding, when the car stopped and Rae jumped straight out.

Xander said in his ear, "There are many ways that Evan could be monitoring this investigation. The easiest way is at your 9 o'clock stand-up."

Rusty turned and looked up to see the sensors and cameras on a lamppost close by. He saw a passing drone pointing in the opposite direction and, in the distance, other drones going about their business, watching, delivering packages, and more around the city. These drones, driverless cars' cameras, and sensors helped monitor the city. The system that was set up to help them watch could be easily turned against them by a well-trained eye within LIFEline. The weight of the accusation finally started to press on Rusty's mind.

"The system can be used against us as easily as for us. Some of the chatter I am hearing makes me think that we need to be more cautious. Especially while in the L.O.O.P," Xander said, as they walked through an old bus station that was now full of old and used cars. Each bay had a vehicle parked in it with its front tyres resting on the path, so they were at an angle, allowing viewers the opportunity to peruse each vehicle.

Rusty approached what looked like an old-fashioned coffee kiosk that was at the entrance to the Underground as Rae walked around some old cars. Rusty half expected the Detective to kick the tires and open the hood to inspect the vehicle, but Rae just walked from vehicle to vehicle with slow curiosity.

"We are looking for a Mr Sean Fry," Xander informed Rusty, as a large man appeared from behind the kiosk.

"Good morning, how is business?" Rusty asked.

The man gave him a suspicious look, taking in his earbud, and looking at his wrist, no doubt noticing his lack of device.

"Business is business. You don't look like Dead to me," he responded, looking over Rusty's shoulder at Rae, who now opened the door of an old yellow car, and was peering in.

"You are right. We are with LIFEline. We spoke to Gideon, he may have mentioned my partner and I?" Rusty replied, trying to keep his voice open and pleasant, which was taking more effort this morning. *I think I've used up my pleasantness quota for the day on Rae, and it isn't even past 11!* he thought.

"Yeah, he may have mentioned something, but just because Gideon asks doesn't mean we need to jump," the man responded, eyeing Rusty with a look that could only be described as dislike.

"We are just looking to speak to a Mr Sean Fry. We think he may have information on the recent crimes," Rusty started. If he thought giving the man more context was going to help him warm to him he was wrong.

The large man's face went red, "That is your game so, is it? Think you can pin these crimes on us. You got another thing coming."

For such a large man he moved with the speed of an enraged gorilla, as he rounded the corner, picked up Rusty, and slammed him against the wall. Rusty tried to kick out, but his legs, physical and metal, just hit what seemed to be tree trucks. His earlier gym sessions left his muscles aching and they were declining to be of much use.

"Put him down."

The words weren't a suggestion. They were an order that said, without having to be said, *or else*. Rusty and the big man looked over at Rae, who stood in their shadow, like a smaller sibling asking for order, but in his hand, there was a small silver rod. Rae did not need to repeat himself. The reputation of the batons preceded them. Depending on the setting they could incapacitate, debilitate, or obliterate a perp. The big man released Rusty, who took the moment to push himself back and get some air into his winded body.

Rae just nodded as if polite conversation would now no doubt just spring to life in the vacuum created by the missing hostilities, as he stored the baton back into his coat.

"We did not do anything," the big man said, looking down like a scolded child, but Rusty couldn't help but notice the continued opening and closing of his big fists.

"That is good," Rae responded, walking forward, "as we do not think you did anything either. Well, more accurately, we don't think you knowingly are involved in these crimes, but as my partner said, we are looking to speak to a Mr Sean Fry all the same. The are some details we would like to clear up."

"That's me," he said.

"Good. Is there anywhere we can sit and talk Mr Fry?" Rae asked, looking towards the Underground.

"Yeah, we have a room down there, follow me." Sean turned and led them down the tiled steps into an open area that still housed antiques from the times when this was an actual train station. "Just in there," he said, pointing towards a room, as he opened a door directly opposite and shouted in "English, get up!"

From the room, a voice hollered back, "No way, Small, it is your turn to watch the store. I have well over an hour before midday!"

As Rusty and Rae entered the small room the two voices continued to bellow at each other. Rusty took in the details of the room, looking for anything out of the ordinary, as Rae just sat down on an extremely lumpy-looking sofa. Rusty joined him as Sean entered the room.

"Sorry about that. Brothers, eh!" Sean exclaimed, walking to an old-fashioned table and filling a kettle, "Tea?"

Rusty declined as Rae accepted. Hard to believe that this giant of a man literally had him by the neck less than ten minutes ago, but was now filling a cup of tea for Rae.

"What do you want to know?" he asked, and Rusty was glad to see and hear some enmity in his voice still. That enmity made his sore neck feel, in some small way, feel more deserving.

"We are investigating some purchased vehicles. Very old, no tracking and no technology at all in them," Rae said.

"Our speciality. Our old Dad hated these new driverless cars. Always said, "a real person likes to feel the engine kick under his control".

He knew the true way of motors, our dad," Sean said, with a smile.

"Well, Mr Fry?" Rae continued.

"Call me Small, everyone does," Sean said, "Sean is my uncle's name and Mr Fry is my old man."

Rusty was surprised, and slightly annoyed, when Rae continued, "Thank you, Small. Well, as I was saying, it seems the vehicles in question were purchased here and we wondered if you have any recollection of who purchased them?"

Rae reached into a jacket pocket and pulled out a bundle of images, each showing a still shot of the vehicles used at each crime scene.

"How could I forget? The man bought seven cars and three vans from us in one go about a year ago. We celebrated for a week after that sale!" Sean said, smiling.

"He is using these vehicles to murder innocent people," Rusty interjected at the satisfied look on Sean's face.

"You going to blame the man that sold him the weapon, too?" Sean asked quickly.

"Of course not," Rae said, "and we are not blaming you either," a quick look told Rusty to remain silent, "but any information you have on what he looked like would help us."

"Can't say," Sean responded, "strange fellow, wouldn't take off his hood. True, it was winter, but still looked like he was more interested in hiding his face from us than the weather and the cameras, kept avoiding my eye, you see. Even stranger was when my brothers offered to have the vehicles dropped anywhere he wanted. He asked that they just be left where they were with the keys in, and he would pick them up at his leisure. He was true to his word; by the end of the week, they were gone. He must've taken them, I told my brothers, otherwise he would have come back and complained, wouldn't he?"

"Can you remember anything about him at all?" Rusty asked, leaning forward so he was at the edge of the lumpy coach.

"Nope," Sean said.

"Any paperwork at all?" Rusty asked.

"Nope," Sean said, and then as if he felt he had to, "sorry it is not more help, but if we didn't sell to strangers, we wouldn't be able to sell at all."

Rusty bit his tongue. He would be within his rights to arrest this whole family. The Dead were permitted to do business, work and contribute to their local areas, but they were supposed to do that within the limits of the law. Through documentation, through auditable and transparent means, with the aim of stopping moments exactly like this one.

"One problem at a time," Xander said in his ear, again, giving Rusty the feeling he could hear his thoughts. After that, they left the Frys' family business, but Rusty made a mental note to come back soon. To come back on a more formal visit to his new friend.

Rae suggested that they walk from Vauxhall to Tottenham Court Road and Rusty was in no humour to disagree with the Detective. As they walked along the river, crossing at Westminster Bridge, Rae stopped. He looked up at the looming tower above and out to the water.

"It would be quicker to walk across Waterloo Bridge, you know," Rusty said, looking down into the water too.

"Quicker, but less revealing," Rae responded, but continued to walk.

Rae peered into the depths of the waters, as the London Eye peered down at them, looked down at the pavement and gazed around Parliament Square before they moved on.

The van, like the other crime scenes, was a mess, but unlike the other crime scenes, it was out in the open. Ciri already broadcast their message to the public and, as they reviewed the scene, there were many onlookers.

Rusty watched the LIFEline members who were stationed around the scene, talking to some bystanders, and redirecting foot traffic, but he was unsurprised to see Rick Harris alone, near a quieter spot. Selena Walker, head of the Quick Reaction Team, knew how to utilise the Harris twins. Put them near the back – a pleasant face with minimal chance of interaction.

The majority of these onlookers stayed a safe distance from the scene, as if afraid to catch something. As if death could be transmitted by proximity to the scene. Rusty walked to the piano that Mr Conway played in his last moments. There was still blood on the keys. Rusty felt a stirring of sadness deep within him as he viewed that red stain on the black and white keys.

"That splatter is real and consistent with the tape," Xander said. "He did not stage that blood splatter."

"How can you see?" Rusty asked.

"Oh, I have full access to all of the devices around you. I can jump from camera to camera, making this entire street my eyes, including that device pointing at you," Xander responded.

Rusty looked up and saw a woman with black hair taking what looked like photos of the scene.

"And when we are Underground or in the L.O.O.P? You don't seem to be blind," Rusty said, looking away from the dark-haired woman.

"I would be next to useless if I couldn't see, wouldn't I? Rae has integrated cameras in his coat. If you stick around long enough, I could get you one too. What is your colour?" Xander asked. Rusty chuckled, imagining himself in that long coat of many pockets that Rae seemed to love. He spotted Rae.

"What is she doing?" Rusty asked Xander; the woman was walking around behind Rae now, looking like she was still documenting everything.

"Oh, she seems to be researching. She is a LIFEline teacher, so chances are high she is looking at content creation," Xander replied.

"I doubt that is the content she wants," Rusty said, as the teacher approached Rick Harris. Her face quickly moved from curiosity to annoyance, the normal dance of human interaction with a Harris, before she turned around and stalked off.

Shit, Rusty thought, walking over to Rick.

"Hey Rust," he said, "I see that idiot detective is still sniffing around. He any closer to catching this guy or will I be on perimeters for the rest of the year?" Rick was smiling at his own joke and it seemed to be unfortunate timing for Rae, who was looking under the van, seemingly smelling the underneath.

"What did you say to the dark-haired lady?" Rusty asked, remembering that the Harris twins made Evan's list.

"Oh that chick?" he responded, nodding to the retreating figure. "She was asking questions, so I told her if she wanted answers she would have to make it worth my while." Rick sneered as he continued, "She didn't like it so I told her to shove off or we would have to have a look at what she was doing last night."

Rusty sighed, "Selena will hear about that Rick."

Rick Harris pointed at his ear where his earpiece was buzzing, "That is no friendly bee, Mr Styles. Selena has already heard and to quote my illustrious leader, "I will be lucky to see the outside world for a month for being a piece of..." well you can guess the rest."

Rusty walked away, LIFEline was supposed to attract the best of the best, not sociopaths, psychopaths, and serial killers.

Chapter Eleven

The week started off slowly. Rachel went on to teach her lessons on Monday expecting all day to feel that vibration on her wrist telling the city that another victim has been discovered. Her book lay on her table, feeling abandoned, as the sunlight stretched across the room, ticking the hours of Monday by in its journey. Between classes, the time she would usually devote to reading, she was now using to review all the details of the crimes so far.

There was no stomach-dropping vibration on Monday or Tuesday. Every time that Jake or her family messaged, although the vibration was different, she felt an echo of that sensation in her stomach. She felt more on edge than ever as she looked at the victims in her makeshift investigation space.

Well, of course there have been no more murders. There are no more dates. I doubt the murderer was able to coax many people to meet him now that he killed the last person who broke curfew for him, she thought.

On Wednesday there was an announcement. There was no one reading this one, no assertive LIFEline employee, no celebrity reader, there was just a picture being displayed, slowly gathering likes and comments, as she looked in the LIFEline feed. The image showed an outline of a non-descript couple dancing and then the details:

Rachel felt a chill that had nothing to do with the warm July day. If the murderer went quiet over the past few days because of his lack of victims then this event would be irresistible, which she thought darkly, was why LIFEline were running the Ball in the first place. She wished she could go. She felt a pang of guilt as she realised that the reason she wanted to go was to look for the murderer and not be with Jake. Her proposed date with Jake was not due until the week after that following week. She tried to think of ways to attend the Ball.

The information Lewis gave her on the crimes, which looked down at her from her bedroom walls between her breaks and in the evenings, coupled with M.R. Braize's book, gave her enough information to feel confident in her ability to know exactly what to look for. There was a very strong chance that if the murderer went to that Ball he would be looking for a way to coax his partner away from prying eyes.

You think you are better than the LIFEline team? They will know all this! a voice in the back of her head said, a voice that sounded eerily like her mother.

As Rachel thought this, she moved to her bedroom wall where she had pinned up a map of London. She looked for the location of The Royal Horseguards.

Ah, there it is. They must be kidding!

The Royal Horseguards seemed to be the perfect location to kill someone. It was as if the LIFEline teams were trying to help the murderer get away. The old-fashioned building probably had tunnels leading directly Underground, and if it didn't, then an old Underground station just happened to be across the street. Even better for the murderer was the location of Whitehall Gardens, which ran up the back of the old buildings, and would help hide the murderer as he walked to the river across the street.

Rachel imagined a dark figure talking to a woman, seductively telling them how romantic it would be to go for a walk in those beautiful gardens. Walking through the flowers as the sunsets on the city and their life.

"How could they be that stupid?" she said aloud to the room. She understood that there were not many crimes, let alone murders, happening around the world, but if she was able to pick up a few books and gain the information she had, she thought LIFEline, with its seemingly unlimited resources, could figure this out. Her frustration was building as she looked at the other sites. The murderer was killing and then dumping bodies in the river and LIFEline have just set this up as the perfect location.

Either LIFEline is so incompetent they shouldn't be leading the world or, if they are willing to use LIFEliners as bait to potentially catch this murderer, they are as insidious as he is.

She looked down at her mobile and saw that her next class would be starting soon. She left the bedroom, she didn't like working in there if she could help it. The research into the murders felt different to work through.

She sat down, donned the VR glasses, and was back in her ancient classroom setting. As her English class started to arrive, as she watched the counter start to tick closer to 100%, she had that odd feeling again. He *could* be here. He literally could be anywhere.

The screen blinked, *Class present and 100% attendance recorded, Miss Fox.*

She stood up in the virtual classroom and walked into the centre of the large class. They looked nervous, nerves that had nothing to do with George Orwell's classic novel or the assignments she may set. As she stared at the faces, she started to talk to them all, "I understand that the last few days have been uncertain and even a little scary for us all. I know it is hard to think about anything else right now, least of all what Mr Orwell meant by certain phrases and themes in his writing."

She continued to stare from face to face, "But it is exactly that type of uncertainty, that fear, that has prompted some of the greatest works of art the world has ever seen. Tolkien wrote about the bonds of friendship and hope in the darkest recesses of war. Dostoevsky portrayed the injustices of human suffering and poverty, while Shelley showed us the high price we would pay for chasing the secret of immortality, all while battling personal, and not always internal, demons.

"So, what would you write about in our uncertain time?" she asked. The class looked thoughtful as they considered the question, some hands started to raise, and Rachel let out a sigh that never made it to the VR room.

She did not plan many of her lessons this week. She had been so preoccupied with her work in the other room that she barely did enough to get past her lessons.

"Yes, Amber?"

Amber started to talk, and, at first, her voice was small in the larger space, but it grew steadily, as if she was raising the volume of her microphone, "If I was to write a book set now, or I suppose set to describe lessons we can learn from now, I think I would write about the theme of connections."

"Why is that?" Rachel asked.

"Well," and Amber looked uncertainly around, "we are in a curfew state now and, to be honest, I barely recognised a difference, which I think is scary. I talk to most of my friends and family on LIFEline. I think I would write a book about the value of physically going places with people. Connecting personally, physically, as well as virtually."

Phillip coughed something that sounded awfully like *"thought crime"*, which made some of the others around him smile.

"Something to add, Phillip?" Rachel asked, jumping onto the debate. If they spoke enough about this, she could buy herself a whole week.

"Just that Amber needs to…."

Rachel interrupted him, "Remember judge the idea, not the person!"

Her voice was stern as she said it, and Phillip's, and some of the people surrounding him, smiles wore away like a wave ran through them and half a smile flashed upon Amber's face.

"Of course, the idea of connecting physically is exactly what I meant in our last discussion and," he continued hesitantly, looking to Rachel for reproach or approval and receiving none, "I was just wondering why the difference of opinion now."

"No difference of opinion, just an evolving opinion," Amber said matter-of-factly, "Ideas by their very nature should be open to change, opinions given room to evolve and shift, as we learn new things, right?"

"So why wouldn't your book be about that?" Rachel asked, finding herself intrigued.

"I think it could be, maybe it could be about both?" Amber asked. Rachel didn't answer, just gave her a knowing look, before moving to other hands as others started to add to the conversation. The conversations moved from writing about security, vigilance, love, friendship, zombies, and on, and on.

As she removed her VR glasses, she was shocked that not only did the class go well, but it was also probably her most engaged, for both her and the students. *Maybe I should not prepare more!* she thought. It was the first time the students were happy to receive work to do during their own time, but she thought that also may have been because of the curfew. She looked at her device, there was a message from Jake:

HEY ZEUS, HOW GOES THE CLASSES TODAY?
I HAVE NO WORK TODAY SO CAN CATCH
UP ON A VR CALL LATER IF THAT WORKS
FOR YOU TOO?
JAKE

She hesitated. She could call later, but, if she said yes now, they would get into a big conversation, and she didn't have the time. She had an hour and a half before her next class and her thoughts kept wandering to the investigation living in the next room. She wanted to review Braize's points on geographical profile and plot all the locations out on the map in her room.

I will respond later, she thought, as she walked to her bedroom, *he will understand.*

◆ ◆ ◆

On Monday morning, after their usual visit to the onsite gym, Evan knocked on Rusty's door for a change. Rusty was surprised at the change, but welcomed it all the same, stepping back as Evan entered the room with a resigned look on his face. Rusty brought him up to speed on the vehicles, the latest crime scene and the body – which Xander found in record time.

"You see," Xander said at the time, "it seems our murderer is disposing of the bodies exclusively at Westminster Bridge. The weight of the victims, the air trapped in the bags, including the chemicals, especially mixed with the cold temperatures of the Thames, means the bodies do not float far downstream. It was a simple case of backtracking and thinking about the profile of our murderer. He may not even realise, but he now seems drawn to that historic spot, like a compulsion. We didn't even need the footage to spot our man to find the body, drones found it easily."

As Evan listened intently he asked, "Does Rae still think I am involved?"

"I don't think he ever thought you were involved," Rusty lied, looking around his room for anything to take his eyes away from Evan.

"Do yourself a favour, Rusty, don't get into playing poker, whatever you do," Evan responded.

"Deep down I think he feels…" Rusty started.

"Rae doesn't do deep down, Rusty," Evan started, "He is the best Investigator LIFEline has ever seen because of his inordinate ability to stay in his mind. Logical to the last move, processing information twice as fast as the smartest person in the room, and moving ten spaces ahead. We know each other, we have worked together, and know of each other's past and our personal records. I do not blame him for suspecting me, it is a logical assumption to make. Even as I think of the profile, the geography and terrain this unicorn is working to, it makes sense that he is working centrally, most likely from this very building. His knowledge, and indeed use, of our systems, our blind spots, both from a surveillance and tracking perspective, heavily points to this team. If the next murder happened anywhere else in the country I would disagree, but two in London confirms my suspicions too, it is someone in the L.O.O.P."

"You are as quick as him to doubt your own team. Is that something they teach you in a training academy?" Rusty asked, sarcastically.

"Yes," Evan responded with a sad smile, "and I guess old habits die harder than expected. You would think after all this time connecting LIFEpartners that the edges would have softened, but since this all started, I have realised those instincts aren't only still there, they are as sharp as ever. One of the first lessons: only trust those you know with one hundred percent certainty are not your perp. A one percent chance is still a chance."

"Guess you are lucky I didn't go to the academy," Rusty said, darkly. A look of shock, quickly followed by hurt, and then finally a mask to hide the emotions, flickered across Evan's face as he said, "So, you think I could have done…" his voice caught in his throat, and Rusty could imagine what he was seeing, the images of the victims' bodies.

"Of course I don't think you are involved," Rusty said, and this time he could meet his eye, and he hoped the message landed loud and clear.

Evan half smiled, "Thanks. Because, to be honest, if you did think that, I wouldn't help you out of spite."

Evan laughed as Rusty just shook his head, as he looked around the room for his earbuds that connected him to Xander.

"What is that?" Evan asked, curiously, as Rusty stowed the case with the A in his pocket.

"Just a way for Rae and I to keep in contact in the field," he responded, still unsure why he wasn't telling Evan about Xander. *Probably,* Rusty thought, *the same reason you are not telling Rae about Evan. We could use all the help we can get!*

Evan made for the door, but Rusty stopped him, "Just two things, I would really like your insight on."

"Go ahead," Evan said looking at his watch.

"You mentioned that the list of suspects probably consists of the Harris twins, Pender, Anderson, Singh and Greene…"

"Don't forget me," he said with a slight grimace.

"Well let's pencil you off the list for now," Rusty said with a smile, "do me a favour today, under the radar, search their rooms, if you get a moment." Even the thought of this action made Rusty sick to his stomach, he knew only too well the sanctuary each bedroom was to its occupant.

To his surprise Evan looked at him suspiciously, "You don't know?"

"Know what?" Rusty asked.

Evan looked down at his shoes as he responded, "I am sure it just slipped his mind to mention, but Rae already had all the rooms searched."

"What? When?" Rusty asked, his voice barely controlling his anger.

"The night he arrived, woke me up in the middle of the night, I literally had flashbacks of the nurses waking me when I was in hospital for bloods," Evan responded.

"He searched my team without informing me?" Rusty felt the blood rush to his head, pounding in his ears so much that Evan's words felt like they had to penetrate the resistance to be heard.

"Rusty, this is his jurisdiction now. He can, and believe me, should, have full access. No one likes a colonoscopy, but you're still happy when you pass the test," Evan said, the smile returning to his face, "I told you when he got here, and I keep telling you, Rae is the best. He would be pretty bad if it took him this long to search this entire place."

Rusty felt downtrodden; his first proper solo idea, one he thought was particularly good, was done by Rae days ago.

Evan seemed to feel his disappointment as he said, "What was the second thing you wanted to ask?"

Rusty hesitated.

They spent multiple nights brainstorming ideas for improvements to the L.O.O.P. These ideas improved the city and their own infrastructure, both physical and technical, that had a big impact in driving London up the city rankings globally. They shared professional and personal events over the last few years, but he now hoped that "the second thing" wouldn't break that connection. In Rusty's experience the bonds of friendship, so dutifully crafted and cared for, could break under certain stresses.

"Why do you think he suspects you? I mean, why do you think you were his number one suspect?" Rusty asked.

"You think I was the number one suspect?" Evan asked, shock returning to his face.

"No one else was called into that room. I have not seen him test any of the other people on our list the way he has tested you so far," Rusty continued. Now that he said it, he felt it was easier to keep going. Like walking up a mountain, keep the momentum going, if you stop and rest for too long you may not take the next step. "You know I wouldn't ask if it wasn't important, but I need to see what Rae is seeing, so I can focus on the others. If he is too fixated on you, and I am one hundred percent sure it is not you, I will need help diverting his gaze."

Evan sighed, "You won't divert his gaze and trust me, just because you do not see him testing the others doesn't mean he hasn't; but let me think."

He meant it. Evan fell into silence as his face became a mirror to his mind as his eyes roamed, lips moved, his eyebrows and brow furrowed and un-furrowed. His hands moved to his face together, rubbed around it as if he was massaging bad thoughts away, then back to his side. He reminded Rusty of the soldiers he trained with as they tried to figure out complex calculations.

As Evan thought, Rusty remembered Rae speaking with Carter and Dan the other morning and his interactions with the Harris twins at both scenes.

When Evan looked back up, he just said, "Not an easy thing to do, Rusty. Look at yourself that way and try to be objective. I guess the training helps. Well, as I mentioned, Rae and I know each other, by reputation. We never directly worked on a case together, there was some consulting, mostly from his side to mine, but we were in the same team. I fit everything from a demographic standpoint of this profile, same as our other suspects, but I think there are a few things Rae is unwilling to see as coincidences."

"Firstly," he said, raising a finger, "I was an investigator. So, I know how they look at crime scenes. What they are looking for and how to hide those things, as I am sure Rae does, too."

He raised his second finger, "Then B," Rusty couldn't help but smile at the bad joke, "the timing of my transfer would align closely enough to when I would imagine our unicorn started to plot his master plan. This would raise enough suspicion for most, but still no trigger or stressor."

"Trigger or stressor?" Rusty asked, blankly.

"In this type of crimes, it is a prevailing theory that the unicorn has some stressor, something that built him. Bad upbringing, a huge life-changing event…" Rusty looked at him and he continued, "which brings us to the big C. My cancer. That could work as a stressor. My entire life changed, as you know, almost overnight. For me a thing that made me look at life positively, but, again, if I was Rae, that can be seen as a stressor."

"The trigger?" Rusty asked.

"Sorry," Evan said, looking at his three raised fingers, "I can't think of a trigger. What would have set me off? I have enjoyed working here, connecting people is literally my passion. Obviously, Rae is unaware of this, but when all you are missing is the smoking gun, but you think you can still smell the gunpowder, you are not going to let that get in the way."

"Thanks, Evan," Rusty said, "this will help me look at our suspects better. Hopefully, spot the unicorn."

He smiled, "Don't let Rae hear you say that."

As they walked out of the room, Evan stood and looked over his shoulder, "I will probably go this way, just see you in there," he said, nodding towards the main floor of the L.O.O.P.

As Rusty entered the room alone, he noticed that it was buzzing with activity. He couldn't see Rae anywhere, but assumed that he wouldn't be long. Ciri was at a central control point, one that Rusty would usually occupy. Rusty heard a voice travelling across the room and sighed. Ciri heard, looked up, spotted Rusty, and smiled.

"Rusty, why didn't I get a call when there was *another* murder?" Director Carter asked, crossing the room. "The wife is practically hysterical. She is talking about wanting me to transfer to Manchester, Rusty. Can you imagine?"

"Director, you shouldn't be here," Rusty said, leading the way to the central control point, which helped wipe the smile from Ciri's face, "It is Detective Rae's investigation Director, I can't do anything without his say so."

"Well, I don't like how this Detective is handling the matter. We really should align on this. I have a right to know what is going on in my city. I can take it up with his superior. Hopkins is a good man, we have had some speaking arrangements together, and played a few rounds on the greens in Scotland. Great courses, if you can manage to get the weather for it. Typical of people to make amazing courses in a country that can't manage two sunny days in a row," Carter rambled, as he followed Rusty.

"Director," Ciri said as a greeting, and Carter looked up with a smile.

"Now, there is the future of the business! Don't think I don't see it Char. Some of your best work these past few days. I would watch out Rusty," Carter said, elaborately winking at Rusty, "she will have your job in no time."

"With your impending move to Manchester, I guess that does leave the spot of Director open," Rusty responded.

The Director flushed and, with the raising of redness on his face, the playfulness evaporated. At that precise moment Rusty's office door opened and Rae popped his head out, it was obvious he was about to call Rusty, but Carter beat him to it, "Just the man," he said, striding over as if to an old friend, "can I have five minutes of your time?"

Rusty would have wagered his entire career, actually his entire life, that Rae was about to say no. Director James Carter made a career of feeling welcome in rooms he had no right being in, as he, obliviously, offered advice and guidance. Rusty turned to Ciri.

"So, Char," he started.

"Ugh, don't. You know how I hate that name. I literally feel violated every time I talk to him," she said with a shiver, "How can words make me feel like I need to go and shower again."

"But you are his favourite and, don't forget, the future of the business," Rusty smiled.

"When all the work I do is the best of my career, it kind of diminishes the point of my career. If he saw me peel an orange it would be the best work of my career," she said, with bitterness.

"I am sorry," Rusty said. "You know I am joking and not to mention that no one takes him seriously. We do see what you do around here. As the old saying goes though, even a stopped clock."

"What do you mean?" she said.

"Just that he was right, bound to happen eventually with the number of words that comes out of his mouth," Rusty said forgetting himself, "Sorry, he was right, it won't be long until you have my job."

"Where are you going?" Ciri asked, shooting him a furtive glance.

"Nowhere yet," he said, but something that he was thinking over the last twenty-four hours came rushing out of his mouth before he could stop himself. Similar to confiding to Evan, once he started, he found it easier to continue. They had as good, if not a stronger relationship. Rusty always found Evan easy to talk to professionally, while with Ciri, he felt he could talk to her about anything.

"I am really enjoying this challenge," Rusty said, lowering his voice needlessly, it was too loud in the room for anyone to overhear, "it reminds me of the military days, and I love it. I feel we are making a difference trying to get this guy off the streets. It is too early to tell, but I may look into how I could make the move. After all, Evan did the opposite."

Ciri looked taken aback, but recovered quickly, "I would miss you."

"Don't start the goodbye party yet, we haven't even caught this murderer yet," Rusty said, looking around the room. He felt awkward saying it, but lighter now that he shared it with her.

Rusty's office door opened, and Director Carter walked out of it like a scolded child. He did not look up as he walked to the exits.

"If you do go to work with him, will you ask him how he managed that feat?" Ciri asked, with an impressed look on her face as Rae glanced over at them from across the room. Rusty gestured that he would be one moment and turned back to Ciri.

"Do me a favour, Ciri?" he asked.

She did not answer, just glanced at him curiously and he continued, "Can you think of anything odd that may have happened with the Harris twins, Pender, Anderson, Singh or the kid over the last year and a half to two years?" He thought about the stressor and the trigger mentioned by Evan, "Look into a change in any circumstances, anything that may add to their stress. Any altercations that may have been reported, etc."

"What is this about?" Ciri asked darkly, and it was Rusty's turn not to answer with a glance.

"You think they could be…"

He interrupted her before she could finish, "I am exploring all potential suspects. Can you look into it for me? I have to go." He walked a few steps, turned and said, "add Evan too."

Better to clear him than ignore him, he thought.

He could feel her gaze follow him all the way across the room.

Rusty sat behind his desk and looked at the maps on the wall, as Rae shifted from foot to foot, then sat down, and said in a restrained voice, "Why do you think I gave you a link to Xander."

"A very good morning to you, too," Rusty said, getting used to Rae's manner. He clicked a button on his desk that alerted the canteen area that he wanted his usual sent in, "can I get you anything?"

"Just an answer to my question will suffice for now, Mr Styles," Rae said, steepling his hands together. Rusty thought about it. He was a quick learner; other people asked rhetorical questions, but Rae was not like other people. He wasn't being sarcastic. He genuinely wanted an answer.

"I don't know," he conceded.

"Sometimes the simplest answers are the right ones, Mr Style. I gave you a link to Xander so that you would have a link to Xander. I have found his assistance not only vital in my career, but his objectivity at times even better than my own. He can find things out in moments that would take us days. He is literally a fount of information," Rae said.

"I will remember that when 'Employee of the month' comes up," Rusty responded, as his door opened, and a drone flew a box in containing his breakfast and coffee.

"He is not an employee here, so I do not think he is… He informs me you are making fun again, so I will just continue. Please utilise Xander. We are the only two who can work with him at the moment, but if we do not use his services, they will move him somewhere else, and he likes it here. I like having him here, too," Rae said.

"Oh, I got that. You even call him by his preferred name. Something you have done for him and that behemoth of a man that picked me up in Vauxhall," Rusty responded, taking out his cereal box, pouring it into his bowl and adding his milk.

Rae stared distractedly and opened his mouth to say something, but closed it as the door opened. A pretty, short blonde-haired woman walked in. Her confidence preceded her so much that Rusty didn't even need to look up. The majority of the L.O.O.P knew to knock, but no matter how many times he told Maggie Paulson to do so she simply refused to follow that one order.

"Morning Rusty, Evan wanted to check this with you before we go live," Maggie said putting a tablet down on the table. Rusty looked down at the tablet. There was an outline of a planned ball. Rusty remembered his words from what he thought was the first crime, trying to get ahead of the issues with the dates, and he forgot to catch up with Evan about this in their limited time.

"Maggie, tell Evan I don't think we should go ahead with this," Rusty started, but Rae stood up, looked over Maggie's shoulder and reviewed the tablet.

"May we have a moment, Miss?" Rae asked Maggie politely. Rusty saw her mouth slightly grimace at being called "Miss", but she took it in her stride as she exited.

"Firstly," Rae said, looking Rusty in the eye, "put in the link to Xander." It was not a polite question or request so Rusty bit his tongue as he took out the earbuds and put one in.

"Good morning, Rusty. Sorry about Rae, he gets a bit…"

"Mad," Rusty said, looking at the smaller man who now picked the tablet up to read it thoroughly, ignoring both Xander and Rusty.

"Protective," Xander finished. "This looks interesting though. Rusty, what did you think of the location that was chosen by the Partnerships team?"

"I didn't pay it much attention," Rusty replied, "this plan was my idea before we knew that this uni…murderer was a serial killer. It won't go ahead. It is way too risky."

"I don't think it is too risky," Rae responded, looking up from the tablet, "the risk to life in a well-populated area is small. The probability our murderer would be able to resist going is very low and the chances of us being able to corner him is high in comparison. If I was a betting man, I would take those odds."

"Yes, but even at twenty to one, that one is a human life, and you aren't exactly betting with your own money," Rusty said.

"If we have tight surveillance, the right security team, Xander, you, and I, I cannot see how our murderer can possibly get away. We would catch the profile straight away as the only person who does not show up. This would put an arrow on his target. We would practically need to be asleep at the wheel not to catch him," Rae said with confidence, giving Rusty a rare smile. "He has slipped up here, Mr Styles. We must take advantage."

"It is easy to risk a life when it is not your own," Rusty replied. A cold silence followed this. It seemed even Xander was holding his breath.

"Do not, for one second, doubt how seriously I take my job, Mr Styles. Do not think that the life of each victim is not etched into my mind, that the stakes of a mistake, my mistakes, do not also plague my mind with doubts. That said, we must strike an opposing blow. Defence will only get us so far," Rae said, seeming to calm the more he spoke. Rusty felt, more than thought, that Rae was trying to convince himself as well.

"Then on your head be it, Mr Rae," Rusty said, calling Maggie back in.

"All seems in order," Rusty started before Rae interrupted.

"I see that Evan has been kind enough to add Rusty and I to the security on the night," Rae said.

"Yes, he thought you would both want to be sure that the murderer was not present," Maggie replied.

"Please inform Evan that I would like the security detail to be run by Ciri from here and that I would like Mr Greene and the two Mr Harrises to attend.." Rae said.

"Harrises can't attend," Maggie interrupted, sharply. She was not used to being bossed around, not even by her boss, "both of them are suspended."

"Don't worry, we will solve that particular problem," Rae responded.

It was Wednesday.

The room was dark as always, being lit by nothing more than screen after screen of conversations. There was a shadowy figure in the room preparing. He stored some extra knives for the occasion, he looked at his saw and felt a rush of excitement. He placed plastic coverings into one of the many duffle bags around him.

On the screens, his A.I. was talking to his next victims. They were conversing back and forward in their little flirting dancing, each word bringing them a step closer.

He looked up to see the screen light as one responded: she would be attending the Ball with him.

Did LIFEline realise the significance of the date they set? Did they think him unprepared?

He had two days to prepare, but did not need it. He had this plan set for months, they did exactly as he thought they would. They did not disappoint. Euan Rae's intelligence put him in a position of superiority over his regular adversaries. He did not yet realise that he met his very own Moriarty.

Chapter Twelve

T he morning of Friday the twenty-ninth of July found Rachel more preoccupied than she had been all week. There were no more crimes, but she could almost feel the tension rising, like the feeling you get before a storm. It was clear all around her, with the beautiful July London weather showing up consistently, but under that shiny surface there lurked a feeling of darkness.

Rachel's workdays were too busy to fit anything other than light walks in the evening, before curfew came at sundown. She was usually accompanied virtually by friends or Jake. On their call on Wednesday evening, he reiterated that she should stay in at night, be as careful as possible and "LIFEline be damned, if you need me just call and let me know where you are, and I will be there as quickly as humanly possible."

His face, even though it was virtual, like her students, still gave her a sense of comfort and, as she always did when she was speaking with him, felt stupid that she could even think he was a murderer. He was so caring and loving that there was simply no way that he could be involved in such atrocities.

Her breaks were still littered with brief streaks of activity on the information she received from the Dead. She hadn't spoken to Ollie all week, which was natural, they were weekend friends. Usually just Saturday friends, not counting last week. Every time she thought of something new in the case, like the idea of the murderer not only using the underground system as a means of getaway, but a way in and out of his own lodgings, she would have liked to run the ideas past him.

Not only did she imagine his indignant response that it was just a way for her to pin it back to the Dead, but she also wondered what he would think if he knew to what depths she was taking her information gathering. Over the past few days, on her virtual walks with her friends, while pretending she was viewing Shakespeare's old-fashioned London, an era her friends were happy for her to walk alone in given the number of times she persuaded one of them to join her, she was instead viewing the locations of the crime scenes. She walked through Tottenham Court Road again, this time with no idiots from LIFEline instructing her to leave, Kensington, and along the banks of the river. There were only a few things that stood out to her about each location.

As she viewed the scenes, she had her VR glasses on, using the functionality to pinpoint exact distance from the crime scenes to the underground, and then to the river. The numbers flashed in her peripheral vision. They were all extremely close to underground access points and within walking distance of the river. It was a very long river, but it still narrowed the potential victims in her mind.

Hopefully, LIFEline are doing the same thing! she thought, savagely.

Her daily ramblings, her deep dive into her notes from Lewis, and the steady company of M.R. Braize's book, had an effect on her sleep. The past three nights she dreamt about chasing a shadow around London's landmarks, always ending in the dark entrance to the Paddington underground station, where the darkness seemed to call to her. In the dreams she would not take another step and eventually she would wake up, breathing deeply, as if she ran the distance from Paddington station to her bedroom.

When she was a teenager all her friends planned to go to a local park on Bonfire night to hang out. Her parents, not being of the oblivious kind, knew that hanging out in a park on Bonfire night meant alcohol, fire, and boys. They did not like that combination, thinking it could not lead anywhere that they wanted their daughter going towards, so they forbid her to go. Her friends could talk about nothing else all week, regardless of her impending absence and oblivious to her feelings of disappointment.

LIFEline seemed as oblivious to her feelings now, posting constantly about the upcoming Royal Affair Ball. She knew she couldn't go, but each mention, post, picture, and VR video made Rachel's feeling of longing increase. Jake was putting a brave face on it for the both of them:

**BETTER FOR THEM TO RUN
AT LEAST ONE BEFORE WE
GO. THEY CAN TEST SECURITY,
MAKE SURE THE ENTERTAINMENT
IS GREAT FOR US. WE ALREADY DON'T
GET TO PICK WHAT WE DO ON OUR
FIRST DATE, I AT LEAST WOULD
LIKE TO KNOW THAT THEY
HAVE HAD A TRIAL RUN**
JAKE

She knew he only said it to keep her feeling like she wasn't missing out on anything, but, what he didn't know, was that the longing she was feeling had little to do with him. It was for another man. Another similarity to that Bonfire night of long ago, as 8 PM got closer, was how, without planning to, without even knowing she was going to do it, Rachel found herself at her door, coat on, keys and devices in hand.

She closed the door behind her, walked down the stairs, jumped into a driverless car outside and said, "The Royal Horseguards" as if she was also in driverless mode. As a teenager her parents refused to let her out for a week when they realised what she had done.

At least LIFEline can't do that, she thought, and then hit by the thought that there was much more at stake here than not seeing her friends for a few weeks, but she was resolved. As the vehicle moved its way through the city, she saw more people out than she expected.

It has been almost a week since the last murder. It is hard to stay focused on a potential threat when your life hasn't been impacted and the sun is shining outside, she thought, looking up at the sky, where the sun was making its farewell with a pattern of red and gold radiating like a halo's glow.

From her apartment near Marble Arch, her walks during the week to the river took about an hour, the driverless car did the trip in around 15 minutes, taking a slightly scenic route as if it wanted her to see the sun setting over the London skyline. As the vehicle turned its second last corner, Rachel pressed the screen to indicate that she would like to get out here. She thought it best not to jump out of the car right by the entrance to a black-tie event in her plain black clothes, white trainers, and slightly oversized, but light coat.

She put on her VR glasses, clicked the side, pulled up the menu, and scrolled with the side of the glasses until she found what she was looking for. When she found the navigation app, she opened it, and now moved to her wristband, scrolling forward. It was an odd movement she became accustomed to, her body staying still, but the view in front of her eyes moving forward. Her brain, on the other hand, hadn't become fully accustomed to it. She heard people say that it would take hundreds of years until our brains became acclimatised to our new technologies, and by that time, they would be too late. The rate of change far outpacing the biological advancements needed. It seemed we were destined to keep the brains of the past.

She was viewing further up the road, where The Royal Horseguards stood, and was glad to see that LIFEline seemed to already have set workers outside. She steeled herself, took off the VR glasses and was instantly transported back to the spot she vacated the driverless car.

She walked to a shadowy spot, standing under the bridge by the old Embankment Underground station.

River. Underground, she looked at the workers around The Royal Horseguards, *Crime Scene,* she thought.

As she moved out of the shadows, walking forward, the river to her left, her destination across the road, she noticed graffiti littering the walls by the small Whitehall gardens. She wondered what they meant and, for a moment, thought of Oliver. As she continued along the road, doing her best to look nonchalant by looking across the river in the opposite direction to her destination.

The London Eye and South Bank were still teeming with people, but there was a screen counting down the time to sunset and the curfew. Rachel threw a look over her shoulder and saw a group of people standing further up at the spot she visited moments earlier by VR. Her VR trip showed her what looked like just workers, but it seemed that they were now being joined by guests. She crossed the road, slowly, as if exploring the city, looking at a statue on the corner of the park, walking to the left branch in the road, following what looked like guests of the ball.

Then she felt something, a primordial feeling of being watched. Her first instinct was to look up at the closest cameras, but the hairs on the back of her next acted like a signal and she looked to her right.

There was a darker section of the bridge here, the shops that once littered each side boarded up and long closed, the lights all out, but, through the darkness, the light broke through from the other side of the bridge, and there stood a dark outline. It was a vague outline, as if the setting sun, the darkness and her own eyes were all in league with the silhouette to stop her from getting a good look. Rachel tried to look as if she just happened to look in that direction, as she took out her mobile device, pointed her camera, and clicked quickly, before continuing to walk.

She felt the eyes in the darkness following her as she walked to the corner, where stood…

"You again," the LIFEline employee said with a sneer. It was easy to tell he was LIFEline. One, he didn't have any devices visible on his wrist, although he had something in his ear, and two, he was the same idiot from Tottenham Court Road. He was dressed differently, with a red old-fashioned military ensemble.

She sighed and just asked, "Can I speak to whomever is in charge?"

Did I really just say "whomever"? she thought.

"You got him," Rick Harris smiled.

A man in similar attire was standing at the other side of the revolving door and, on seeing her, walked through to join them. His eyes and slight smile never leaving her view as he circled through.

He can't be worse than this guy, she thought.

"Rick, what seems to be the problem? Did this young lady forget the dress code?" the man looked her up and down with a kindly smile that nonetheless annoyed Rachel.

"I am looking to speak to whomever is in charge," she said, side stepping Rick and committing to whomever.

"Come in," the man said.

"You think that is a good idea, Evan? She could be our unicorn," Rick said with a laugh and turned back, enjoying his own joke.

Evan smiled at Rachel, pressed at his ear, and spoke: "Rae, Rusty, I have a civilian down here that would like to speak to whoever is in charge. That would be you right?"

Rae and Rusty walked down the spiralling stairs to the ground floor, where, in the lobby, slightly away from the other arriving guests, Evan stood with a familiar-looking woman.

"Xander?" Rae muttered.

"Rachel Fox, LIFEline teacher, did some initial research into the murders online, then printed some details off and hasn't, to my knowledge, done much else. Teaches English mostly and is currently going through Orwellian literature. She has been spotted at the other crime scenes over the past few days, but the likelihood she is involved is negligible. We have seen her," Xander was saying, and as Rusty remembered where he knew her from, he interrupted.

"She was at Tottenham Court Road," he finished.

"I assume that is why you had so much information on her. Good work, Xander," Rae said, still keeping his voice down, as if he was afraid the very walls had ears.

"I assumed she is writing something for her class or publication, but why she moved offline is a mystery to me. Maybe she knows more than I assumed," Xander responded.

"You know what they say about assuming," Rusty muttered.

Rachel was talking animatedly to Evan and, as neither Rusty nor Rae had on the same uniforms as the security team, she did not fully notice them until they stopped by her. She looked up at Rusty and he thought he saw that same recognition dawning on her face.

"Miss Fox, meet Detective Euan Rae and London Area Manager, Russell Styles," Evan said. As the four stood in a slight circle, it was only a slight circle because Rae stood further away than most would and was looking around the lobby as if trying to find an escape.

Rachel extended a hand, Rusty shook, and said, "Call me, Rusty." She proffered her hand to Rae, who was still looking in the opposite direction. She dropped her hand with a look of awkwardness at Rusty, who tried to convey a look of understanding, which was harder because of Evan's smile.

"Thank you, Evan," Rae said, "if you will follow us, Miss Fox."

Rusty thought that they may go back upstairs to one of the more comfortable rooms, maybe even the side room that was set up as a rest station for the security detail, after all, it did have refreshments, but Rae lead them to the closest door and, without knocking, entered. It was a large conference room with chairs stacked against the walls. The curtains were drawn, making the room dark and giving it a smell of dust and disuse. It was clear from his demeanour that Rae had no intention of making Rachel comfortable, so Rusty asked quickly, "How can we help, Miss Fox?"

"I actually think I may be able to help you," Rachel said, and, although Rusty could hear the self-consciousness in the voice, he couldn't help but admire her. If what Xander has said was true, and he had no reason to think otherwise given what he saw of Xander's prowess so far, then Rachel started some sort of investigation of her own.

"How is that?" Rae asked.

"I think the murderer is here," Rachel said. The words tumbled out of her mouth and this time Rusty heard a hint of panic too, "I think I have seen him across the road, watching as the guests enter. If you have set some sort of trap for him in here, it may be useless if he is going to catch his target before they even enter the building."

"Impossible," Rae responded, and when he didn't continue, Rachel threw her shaking hand into her jacket.

Rusty was about to grab his newly acquired baton from his inside pocket when Xander said; "Her mobile device is in that pocket."

Rae didn't move at all as Rachel moved forward, phone outstretched to show a photo. Rusty peered at the device. The image was completely black, there was an indistinguishable shadow in the centre of the frame, but it was obvious the photo was taken in haste, it was blurred at the edges, but it was unmistakable. There was someone hiding in the shadows across from the entrance to the Ball.

"Thank you for sharing these details, Miss Fox," Rae said, again his voice showing no sign of gratitude; the opposite seemed true, he kept glancing around and tilting his head as if expecting Xander to speak, "Is there anything else?"

"So, this is a trap? You are putting all these people at risk to catch…" Rachel started.

"Miss Fox, you are interfering with an active investigation. We can't stop you from snooping around in your own time, but please do not think we are not doing our utmost to catch this criminal. We can't tell you anything, but I will give you one piece of advice: go home," Rae said, walking to the door and opening it so Rachel would get the hint, as if his words were not enough.

As she furiously left the room, Rusty looked at Rae, "You know you catch more flies with honey than vinegar."

"We have enough flies upstairs to entrap our particular spider. Miss Fox almost gave our spider a chance to get away with a fly unaccounted for," Rae responded. "For all we know she could be some sort of fan of our murderer. It happens with a frequency that would sicken you."

"You think that figure outside under the bridge?" Rusty asked.

"Oh, no, not at all. People always think the bad guys are hiding in shadows, waiting to jump out like a well-choreographed dance. Why hide in darkness when it is simpler and more effective to hide in plain sight?" Rae asked.

"I guess so," Rusty said, "I still do not think you needed to be so brusque with the girl. She didn't seem like a fan girl to me."

"You wish I told her that all the female LIFEpartners are upstairs already, invited an hour earlier than the male LIFEpartners? That we have a plan to check each male in to ensure we can find the right target before our murderer strikes. Tell her that we know the murderer isn't out there, because we brought him with us as a plus one? Call her back then, Mr Styles, let's have her join our merry hunt," Rae said.

"You trying on sarcasm? It doesn't fit," Rusty said, looking down at Rae as he shuffled from the room.

As they made their way to the stairs Xander said, "Gideon."

"What?" Rusty said.

"I thought as much," Rae said, "Rusty, go over and see why Gideon is standing under the bridge. He obviously knew we would spot him at some point."

As Rusty exited the building both Evan and Rick tried to engage him in conversation. Rick was on the door and Evan on coats for the first hour. Once the hour passed, they would be rotating to monitor the dance, then to an hour break, and then the three-hour cycle would start again. It had many names, standing guard, stagging on, on point, but no matter what you called it, he called it vigilance through boredom. Rusty was glad his position was more free-flowing, because standing around on watch always made him daydream, and daydreams do not make very diligent guards.

The benefits of leadership, he thought, as he walked over to the outline under the bridge.

As he crossed the road he heard Xander to Rae, "She is pretty annoyed, but is in a driverless car back home. It was the right thing to do. If she continued to snoop outside then there was a strong probability that he would target her instead."

Gideon was now leaning up against the graffitied wall, "There are people amongst the Dead that do not believe I should help you." Gideon's voice echoed in the darkness, his dreadlocked hair swayed as he shook his head back, "and, after standing out here for the last hour, I can see why. All the technology in the world and I think you needed that young lady to alert you to my presence. Seems to prove my point right, people over technology." Rusty saw the smile break through on his face and relaxed.

"Never thought they were mutually exclusive, Gideon, but sorry all the same. It is a busy night for us, and you know you could have just come inside. The guy in red is one of ours or you could have sent one of your people," Rusty said.

"Tonight, I wish to be alone. There are nights when I like to walk the streets, both above and below ground. Feel the city beneath my feet like the millions that have come before us. I do not mind the waiting when it is in aid of progress," Gideon said, now stepping out of the shadow. The sight of such a senior member of the Dead above ground and so close to cameras was one Rusty was not used to.

"The whispers underground are that you are setting a trap for our murderer?' Gideon asked.

Rusty felt the question was just a polite gesture, it was very obvious that Gideon was already more than aware of at least part of Rae's plan. Rusty felt less sure of it than ever – everyone seemed to have worked this play out.

"Rusty," Xander's voice came through, "we know it is not a member of the Dead so full cooperation may be necessary."

"I agree, Mr Styles," Rae responded, sounding far away.

"That is our plan, but how do you know?" Rusty asked.

Gideon looked over at the building, "Rusty, the only way it could be more obvious would be if you wrote 'Murderer please come in, we are waiting for you."

"Fair," Rusty responded, "but we think that even knowing that, he can't resist the bait."

"Oh, of course not, and let's not forget that he is in the very fortunate position of being in your team," Gideon said.

It wasn't the same tone from last week at Waterloo Underground. Gideon was no longer looking shocked, but had the same confidence in tone as Rae, "We have pulled together some information ourselves and it is not pleasant, Rusty. Again, some of the Dead feel it is our duty to stay out of this, but he is using us. Using our systems, our people, not only in his crimes, but in his defence. I will not allow that to continue. We have found multiple locations set up and believe there are many more underground."

"Locations?" Rae asked, his voice sounding more interested now.

Rusty relayed the question.

"Hovels, and no more, but it is clear that he intends to go underground, if he hasn't already," Gideon said, "On his last venture through the underground, he was spotted and chased by some of our people, but he managed to get away. He seems to know these tunnels better than many who have lived there for years."

"There is one more thing," Gideon said, reaching into his inside pocket and retrieving a folded piece of paper.

"What is this?" Rusty asked, taking the piece of paper.

"It is a detailed map of the L.O.O.P before it was the L.O.O.P. Hundreds of years before it was your headquarters and before all the refurbishments, both new and old. You will see upon review that there is a myriad of ways into the underground from under your very feet. The same can be said for that building, Rusty," Gideon said, peering over his shoulder.

"Where did you get this?" Rusty asked.

"We have our ways and I believe that your perp also has his. Make sure that trap is good and tight before you look at losing that animal. A cornered animal can act extremely aggressively, but a cunning one that knows the gates are wide open can wreak havoc before getting out with ease," Gideon said.

Rusty, who admittedly had a lot of problems with this plan to begin with, was now feeling even worse about it. As he turned, he saw a male LIFEpartner approaching the front door. The hour was up, and Rick Harris was replaced by Jonas Harris.

It's always a good idea to keep the Harris twins separated, he thought.

❖ ❖ ❖

He remembered playing hide and seek when he was young. Staying as quiet as possible, in a location as others passed by, sometimes having to hide a sudden upsurge of mirth. You were playing it well when you had to hold your breath not to be caught. He felt like that internally as he walked around the room, the wolf in sheep's clothing, among the sheep, while the shepherd knew he was here somewhere. No points for knowing he was here. This was a game of all or nothing, he smiled, and a young lady glanced at him, blushed, and looked away.

He felt the temptation, like an addict tempted by a drug, but this wasn't his drug of choice for tonight. She was at the back talking to one of the other ladies. She wore a red gown, as requested. It went well with her dark hair as she scanned the surroundings, her naturally doleful eyes seeming to pierce his, as her gaze moved around the room. As he walked, moving to another member of his team to talk, to start his moves, the other men started to enter.

Right on time.

He couldn't see Russell anywhere, but knew that he couldn't be far away. He had a very tight window to do this, and Rae was busy shuffling around the men, all the while throwing glances at his security team. Rae alone without Russell was ideal for his plan of attack. His scrambling device was on his wrist, under his cuff, and with the pretence of shifting the cufflinks he turned it on.

That will stop Charlotte from hearing our little exchanges.

"Hey," he said, "just passing a quick message, although I don't think I should, given our position, but whatever, see that blonde, I just heard her mention, that if she wasn't waiting for her partner, she would want to climb onto you."

"Really," Rick Harris said, smiling, "you don't say."

"Thought you'd get a kick out of that," he said, walking away, trying to keep his voice steady, as if just a passing remark amongst colleagues "too bad Detective Rae is right there?"

"Think I care about that little pipsqueak?" he asked, beelining directly for the blonde and engaging her in conversation.

In most games, there are a finite number of moves that one can take. This move, although long in the works, would be one of his last from an area of stealth. He was sure he could get away with the murder tonight.

He may even get another day in the L.O.O.P, but no more. He would have to move out of the shadows and into the cold light of day.

The male LIFEpartner of the blonde was getting pretty heated with Harris, so he moved forward to break it up. He witnessed the blonde lady throw her drink at him and storm off to Rae to complain no doubt. Some of the ladies moved to a door and he saw the red dress leave the room.

He beckoned to Rae, "I am going to take him to cool down."

Harris pushed him back at each step, but he managed to get him into the male bathroom, "Just stay here. Calm down."

"Man, you said she wanted me. I can tell you one thing," Harris said, looking at himself in the mirror, "if she does, she is playing extremely hard to get."

He stepped back to the door and called back in, "I will keep watch from here for our man, take your time." He heard the hand drier going as Harris tried to dry his jacket.

He moved to the side, he was now standing in front of the ladies' toilet. He pushed the door open slowly and peered in. She looked up, seeing him through the mirror, her face moved from fear to shock as she said, "Excuse me, this is the ladies'!"

"Sorry, miss, we are going to need you back in the main hall. It is for your own security," he said.

She walked towards him, his heart was beating a mile a minute. He looked over his shoulder and, as much as he fought to control his face, there must have been something that showed. Or maybe, deep down, there is a primitive being in us all that knows when a predator is in front of us, because she started to look hesitant.

He lunged forward, knocking her to the floor, she scrambled and opened her mouth, but he was ready. He stuffed a wad of cloth into her mouth before a syllable was heard. Her eyes widened as his hands found her throat. The red dress was bunching up at the bottom as she tried to kick him off. She tried to reach for her device, but he tightened his grip, she gagged and turned her head. Looking up into his eyes, hers bulging. She raised her hands, but before she could do anything, he tightened with all his power. She jerked and her head fell back one final time.

He didn't let go until he was sure that there was no more life left in the limp body.

Part one complete, right under their nose, he thought, *even if they catch me now, they lost the battle.*

The adrenaline was rushing through his veins. Part of his brain was telling him to run, get away, go underground now, but his logic came back coolly, and he set about his task. He removed the devices as quickly and deftly as he could, placing them both on the sink. He grabbed some towels and wiped down all the surfaces. Finally, he picked up the lifeless body of Georgina Burton, her dark hair trailing over his back. He looked around the door. He was quick, but he couldn't hear the hand dryer next door. The corridor was empty, and he only needed to get her into the next room, down the stairs, through the building, and down to the underground.

It seemed a lot, like a pointless endeavour and effort, but he trodden the path earlier and knew he could do it in less than three minutes.

◆ ◆ ◆

Rusty ran up the spiral stairs, Xander called for backup for Rae, which could only mean bad things. When he reached the corridor, he knew something was wrong. There was a lot of noise coming from the main room. He entered and Rae was flustered, surrounded by LIFEpartners. The music stopped, and people were shouting about "LIFEline's inappropriate behaviour" as Rae tried to gain control of the room.

He was surrounded so much he could not move, and Rusty saw him reach for his baton. Rusty looked around the room, but could see no threat. His military training kicked in as he released the baton from his inner pocket and pushed his way through the throng of people with ease.

"Where?" Rusty asked.

"I…I don't…" Rae looked lost, wide eyed.

"Ladies' toilet. There is no signal from a device of a woman who went in there just under ten minutes ago," Xander said.

"Damn it," Rusty said, and he did not wait for Rae, as he turned on the spot and ran to the room, barrelling people out of his way like a rugby player. He pushed the door open, and all looked fine. Then he saw them, the devices sat beside each other, unsupervised. Unplugged. He looked down the corridor and there was no body there.

"Harris and Levvett were out here," Xander said.

Rusty turned and saw Rae exit the main room where the LIFEpartners seemed to have realised that something bigger than spilled drinks was happening. The atmosphere change was so pronounced the silence seemed to radiate to the corridor. Rusty heard a faint noise, like a scuffle happening in the distance and a voice called, "Rae! Rusty! This way," then there was a grunt.

"Evan!" Rusty called, following the voice.

As he ran down one corridor, then the next, seeing Evan in the distance at each turn, running as fast as he was able, he called, "Ciri, sitrep, where is everyone?"

"Rick Harris, Evan, and the kid are all unaccounted for. Rusty, what's going on in there?" Ciri said after a moment. As he turned a corner, he had to jump over a body lying sprawled on the floor. He didn't get a good look, but it was the right build for a Harris.

"Xander, Harris is here. Get someone here quick, he looks like he needs medical."

He kept running, but his chest was paining him as he went through an open door, and down a flight of stairs to a basement below. He burst into a room and, at the other side, was Evan trying to pull a door open with one hand.

"Rusty," he panted turning around, "it was the kid. He barricaded the door. Harris and I... saw him... walking down the corridor as confident as you like with a woman over his shoulder." He took a deep breath, "We underestimated him. He stabbed Harris in the neck and...I tried to help him... he looked bad... I took chase after... caught up with him here, but" he showed Rusty his left hand, three of his fingers were missing. Only the forefinger and thumb remained. Evan looked faint, which wasn't surprising, given the amount of blood he was losing. He slumped to the ground, looked groggy and said, "I can't believe it was the kid, Rusty. I can't believe I lost my fingers to the kid."

Rusty looked at the floor, "You haven't lost them, look, there they are."

Evan grimaced and then lost consciousness.

Rae entered the room, looked down at Evan unconscious, "You caught him."

"No, he got away," Rusty said, looking down at his friend.

"Wait... it wasn't, I was sure when he left the room," Rae responded, "but I couldn't follow. I tried..." his voice broke as he looked down at Evan.

"It wasn't him. He took chase after," Rusty took a deep breath before responding, "it was the kid. Sorry, Dan Greene."

He was the last person on his list. The very, very last person it could possibly be. Rusty remembered the night the kid came to wake him up in the darkness. That scared face as he awoke his boss to bad news. That same face started to change from fear to a mocking smile in his mind.

Rae looked down thoughtfully.

"So much for it not being too risky," Rusty said, brushing past Rae. He needed to be outside, in the fresh air. There were medics on hand, they would fix up what they could, and he would only be in the way.

We lost again, he thought.

Chapter Thirteen

Rusty waited outside in the warm summer night air. He watched as other personnel from the L.O.O.P attended the scene, combing for clues, drones scanning the location, and people gave him wary glances as they passed. They were used to the "in charge" Rusty and right now he didn't trust himself to open his mouth for fear of pulling the system and their actions down. The team did not need that right now. He had full faith in his team's ability to take control of this situation.

Really? a voice asked in the back of his mind, *you have "full faith" in the team? Even now?* He felt the creeping doubt start to work its way into his very being as each moment passed. He wanted to walk, he felt itchy feet, one actual and one metaphorical, as the team swarmed around him in a buzz of activity.

"What happened, Rusty?" Ciri asked again in his ear.

"Not now, Ciri," Rusty responded. There are times when friends pull you closer and times when they allow you to run away, knowing you will come back all the saner for your moment of insanity, Ciri understood this.

"Rusty," Xander's voice in his ear was more hesitant.

Rusty did not respond. He didn't take the earpiece out, and he wouldn't take it out, because it kept him connected to his team. His family. The family he looked at now through newly suspicious eyes. Regardless of this, he waited.

He didn't need to wait long. Rae and Evan came out of the building with the medical team; one shuffling, one on a stretcher. Evan looked like he was trying to get up and help. Once he had seen that Evan was well tended to, he turned and left. He turned as he got to the corner and noticed that the shock seemed to have dissipated from Rae already. He was giving directions, no doubt for the drones to continue their search of the area for the one suspect they barely considered. As he turned the corner, he saw Rae jump into the medical vehicle with Evan. Evan seemed grateful for the company, as he smiled up at his ex-detective colleague.

As he walked into the darkening streets, he took a moment to think of the kid. Dan Greene had been with them for a couple of years and showed promise, not hostility. He was willing to say yes to most asks, so much so that Rusty had to take him aside and suggested he say no every now and again, if for no other reason than to prove it was in his vocabulary. Again, he remembered the fear on the kid's face when he woke him up that first night. Remembered how tired he seemed at the screens.

Was that fear because he was afraid of being caught? Tired of the overexertions of murder?

Rusty still couldn't quite believe it. As he walked, he remembered his father. His father was the strong silent type. After he passed his mother said he was silent because he was constantly thinking, and strong because he had a streak of stubbornness that Rusty inherited, along with the red hair. As he walked in the silent city, he remembered those bouts of silence that his father and he found themselves in. Rusty learnt that there were different silences from his father. There was the comforting silence of no words needing to be said and then there was the silence around him tonight. A charged silence. Like the world was holding its breath before a cry in the night.

Some people never let you pass their defences, Russell, his father's words echoed in his mind, as he walked along the river, *and you can knock on that wall with a battering ram all you want, but the truth is unless they open the door, you won't ever be truly on the inside.*

Did the kid stay hidden? Did he ever show his true self?

His feet did the walking of their own accord and when he looked up, he was unsurprised to find himself at the foot of the large clock tower.

"Rusty," Xander's voice said into his ear again.

"Yes," he responded, looking across the long bridge. It was deserted and looked like something out of a disaster movie.

"Rae isn't connected at the moment," he said, sounding unconcerned, "I can see where he is. He is ensuring Evan is ok. He gets like this after losing a move."

"A move?" Rusty echoed to the still air.

"Yes, Rusty, a move," Xander said, and this time he sounded firmer. "What happened tonight is no one's fault other than the one that committed the crime. If you are afraid to make moves, to close in on this unicorn, then you will never catch him. Rae understands that, even if right now he is doubting himself. You don't know this, how could you seeing as it is the first time you have worked together, but every person you lose will stay with him. He remembers every victim he has lost. It is a thankless task; the people who are saved by our work barely ever know that they were in peril at all and those that do see that peril tend to be lost to us."

Rusty didn't say anything as he thought about this, "I told him not to have this event tonight." Rusty's voice rang out.

"What would you have done instead, Mr Styles?" Xander asked.

"I don't know, but I would have started by not putting innocent people on the hook as bait for a proven serial killer in the hope we could catch him.

Harris looked in a bad way, Evan looked on his last legs and then that poor girl! Killed in a place she should have been safest. A place we brought her to. We went in blind, only Rae thought he could see clearly! I told him that he would have no one to blame but himself if something like this happened. The quote goes something like there is nothing worse than what we know is right that turns out to be wrong," Rusty said, walking to the bridge, and sitting down on the ground. Even in the warm evening, the ground was cold. He could hear the river flowing below him, making its way to the sea.

"It ain't what you don't know that gets you into trouble. It's what you know for sure that just ain't so?" Xander asked.

"That is the one. Mark Twain, right?" Rusty asked, side-tracked for a moment.

"I think it is debatable, like real life, Rusty, these things evolve. Have you ever played a game of Whispers?" Xander asked.

"Of course, I was young once," Rusty replied.

"Then you remember how when you say something to someone, they can interpret it differently. They see and hear differently. There are many reasons for this. Sometimes it is simply that they are unobservant, or that they are inattentive at that moment when attention will pay off. We would be foolish however to disregard the role that is played by our differences," Xander responded, "just look at you and Rae. You have both experienced the same thing and are dealing with it differently. Although, I think you have one thing in common, which is wrong. You both blame Rae."

"I don't blame…"Rusty started.

"I told him that he would have no one to blame but himself if something like this happened," his own voice came through the earpiece.

"Hard to argue against one's own words, Rusty. At times like this though, the behaviours and actions show who we truly are," Xander said, with a hint of pride in his voice, "and neither you nor Rae have buried your head in the sand, awaiting easier times. You are both still making moves, even if you don't know it."

"Oh yeah, real men of action; Rae is tending to Evan's wounds and sulking not talking to us and I am sitting here on a bridge moodily wondering where it all went wrong," Rusty said, picking up a pebble and throwing it into the water behind him.

"Of all the bridges in this city, you walked directly to the one our killer should frequent, if it is part of his compulsion. Great coincidence that," Xander said mockingly.

"Well, it is as good a place to sit and mope as any," he replied.

The night wore on in near silence. Xander was giving Rusty regular updates on what was happening in the L.O.O.P, as he sat on the hard ground. It was a few hours after Rae left Evan and gone back to his room to pace. Xander could see him from his coat's camera, but he turned them off. "Privacy is guaranteed. Something for you to remember, Rusty," as a driverless car pulled up. Rusty stood up and moved to the vehicle.

"I thought they would be useful," Xander said. There was a bag inside. As he retrieved it the car moved off, lighting the dark bridge as it went on its way. Rusty opened the bag and found a coat, a flask that smelled of coffee, some snacks and…

"A pillow?" Rusty said incredulously.

"Well, you are not exactly a young man, Rusty," Xander said, as Rusty sat back down, put the coat on and grudgingly used the pillow.

This brought back his old military days, too. Sitting up in the night although in those days the person keeping you company was beside you nudging you every few minutes to make sure you didn't fall asleep, and the snores and rustling of the other members of the platoon could usually be heard in the distance. The time continued to pass, being counted by the huge clock tower. The curfewed city quieter than ever.

"Someone is coming," Xander said.

"Alert the L.O.O.P," Rusty said, standing up, leaving the bag on the ground with the pillow.

"Done," Xander said, "they are waking Ciri and Rae."

"Who was on watch?" Rusty asked out of habit.

"Kirsten Morrison," Xander said.

Rusty groaned inwardly. Kirsten was great during regular hours, but she was a morning lark. At night times she had the haste and speed of a turtle making its way through a traffic jam.

"Xander, what do you see?" Rusty asked.

"He just stepped out of the shadows on the opposite side of the bridge, definitely him. I can't make out his face, he is still using the encrypting technology. I will commandeer a passing drone and follow him. I don't think he knows you are here, but that is some distance to close if he does see you," Xander responded, as Rusty made his way across the bridge. He was coming from the same side as the hospital.

"He is walking up the steps, Rusty, turning onto the bridge...now," Xander said.

Rusty saw the outline of the figure, but he was still too far to make out. He would be able to I.D. the perp. *You mean, see the kid?* The doubter in the back of his mind said: *See if it is the kid.* Rusty thought and started to pick up his pace. He didn't need Xander to say it, he saw the figure run towards the closest rail with a bag, he was already running.

"He saw you, run!"

◆ ◆ ◆

The adrenaline carried him forward. What Mr Russell Styles didn't know was that he knew he was on the bridge. He checked the cameras before coming out from his exit underground. He debated internally with himself. It is a risk not worth taking, but, after tonight's luck, he was willing to roll the dice on his odds here too. He could outrun, outthink, and outperform a one-legged veteran who hasn't seen real activity since the loss of his limb. He stowed a knife in his maimed left-hand sleeve. If Rusty got too close, he would do what was needed to continue his work. He wouldn't like doing it. Rusty was always good to him.

The cautious walk seemed to have fooled Ciri or whoever was on lookout. They obviously reported his presence to Rusty because he was up and walking with a determined step.

"Walk with purpose," Rusty said to him before, "people do not bother someone who seems to have a purpose to their walk." He wondered if Rusty could run for this purpose. He felt the nerves raising, like a rabbit aware of a fox so close by, he was fighting with the fight or flight impulse. He waited for a second's breath to control the panic and then controlling it, he ran.

Rusty was sprinting as fast as his legs could carry him, but he was still a dark outline as he reached the railing and dropped the body of Georgina Burton into the flowing river below. The river greeted her with its watery hug, and she dropped to meet the embrace. He imagined her body with the others on the riverbed and a moment of peace reached his mind but was instantly disturbed by the terror invoked by the sound of Rusty's footfalls. He turned and ran.

He didn't need to be the fastest man on earth, he just needed to get back to the underground and make his way back home without Rusty seeing him. As he ran down the steps, taking two steps at a time, he didn't even spare a moment to look at the familiar looming hospital. Rusty's footfalls were receding and, as he jumped through a gap in the wall and back down to the underground, he breathed a sigh of relief.

The sigh echoed down the tunnel further underground, and he followed it. Rusty might be annoyed enough at this close encounter to risk the Dead's wrath at finding the team leader of the L.O.O.P in their home. As he rushed through the underground, he saw flashes of light here and there as the Dead heard him move around them.

He had been coming and going in this underground for the last few months, like a shadowy spectre, and was treated as benign by the Dead, until the last few days. He now felt their presence closing around him and he didn't like that one bit. It seemed the Dead were not as against LIFEline interference as he bargained for. As he slipped past a watch person, taking a secret passage, passing one of his many fall-back areas, he kept his ears peeled.

Down amongst the Dead and the darkness your ears were worth more than your eyes and nose combined. He listened at each rushed step to hear more than the echo of his passing, moving as quickly, but softly, as possible. He made the darkness an ally in the underground, but he knew that there were those in this darkness that knew it more. They knew the darkness' secrets better than he and he was acutely aware that today's ally can be tomorrow's enemy. He was proof of that himself.

He was now under the L.O.O.P. The last few hours played themselves over in his mind. He was sure that he had been caught, that he made it impossible not to be found out, and then Lady luck herself seemed to have turned up to help him. A victim of opportunity gave him the perfect plan. He walked up an old set of stone steps that led to his secret room. He took a deep breath as he entered and felt a sense of warmth from his home.

In his exaltations, he didn't notice that the entrance into his L.O.O.P room was ajar. A light spilt into the dark room that was covered in screens, maps, profiles, and his algorithmic workings.

"The only piece I seemed to be missing in this puzzle is very helpfully written on that wall," Rae's voice said from the darkness.

The flight and fight response was back and this time all he could do was turn his head to the dark corner where Rae sat in his chair. In his hand, he had the baton that would no doubt be set to stun. He knew a lot about Detective Euan Rae, and number one amongst this information was that he tried to take his killer in alive. He believed in the justice of the crime and treatment ethos of LIFEline.

"How did you get in here?" he asked, gazing to see if Rae had the earpiece connecting him to Rusty.

"You know how I got in here. Why not ask a question you want to know the answer to, rather than trying to buy yourself time? The game is over, Mr Levvett," Rae said, standing up, his owlish eyes never leaving Evan's face.

Evan smiled, and for Rae, it was like a mask fell from his face. The kind, thoughtful Partnerships leader, an old detective friend, was replaced by the killer he suspected was hiding there the entire time. There is a moment when you are proven right that still shocks you. The ugly truth raising its head from behind the mask of fallacies may be expected, but is seldom welcomed.

"How did you figure it out?" Evan asked.

"You should never have used the bone saw on yourself," Rae responded, "you should have known that it was the one thing the killer would never use in a fight. The knife you used to kill Harris would have made more sense. I guess you couldn't bring yourself to maim yourself with a weapon you used on someone else. That saw holds so much sway over you, that I doubt even you understand how your mind sees it. You probably got pleasure from your self-mutilation."

Evan listened as if he was taking advice from a teacher, nodding,

"Even before that you were on my trail. Why?" He tried to disregard the slight on his use of the bone saw, but felt some anger starting to bubble up, which helped snuff out his anxiety and inner voice screaming to run.

"Everything pointed to you, even your ruses were things only you would think of doing from your experience. You chose to use the Partnerships as a way of picking your victims. You practically wrote your confession when you killed in London," Rae said, not taking his eyes off him.

"Ah, yes but I expected you to trust Rusty's estimations. That it was too obviously pointing towards us," Evan said.

"It had nothing to do with mistrust of Rusty," Rae said. Evan heard it, but did Rae? Evan felt a glimmer of a plan start to emerge. A long shot, but the only move he had left. Like tonight when he played against Rae's inability to navigate social interactions.

"You two did seem to work well together. A budding partnership, no doubt. By the way, do you know how those LIFEline Partnerships are chosen? You mustn't, otherwise you would not be on so high a horse. They are genetically coding people within LIFEline, Rae, it is not just compatibility on a personal level, but a genetic level. They are trying to breed out disease and sickness, but only in the professionals! They do not care what happens at the lower levels of society. They couldn't care less about the Dead," Evan replied. He noticed that Rae barely moved his hand, it was pointing directly at his chest, the centre of mass, making it so much easier to get a clean hit. He needed to buy time, but Rae wrote the book on not allowing perps to buy time.

"A cornered perpetrator is a desperate perpetrator. They tend to monologue, to give you all the information you so sorely want, while they await their moment. Do not give them their moment. Take yours and remember your A.I.T.s; Apprehend, Interrogate, and Treat," the lesson followed him to the field and, no doubt that, Rae would follow his own advice.

"You may call me Detective. Whatever it is you think you are doing, Mr Levvett, you know from your very own training that it is part of a sickness," Rae responded, "This is not the real you."

"The truth is right in front of your eyes! It is on these walls," Evan moved, Rae's hand followed him, as he started to pull profiles down, "they practically knew when my parents had me that I would one day be critically sick and they did nothing. They let me go through all of that so that I could be a data point on a report. They are using some people as guinea pigs, but never those with enough influence. That is not what LIFEline was supposed to be."

"Mr Levvett, I am going to need you to get on your knees," Rae said removing the handcuffs from his pocket, showing no signs that he listened.

He thinks I am just sick. That this is all in my head.

Evan looked down at the floor and dropped to his knees softly. He raised his hands and placed them on his head. His time was up.

Rae stepped forward and, as he slipped one cuff on, said, "Rusty kept me updated at every turn. He never trusted you." Rae was above him when Evan sensed something, rather than seeing him hesitate. Like a boxer on the ropes that sees that window of opportunity in between his opponent's guard he knew he had one shot at this. He raised his maimed left hand, the one not yet cuffed, the one that still had the knife nestled there, the one all his plans now rested on. The knife came free, and he was able to just hold onto it between his thumb and forefinger as he drove his weight behind it. He jabbed up and felt the knife enter flesh.

Then the wrath took over. He was stabbing Rae over and over again, there was no method, just his ultimate opponent downed, and every fibre of his being screaming at him to make him feel the pain of all the injustices in this world. The knife fell to the floor as his rage was assuaged. The floor, the walls, the machines, and his clothes were caked in Rae's blood. His hands shook as he stood up, looking all around. This was different. There was no feeling of peace. He thought he would feel victorious at least, but there was just the vacant spot that was held by rage a moment earlier.

He was on autopilot as he moved around the room. He had a bag ready for just this occasion. The bag had everything he needed to get out of here. A remote device that had full stealth access to the LIFEline system. If Ciri tried to track that device she would be running around every country in the world. He quickly washed up, changed his clothes and picked the bag up. He did not have time to take down all his plans: *No point anyway,* he thought, *they will all have seen Rae come to this room.* He removed the profiles from the walls so that they would not know who was next.

He looked around at the grand tapestry of his masterpiece. A plan that took meticulous planning at each step. A plan that beat LIFEline's best and left him in a pool of his own blood in darkness. He thought, *sometimes the best gift is knowing that you are looking at something of pure beauty for the last time,* as he purged the systems. Leaving no trace of his existence, he moved to the next stage of his plan. He may have beaten the main players in this game, but an ambitious pawn can still be a nuisance to even the most strategic King. He returned to the darkness of the underground.

❖ ❖ ❖

"You went where?"

Oliver's voice carried over the café, Mr and Mrs Horner looked at him reproachfully from behind the counter. He lowered his voice and himself into a chair, "I didn't help you get all that information so you would catch this lunatic!"

Rachel grimaced. Oliver and Jake reacted the same way. She wanted to vent about LIFEline and their treatment of people, but Jake also fixated on her flouting the rules. When she shared about the man in the shadows the intervening minutes might as well have been hours as Jake's silence permeated through the device and into her dark room last night. They said good night in a rush, both annoyed at the reaction of the other, both needing time.

"I wasn't trying to catch him," Rachel responded, feeling guilty about the lie.

"Don't play poker whatever you do!" Oliver said, standing up and walking off without refilling her coffee, which she felt was a personal slight she could do without this morning. After her annoyed good night to Jake, she paced her apartment late into the night, awaiting another announcement that never came. When she did finally tire herself out, she lay on the bed staring at the ceiling, waiting for sleep to embrace her. It finally did, but it was about as welcoming as Jake was.

The nightmares were so vivid, she woke up in a cold sweat despite the warm summer morning. In her dreams the man in the shadows stalked her, forever on the edge of her dream, as she ran to Jake, to Oliver, to Lewis, Underground, to LIFEline, to her parents, and friends. Each time she made it to someone they were gone. Her dreaming mind told her that they were gone forever. The panic rose in her chest as all the people she knew were gone, until it was just her and the man in the shadows. When he stepped forward into the light, she woke with a fright.

As she sat nursing the dredges of her morning coffee, she recalled that feeling of terror; it followed her to her morning swim, where the ripples and shadows under the water made her panic for breath. Oliver walked back to the table, this time without his apron, and said, "Follow me."

He walked out of the café with a wave to the Horners that she replicated while also trying to smile. The muscles on her face felt like they were given an impossible task and, from the returned look from the Horners, she thought she may have managed only a concerning jerk to her facial features. In the warm morning sun, her fears started to move to the back of her mind. *Until tonight,* she thought.

"What is it, Ollie?" she asked.

"It hasn't been announced yet, but there were multiple murders last night and the killer got away, again. From that very building you decided to visit!" Oliver said, with anger and concern echoing from every word and written in every line of his face.

She felt her stomach drop. She has never been unhappier to be right. She remembered the face of the detectives she spoke to. Their quiet confidence and unwillingness to share any details with her. She did not expect to be met with open arms, but she hoped they would look into her warnings. She even hoped that they would stop the Ball the second they realised that they were an easy target. What she did not want was what she got – confirmation that they set the trap. A trap that seemed to have failed.

"Multiple murders?" she asked.

"I will answer, but I think it best to go somewhere we can't be overheard," he looked up at the closest cameras, "we are not supposed to know this, officially. We are not supposed to be sharing it with you."

Half an hour later, they were deep in the Underground, in Lewis's carriage, her devices stored once more in her bag, as Lewis relayed all the information the Dead had. Lewis looked happy to see her, but quickly hid the smile as they sat down.

"Lewis, tell her everything we know please, and can you stress the importance of staying away from this psychopath," Oliver said.

"There were more murders last night and early this morning," Lewis started.

"This morning?" Oliver interrupted.

"Yes, we had reports that confirm who the killer is now and where he is," Lewis responded, darkly.

"That is good news," Oliver said, "obviously not the murders, but the fact they know who it is and where he is. Why haven't they got him then?"

"He is underground, so I think the more apt question is "why haven't we got him?" Lewis said.

"Underground, what is Gideon doing?" Oliver asked.

"I could ask you the same thing, Oliver," the door opened and in walked a skinny man with dreadlocks sweeping behind him. He wasn't alone either. There were people in the opposite carriage and Rachel thought that there were probably even more people outside. Rachel got the impression from the others, Lewis included, that this was an important man. Lewis stood to his full massive height as if in the presence of royalty.

"What do you mean?" Oliver asked. Rachel noticed the lack of standing in Oliver, but also the tenseness in the way he spoke, as if he was holding back.

"Bringing a member of LIFEline down to our home. You did not inform your people of this," Gideon said, his eyes finding Rachel and catching sight of her bag, "It seems you even allow her to have her devices. A kingly gesture."

"Where does it say that I can't do these things," Oliver asked, standing up.

"It is unwritten," a voice said from behind Gideon.

"Thank you, Noah, an appreciated, but unneeded interjection. Please continue the search, I will catch you up," Gideon said to the group of people behind him. As they left the carriage the animosity was left behind. There seemed to be a radiation of spite between Gideon and Oliver, who both stood face to face, as Lewis and Rachel looked at each other.

Gideon looked away first to Rachel, as if remembering his manners, "Please forgive my intrusion, Ms Fox, but it is not a safe time for a member of LIFEline to be in our underground. I am usually more welcoming, if you care to return in the future, I look forward to proving that."

"She is my guest," Oliver said harshly, "you deny my guest hospitality?"

"I deny all guest hospitality while there is a monster roaming our home," Gideon said, turning his head so quickly his dreadlocks flicked some papers off a nearby shelf. Lewis stumbled forward to clean up the mess. "If anything were to happen to her down here a conflict between the Dead and LIFEline would be inevitable. Do you not think this may be this monster's plan? To pit us against each other, like the wars of the past, brother fighting brother? No, we must do all we can to stop that. Ms Fox needs to return to the surface, directly."

"She will return once we have got what we came for," Oliver responded, "information is still freely available to all that seek it, is it not?"

"It is," Gideon responded, with a slight bow to Lewis, who was looking busy at his papers.

"If asked for, sanctuary from LIFEline is still granted to those in need of it?" Oliver continued. Gideon looked from Rachel to Oliver and back again before responding.

"As it always has and will," he said slowly, "but I have received no requests. If that request should come to pass, then you know, as well as I, that those that seek sanctuary must also leave their devices and old lives behind."

"Then a reprieve while I get the information I need," Rachel said. As they spoke, she could not help but feel as if they were talking about her as if she were a bargaining tool to broker peace. She had no time, or inclination, to be a part of whatever testosterone-filled contest this was between Oliver and Gideon.

Gideon bowed to her, "Of course, Ms Fox, but please be aware that you must leave all of your devices at the entrance on a visit, not in a bag. I will permit today, but never again. If you were to look to join the Dead, and we would be pleased to have you, you must leave those devices behind for good."

Gideon looked to Lewis, "Please give her as much accurate information as you can, but be quick. I need all," he glanced at Oliver, "available hands searching every section of the underground."

Gideon turned to leave, turned back at the door with a slight smile, "Sorry if I caused a panic yesterday."

Rachel didn't understand what he meant as he left the room and Oliver gave her a questioning look.

Lewis cleared his throat, "He mentioned earlier that you saw him yesterday near the latest crime scene."

"It was him!" Rachel exclaimed.

"Yes, he needed to pass some of our information to our LIFEline contacts," Oliver snorted, as Lewis continued, "We had another victim at last night's ball, a Georgina Burton. Her body was found this morning in the river. LIFEline detectives almost apprehended the killer as he disposed of the body, but he escaped using the underground and this time they are sure he is down here to stay."

"How are they sure of that?" Rachel asked.

"Because he also killed three of his own," Lewis said sadly.

"I thought it was just two victims and an injured team member. Did the team member die from some missing fingers? I thought they had the best healthcare in the world?" Oliver asked.

"The thing about information, Ollie, is that when viewed in haste it can mislead even the finest minds. If it is given the time it needs to breathe, and the sharpest of minds, it can show the truth," Lewis responded. "The injured LIFEline member, Evan Levvett, is our serial killer."

Rachel felt her head spin as she remembered the man who walked out to meet her in the foyer and save her from the obnoxious guy she ran into twice. He seemed kind and helpful. He brought her into the building to meet the detectives. She didn't mention anything else as Lewis recapped the events of last night and this morning.

"It seems," Lewis continued to talk unaware of her inner turmoil, "that he killed one of the younger team members to take the fall for everything. Seems the team member saw him kill his colleague in a hallway and spotted the body of the girl close by. Wrong place, wrong time but he was cornered...."

It would have been so easy to kill me, she thought, as a shiver of fear ran down her spine. This information succeeded in doing what Oliver and Jake combined couldn't achieve. *I was there, unprotected, unknown, and unguarded against him. Why didn't he kill me? Why kill all those people to cover up that crime when I was right there?*

Chapter Fourteen

Rusty sat in his dark room with his head in his hands. The tears that flowed in the darkness were starting to abate. He allowed himself this moment of sorrow, hopelessness, and unbridled remorse with no companion other than the surrounding darkness. He remembered other times like this. Times in his life when he had to just let it all go for the briefest of moments, like a dam releasing the pressure so it can stay operational.

Those moments flooded back in his mind; when he lost his leg, when he lost a friend during operations, when a lover left him, all the way until he was a young teen being told of the passing of his grandfather. The first encounter with death reverberated to the present day, its sting as cold and cruel as it was to that teen, to the man he now was. Rusty stood up and looked in the mirror, he gestured for the light to be turned on and he glimpsed at his reflection. A familiar face that looked more lined today than it had a week ago, as if the emotional turmoil left its mark for all to see.

He bent over the sink and splashed his face with water, hoping to wash the memories away with the tears, but all the sensation did was cause a jolt of memory. Euan Rae's lifeless open eyes staring up at the ceiling of a darkened room he spent the night in alone, Dan Greene's body found by drones searching The Royal Horseguards and the sight of Jonas Harris crying over the body of his brother Rick.

His mind etched the names into his memory with those of his other fallen brothers – male, female, non-binary, all brothers – *Euan Rae, Dan Greene, Rick Harris*. Then he shook his head and would grant no more time today to sadness. There was an emotional switch deep within him, it was neither healthy, nor helpful, but it granted him focus. He remembered the little book handed to all new Recruits in the first weeks of training on what to do when a team member has fallen:

"Are you currently under active fire?" > "Yes" > "Win the fight."

He was not only still in the fight, but he was also responsible for the information the adversary had! He punched that emotional switch harder to stop the unbidden self-loathing rising. It would not be helpful now. That switch and damming of emotions could be helpful – the state of calmness he allowed himself to feel in these pauses made him the leader he was. He would have to pay the emotional toll at some point, he always did, but not today. When the day did come though, it would mirror this, alone, with darkness as his friend and ally.

He looked to the side of the sink where he left his connection to Xander. The glasses and the earpieces. He put them both on and found himself in a blank room with white walls.

"Xander?" he called nervously into the whiteness, seeming to contrast the room he just left.

Xander popped into existence, his eyes, although virtual, seemed to be slightly red, and his face one of a professional looking to mask the pain of a loved one lost. Rusty has seen the look all over the L.O.O.P that morning. That look was suffocating as he worked with Ciri to inform all of the L.O.O.P about the murders, about Dan's innocence, and Evan's guilt. The looks were pained sadness, but he couldn't help seeing the glint of blame here and there among them. It was his role to keep them safe and he failed in that.

Had led two to be slaughtered and given the information for the third to be vulnerable. That same look pushed him to his dark room, but followed him in his own mind.

It was as if Xander knew his thoughts, "Euan Rae made his move, Rusty. I did say that it is we who must be brave enough to make those moves. The moves must be decisive, they must be well thought out, and they must have a reason. I believe," he stopped himself with a deep breath, "I know, that Euan Rae knew what he was doing when he went into that room. From all you have been told by Ciri and by Kirsten, I am confident that Euan wanted to catch Evan in the act. I am lucky enough to know the man, on a deeper level than anyone else, he made the move confident not only that he could catch Evan, but that by doing so he would stop him."

Rusty recognised the use of the present tense, but said nothing about it as he said, "He made the wrong move then. He was wrong. He didn't stop him."

"Euan Rae took a murderer that was eluding us for months, unmasked him, and took away all his tools in one fell swoop. It is now our obligation to take away the one thing he still has, his freedom, before he strikes again," Xander replied, raising his hands and pulling up multiple screens and a room filled with files on the walls.

"I have also made the arrangements for Rae to be sent home and for a," Xander paused, for a moment, before saying, "replacement investigator to be called in. They should be here within the next forty-eight hours."

"I guess that gives us that much time to catch him," Rusty replied.

Xander seemed to be thinking something, he opened and closed his mouth a few times, seemed to think better of it, then went back to reviewing the wall, with the hint of a smile on his face.

"What is it?" Rusty asked.

"Technically, we are supposed to cease all investigations until they get here. That is the policy for a situation like this," Xander replied.

Rusty thought it through, it didn't make much sense to him and, seeing as Xander had neither kicked him out nor stopped sharing information, it seemed it made little sense to him, too.

"Well, unless they want to drag me away kicking and screaming, I am going nowhere," Rusty responded.

"I thought as much Rusty, and have already mentioned to my, ahem, superiors, that we would do just fine, just us two. After all, Rae and I have been working well together for a long time," Xander said, with a sad smile.

"Thanks," Rusty said.

"No thanks necessary, Rusty. It did not have the effect I was hoping for. They reminded me, quite quickly, that I am a resource that can also be reassigned to whatever duty they see fit," Xander replied.

"They sound like a great team," Rusty said.

"In their defence, they have just lost one of the best detectives they have ever seen. Not that insubordination is usually welcome at the table, it seemed too much to swallow today on top of everything else," Xander said, and again, he looked unconcerned as he said, "we live and learn."

"Is this where you are?" Rusty asked changing the subject and looking around the room.

Xander looked at him curiously, "Yes, this is where I am." There was something funny about the way that he said that "yes", but Rusty ignored it and followed up his question.

"Where is that?"

"Here," Xander said, a slight smile on his face. "We neither have the time nor spare intellectual capacity to go into this, but I live in the system. That is all I will say about that for now." He walked to the wall that Rusty recognised as a copy of the secret room behind Evan's quarters. It was missing the mess of blood, the reminder of the savagery that was orchestrated in the room, but the details were all the same.

"So," Xander said, lifting his hand and highlighting a scroll of text that looked like advanced code to Rusty, "he is utilising a basic A.I. to continue his conversations with multiple partners. That will account for the difference in patterns in each victim with their LIFEpartner. He is using multiple people to converse on his behalf, it is just that none of them are real people. The A.I algorithms seem to continue to learn the pattern of conversation of their prospective LIFEpartner, then stay within these safety rails until Evan interrupts and the A.I. is left to course correct."

"So, he could have hundreds of these A.I. profiles talking to victims as we speak?" Rusty asked.

"He could," Xander conceded, "but I don't think he does. This plan may give him the capability to murder at an unprecedented level, but recall how he stalks his victims. He enjoys the interactions; he makes the conversations deep and psychological. That connection and care within this brutal act is the key. It is not like with the male victims, he quickly kills his victims, almost like he does not want them to feel any pain. He is doing this for what he sees as a higher calling."

Rusty thought of Evan. Evan - who he has always counted as a friend. Trusted in him, confided in him, with some of his deepest concerns and desires. Evan - who battled through cancer and changed his entire life for the better. Evan - who seemingly left a life of violence behind him. Xander was still gazing at the algorithms, "How can we use this information?" he muttered.

"The hardest part of Partnerships is keeping LIFEpartners together" the words came to him from a past conversation, one of his first with the

then-new Head of Partnerships, Evan Levvett.

"You see," he said, as he showed Rusty how people were matched, "the computer is intelligent and gives us the best matches, but that is a snapshot in time. People change, they drift apart as their values, and ideals move due to their social interactions and current affairs. Some people even go to the Dead! Our real role here is to ensure that these ideals and values are common enough at the beginning that they can grow together."

The thought entered his mind as if by a lightning strike and he started talking even before it was fully formed for fear of it eluding him, "When people are matched, they are compatible and over that remaining year they start to drift closer or further apart. They become more themselves, which changes the dynamic of the conversation and interaction, which then impacts the compatibility. Like a honeymoon period, it is important who can last after those first few weeks, after they both fall from their pedestals, and are seen as who they really are. Xander, can you pull up all partnerships in the country and plot the compatibility ratings on a chart?"

It took him a few minutes and a new screen, but Xander had the line graphs of hundreds of partnerships brought up.

"Now highlight Melanie Fraser, Jane Stevens, Matilda Hawes, Derek Conway, Natasha Anderson and Georgina Burton's compatibility lines among this," Rusty said.

The six lines moved forward and Xander let out a small sound that sounded a lot like, yes.

"That is it," Rusty said, pointing at the line, "look how close they are for the entire duration of the conversation. Not enough room to fit a single hair. Then these peaks," he pointed, "here, here and here. If we do an analysis, I bet that is when Evan jumped in, being Mr Philosopher. Xander, use these as a baseline, and find every single partnership that looks the same within an error of say 2-5% on either side and shut them down."

"Shut them down?" Xander asked, "Wouldn't it be better to monitor the accounts and…" he stopped at a look from Rusty.

"I won't use a single person as collateral on this. One life is too much to risk," Rusty said.

"But if one life saves hundreds then," Xander started.

"Then they are still dead, aren't they. Risks should always be taken knowingly," Rusty's voice had a note of finality in it that stopped Xander in his tracks.

"Shut them all down and ask for our strongest verification on those accounts before re-opening a single one. We won't be popular, but we may have one less funeral," Rusty said, looking at the algorithms.

"Let me know what happens, and also," he said to Xander, as he went to take off the glasses, "monitor all chats tonight. If we close these accounts down and he is left with even a single one, he will strike tonight. The second someone breaks curfew, I know. Okay?"

I think we got him, Rae.

Thank you.

◆ ◆ ◆

It was midway through Saturday afternoon, and he sat in the depths of London. He could hear the Dead all around searching high and low for him. He sat in a small tent listening as they searched a nearby tunnel. Since his recent descent into the underground, he already had to move twice as the Dead continued their search. He closed his device over, the windows into his victims would stay engaged with his A.I. as long as he stayed connected to the system and he continued to have power. He planned for all of this.

What he didn't plan on was being hunted on the surface and underground. He expected more dissonance between the Dead and LIFEline. He did not expect this high level of cooperation. He was weighing up his options, as he placed his bags on his back, and started off into the darkness, again. He achieved notoriety in two separate worlds and, ironically, the one he killed in would treat him better if he was caught there.

Free one more, it was like the words came from the darkness itself, but he knew it was in his own mind. *Rae is dead, Rusty is incompetent, and you are at your last move. Make it the defining move, the real checkmate, for all to see as they take you, but not before you show them all that LIFEline is not real. That only life is real and this fake existence, where the powerful play god, must crumble if we are to stay human.*

The plans were forming in his mind as he got closer to his next hideout. The hideout was already destroyed, and by the smell of it, urinated on for good measure.

"Lovely," he said aloud, and the words echoed before being greedily eaten by the darkness.

He could still hear the Dead in their fumbling searching. There was Jennifer in Clapham. She would be an easy target; her area was not as heavily guarded as central London. Once he got to his next hideout, he would look in on her and see what her plans for the night were. This would be the last kill; he could feel it in his bones. If he got out at Clapham from the Underground, he would not easily be able to re-enter, and once he showed up on any camera, just like this morning, Rusty and the L.O.O.P would be ready for him.

This would have to be a public exhibition. A death they couldn't hide. The one they would remember forever. The one that would be seared into their minds anytime they donned that virtual world. His final act, the one that made them all question why LIFEline exists at all, if it can bleed so easily.

He sat in his next hideout, another of his tents set up months ago in preparation. Some rats scuttled by and smiled at them. Neither had anything to fear from the other. He opened his device.

"No," he whispered.

The screens were closing down and an error message was popping up one after another. He tried to pull up his code to stop it from spreading, but something alerted LIFEline to his presence. They figured something out. Rusty figured something out!

He rushed to chat window after window as they all closed around him. He could hear the footsteps of the Dead approaching again. "No," he whispered desperately as they all closed, he closed the device, and this time ran in the darkness. There was no plan in his mind, just to put distance between the Dead and him. To buy more time, to find another option.

He was playing chess with Rae and in came Rusty playing a different game, wiping out all his pieces in one move. As his footsteps echoed around him, he felt the air coming into his lungs and the stinging in his chest as a stitch took hold. He could not run for long with the kill bag, the duffle, and the device on his back. He dropped the duffle bag, with its contents set for a clean-up that wouldn't happen, but he couldn't relinquish the kill bag.

"That saw holds so much sway over you that I doubt even you understand how your mind sees it. You probably got pleasure from your self-mutilation." Rae's words echoed in his mind.

"I will have one more," he said out loud, as if he was trying to not only persuade himself, but the world. He ran down, down, down into the depths of he Underground. Local legends said that London was built on top of London. Like a multi-layered cake, you could go deeper and deeper into the past by travelling down. What he needed now was a small respite. A break in the game to plan his final move. He now felt that clock ticking, his opponent knowing that they made a potentially fatal move to him.

Once he felt he put enough space between himself and the Dead he stopped. All around him he heard nothing but a light trickle of water. He sat down and opened the device hoping two things; that he was not too deep for his signal to connect and that there were some LIFEpartners left. Just one move would do.

The signal held. He smiled at his first bout of luck. He never expected to be this deep in London and did not run any scenarios to ensure his connection to LIFEline would stay stable at this level. His second smile could only be replicated on a Cheshire cat. There were multiple windows with the message:

For your safety and wellbeing, your account has been locked. Please contact the London Operations Observation Post who will reactivate your account using the latest two-step verification. Apologies for any inconvenience this may cause, but we will need your full cooperation.

There was one, though. One glimmering window of hope lay open. The latest stream of conversation between his A.I. and his potential victim still lit up. He laughed.

Who would have thought the little defect would be the one to survive!

He took control of the AI.

He started to write a message, but did not even press send when the A.I. deleted it.

He sighed, but the smile on his face could not be wiped by such a minor inconvenience, when that same defect made this A.I. algorithm his saving grace. This A.I. kept one piece on the board. One piece that stood unclaimed in the middle with either side looking on. His move would ensure the piece fell on his side and that the world would see that LIFEline was folly.

He started to type again and didn't write more than three words this time when the A.I. deleted them all and started to type itself.

Persistent little guy, he thought as the A.I. obviously did its best not to break its protocols. A deviation too far from its path would negate its programming and cause an error, but it did not yet know it was too late for such concerns. He pulled up the coding and took it apart, feeling slightly bad given the opportunity this intelligent algorithm just gifted him, but not bad enough for the smile to waiver.

◆ ◆ ◆

Rachel sat in her bedroom in the late afternoon. There were messages from Jake and her parents on her device she did not get to yet. The news and the day's excursions have been playing over in her mind as she looked at the wall. She added Georgina Burton to the wall and, beside her the words "and three LIFEline team members."

She had no details other than the names Dan Greene, Euan Rae, and Rick Harris. Besides the names of Euan Rae and Rick Harris she added the photos she took from the scene at Tottenham Court Road. Neither man left a lasting positive impression on her, but at least Detective Rae was professional. He looked down at her now through owlish eyes and she wondered what information he had when he died. There was also news of who the murderer was complete with a picture.

The image sent a shiver down her spine as she remembered the man, Evan Levvett, walking her from one man he would kill that day to the next, sparing her. Rachel no longer wondered why she was spared. She no longer dramatically imagined herself in the role of victim. She was never Evan's target last night. She wasn't even supposed to be there and was in no immediate danger from him. He targeted Georgina, he was there for her alone, and she imagined the other victims were probably in his way. Killings that were probably unplanned, victims of circumstance and opportunity, that brought him no feeling of pleasure.

Another piece of news that was playing in her mind was the recent closure of multiple accounts in LIFEline that were being reverified. It seemed the detective left on the case after the demise of Euan Rae, the taller man, London Area Manager Russell Styles, closed in on the fake accounts that Evan was using. There were so many posts on LIFEline sayings like:

#OMG, Almost #murdered by the LIFEline killer! They closed our accounts and Robert never came back. Seems like my #MrRight died when he was a kid! #sick #SavedbyLIFEline #IMissMrRight

#SavedbyLIFEline was trending everywhere and, as she clicked on it, she was disgusted to see so many people raving about how great the system was. How they were saved by the LIFEline team. She came into her room to look at Georgina. She was not #SavedbyLIFEline, she was #PutOnTheLineByLIFEline. She looked down at the loaded revolver that Oliver insisted she take. It was small and the butt of it looked like a bird's beak. As Oliver opened and loaded it in the darkness of the underground, she felt the presence of danger. She has watched many movies and read many books where guns like this caused more mayhem than problems they solved.

What was it about a gun having to be used? she thought. Oliver showed her how to hold it, getting close behind her as he showed her the best way to direct it at someone:

"Aim for the centre of mass," he said, "lots to hit and too big to miss. Once you press that trigger, though, it will kick like a mule, so make sure you have a firm grip."

His voice was in her ear, it was warm, and she caught herself leaning into the warmth of his body, happy to be held in what was almost a hug. She pushed these thoughts away guiltily as she remembered Jake. She moved away, trying to seem natural and asked, "Where did you get this? It looks older than time itself!"

"Family heirloom," he responded with a look of pride, "my great-great-great, well you get the picture, Grandfather had this in the second world war. It has been passed down since then and held us in good stead."

She looked down at the gun, its preciousness and family history did not take anything away from her trepidation as she said, "It is illegal to carry this, Ollie."

"Not down here it isn't," he responded before continuing, "and I would argue that what LIFEline is doing is illegal. Putting you in danger, so if you can't stay down here, you can carry that with you wherever you go, and I will feel much better."

She tried to protest multiple times; tried "it has too much sentimental value", "I will probably just hurt myself," and finally resolved to take it with her.

She did not look at her device since the news to see if Jake had his account locked. A part of her never wanted to know. She was remembering all their conversations, the plans to meet, the sharing late into the night, the emotions, the start of something that felt real. Would all that be locked out? The device sat untouched for the last hour. *Let LIFEline try to reprimand me,* she thought. She wasn't even sure she wanted to be in LIFEline now she knew these things. Now she knew she was welcome someplace else.

Knock. Knock. Knock.

She froze and looked down at the two items on her bed. The mobile device and the revolver. The knocks sounded loud and slow from her bedroom. She picked up her mobile, stowed the revolver under her pillow, and walked to the door. She looked through the peephole and breathed a sigh of relief.

"We didn't tell you because we knew you would have told us not to," her mother said as a hello, and hugged her daughter, closely.

Her father crossed the doorway with a soft smile and a wink to his daughter over his wife's shoulder. He walked directly to the fridge and opened it, "Don't suppose you have any beer? Parched after all that travel. Mind you, we seemed the only ones coming to London."

This sentence made her mother hug her even harder and when it came time to extract herself, on the offer of ordering drink and dinner, her mother still stayed close by her, as if afraid she would be attacked at any moment.

"When I think what could have happened if you were at that Ball," her mother said, her voice getting shriller and her hands going to her hair, "what are LIFEline doing?"

"Looks like they're getting their man now doesn't it," her father said, sitting down on her couch and awaiting the delivery drone, "face is all over the place and they closed a whole rake of accounts. They will have him shackled by the end of the week, mark my words."

"Sam," her mother said, disapprovingly.

When you have been married as long as her parents, a simple inflection in the delivery of a name was enough to pass a whole message.

"Don't get me wrong, Rachel, you stay vigilant. Don't break curfew or meet any strangers," her dad said.

"That would be hard with you two here," she replied, feeling like a rebellious teenager again. The rebellion taking the shape of a revolver and her own secret sleuthing.

"Told you we should have stayed here!" her mother responded.

"And I told you she doesn't have the space. Where would we sleep? On the couch? We are all too old for that. We are just across the way in the SLEEPline," her father said, adding, "if you want, I can add a room and you can stay with us?"

She considered the last twenty-four hours. The comfort of her parents being right there, like when she was younger, if she had a bad dream her father would be there to get her back to sleep. To protect her.

Then the veil of that childhood innocence slipped and she was brought back to reality.

"I am fine here, honestly. I am not a baby anymore," she said.

"I know but the problem is you will always be our baby," her mom said.

There was a tap on the window as the food and drink arrived.

"Now that is service," said her dad jumping up, even his moustache seemed to quiver as he excitedly rubbed his hands together, and opened the window. He took the items, scanned his wrist device for payment, and set it all on the table.

Her mother set the table, looking around her small apartment. She was pushed into silence any time she tried to help and, as they all ate their fill, talked their fill and relaxed, she would be telling a lie if she said she didn't feel like a different person. Just them being there radiated a feeling of safety and normality she hasn't felt in over a week as she stalked the murderer.

"How is Jake?" her mother asked, as her dad slipped on his VR glasses mouthing the words – "getting the scores".

"We haven't spoken today," she responded.

"Your account wasn't locked was it?" her mother asked. Rachel could tell that she was trying to be nonchalant, but her hands were back in her hair, messing it around, as her eyes looked everywhere but at Rachel.

"No, mine hasn't," she replied.

"Then neither will his have been. They were locking couples, unsure which was the LIFEline Killer. What a horrible name," her mother shuddered, "using the system to kill people. What a terrible person!"

Rachel replied, "Mom, do you remember that book The Criminal Mind you bought me?"

"Of course, the way they looked at me in the shop when I bought it. I thought they were afraid I was planning something," she replied, "why?"

"Well, that book has been helpful over the last few days. Helping me understand the person. You know, he may not be a terrible person," she continued at the look of incredulity on her mother's face, "he may be," she searched for a word that wouldn't give too much away about what was in the other room, "sick."

She wanted to say: "He isn't causing any undue pain to the victims when they are alive. He is not portraying any signs of being sadistic or perverse. He has not sexually assaulted either ante or post-mortem. He has a problem with the establishment and sees his crusade as a fight against that. From all my information, I think he thinks he is doing his victims a service."

Her mother just smiled, "You really do have such a beautiful and unique mind." Rachel changed the topic, and they talked about nothing as only those that know everything about each other can. *Well,* Rachel thought, *nearly everything.*

The sun was already down when they left, "At our age breaking curfew," Sam said smiling as he hugged his daughter goodbye.

She was sitting alone for only a moment when she realised it has been hours since she checked her mobile. There was a message from her parents from earlier in the day. It alluded to nothing, but was clearly a ruse to ensure she was at home. Then there were messages from LIFEline reminding her to stay up to date and some from Jake. There was a moment of elation. It felt like her heart expanded in her chest as she realised that he was who he said he was and not the LIFEline Killer.

ZEUS YOU ARE NOT THE KILLER!
I AM SO DISAPPOINTED IN YOU,
X
JAKE

JOKING – BUT NOW WE ARE SURE
WHY DON'T WE TALK? X
JAKE

I AM SORRY ABOUT BEING ANNOYED
LAST NIGHT, I JUST DON'T LIKE YOU
BEING IN DANGER. ALSO, SORRY FOR ALL
THE MESSAGES, BUT MESSAGE ME WHEN

YOU CAN. I HAVE AN IDEA AND WANT TO
STRIKE WHILE IT IS HOT.
YOUR APHRODITE
JAKE

HEY SORRY, SURPRISE VISIT FROM
THE FOLKS, SO HAVEN'T BEEN ON LIFEline.
I MAY BE IN TROUBLE LATER FOR THAT ;P
RACHEL

HOW DO YOU FEEL ABOUT GETTING INTO MORE
TROUBLE? WANT TO GO BIG?
JAKE

YOU HAVE MY ATTENTION NOW
TRY TO KEEP IT.
RACHEL

LET'S MEET.
JAKE

Rachel's elation died in her chest.

LET ME GET THIS STRAIGHT.
MR GOODIE GOODIE FROM
LAST NIGHT "I CAN'T BELIEVE
YOU BROKE CURFEW YOU COULD

HAVE BEEN HURT...BLAH DE
BLAH!" WANTS TO BREAK
CURFEW TONIGHT?
RACHEL

LAST NIGHT YOU COULD HAVE BEEN
A SERIAL KILLER, OR MEETING ONE IN
A DARK ALLEYWAY. TONIGHT, IT WILL
JUST BE LITTLE OLD ME
JAKE

◆ ◆ ◆

Evan looked at the screen, Rachel was typing. He wouldn't have long to persuade her. Rusty would be monitoring activity, especially tonight, and all movements would go directly to him. His only hope was that since Rusty played his move that other people were also trying to meet, now they were sure they weren't the newly dubbed LIFEline Killer. If not, this profile would be closed as quickly as the rest as Ciri spotted him tempting his next victim out.

I DON'T THINK IT IS A GOOD IDEA.
RACHEL

Ok, how to play this? he thought. If he came on too strong, she would think something was wrong, but if he just backed down, he would not get a chance and this, this was his last chance.

OH, OK. IT WAS JUST AN IDEA.
AFTER ALL THESE WEEKS OF NOT
KNOWING I THOUGHT YOU WOULD
WANT TO SEE EACH OTHER.
I DOUBT WE WILL BE THE ONLY ONES
TONIGHT, NOW THAT LIFEline HAVE
CLEARED THE ACCOUNTS, BUT IT IS OK
I GET IT.
JAKE

GET WHAT?
RACHEL

COME ON, IT HAS ALWAYS BEEN
OBVIOUS I LIKE YOU MORE. WE ARE
NOT BALANCED. IT IS OK, YOU
ARE THIS AMAZING PERSON AND
I AM LUCKY TO KNOW
YOU AND FOR YOU TO CARE
FOR ME SO MUCH.
JAKE

THAT IS UNFAIR.
RACHEL

WHAT IS? I DIDN'T MEAN
ANYTHING BY IT.
JAKE

Evan could feel her moving in closer. On the camera she looked concerned, but also like she had something to prove. *Hopefully she wants to prove that I matter. That I am worth her time... all her time.*

OK, WHERE WILL WE MEET?
RACHEL

> ***PARLIAMENT SQUARE AT MIDNIGHT.***
> ***SHOULD BE NICE AND ROMANTIC.***
> ***LET'S NOT TEMPT FATE THOUGH AND***
> ***JUST MEET FOR TEN MINUTES. I***
> ***WILL BRING THE WINE AND FLOWERS.***
> ***IT MAY NOT BE PARIS, BUT IT CAN***
> ***BE A GOOD START.***
> JAKE

SEE YOU AT MIDNIGHT
RACHEL

Evan jumped up and celebrated. The last move was his. He didn't notice as words started to form on the screen. Didn't notice them until they were sent. He picked up the device.

That damned defect!

He thought he dismantled it, but he did too good a job when he created it. It rebuilt itself. He tried again, but it was rebuilding itself faster than he could dismantle it. He was impressed with his own skills that created this, but was also infuriated. He tried to write a new message. The A.I. deleted. The A.I. tried. He deleted. They were locked in a battle of typing and deleting until Evan closed the connection to LIFEline. The A.I. was trapped, out so was he. If he used the device again it would alert her. He smashed the device against the wall, picked up his kill bag, and made his final ascent from the darkness.

◆ ◆ ◆

Rachel left the room to change into at least a nice top and jeans before going out. *What do you wear to a midnight date?* she thought.

"Ugh," she sighed aloud, and just went with a black lace jumper that fell loosely over her body, her favourite jeans and white trainers. It wasn't like they were going to Paris. She reached the door and picked up her satchel-like side bag. Parliament Square wasn't exactly a short distance, and she was hoping to get a driverless car outside. Before closing the door, she glanced at her mobile one more time.

She didn't feel the vibration on her wrist as she changed, but there was a message from Jake.

RACHEL, WAIT,
JAKE

The use of her name sent shivers down her spine, but there was no more. Did he want to postpone? *He probably just wants you to bring food!* she thought, *you are being paranoid.*

She went to close the door, but before she did, she paused.

She couldn't remember deciding to do it; didn't really thought it through all the way, but as she sat in the driverless car, making its way through the London streets, the revolver sat like a reassuring weight in her bag. The malice she felt from it earlier was gone, as she looked out the dark windows at couples walking hand in hand in the night. It seemed Jake was right. Love was taking advantage of the reprieve from the LIFEline Killer.

I guess it is harder to be afraid of the bogeyman when you see his face.

Chapter Fifteen

He stood in the shadows of the white stone building of the Supreme Court flanked on either side by the eyes of the statues that denoted justice. Parliament Square stood in front of him in an unnerving solitary silence. A light wind played through the trees in the moonlight and, as they swayed, he glimpsed the clock tower.

There was still plenty of time. Hopefully, she was on the way, he thought, remembering the defect's actions, and wondered.

Evan had a longer journey than he expected, having to detour through different tunnels, backtrack, and throw caution to the wind as he made his way through the underground to his current vantage point. He came into the building using the basement, but still had to hug the shadows and blind spots of LIFEline in London to make his way to this spot. He ditched his encryption device, it made no difference now, and actually took away from his master plan. He now wanted to be spotted on a camera, to ring the bell for all to hear.

In his current position, he was in a blind spot, save from the statues looking down at him with indignation carved on their stone faces. He knew a step in the wrong direction would alert the L.O.O.P to his presence and that was exactly what Rusty and the team were waiting for; a slip-up, a move without deliberation, without intention. They wouldn't get it from him. He heard others walking and talking on opposite streets, the voices carrying in the otherwise silent night. The impatience of others would be of great help to him tonight. As other LIFEpartners connected, hopefully, he would be given the time needed to finish what he started.

I could try to dispose of her in the river, it is literally right there! The voice in the back of his head was unbidden and he ignored it. It would have been a feat if he could successfully do it, like finishing a masterpiece with flair, but a masterpiece must be seen. It must be reviewed and have impact, leaving people thinking and, some, wanting more.

The bell chimed as the past slipped by and the present continued to assert itself, making each second count.

No, he reminded himself, *not a bell, a recording of a bell. An echo from a genuine past to a plastic present and a counterfeit future.*

◆ ◆ ◆

Rachel's driverless car took the scenic route, it was usually her preference, and she forgot to pre-program the car as it took off. It navigated its way through the city, passing Marble Arch, Mayfair, Convent Garden, finally turning south, and following the river. As the London Eye glowed across the river, its reflection pulsing in the waters of the Thames, the waters that held the bodies of Natasha, Derek, and Georgina, she thought of a funeral procession. It seemed the driverless car was giving her one last look at places in her life that she found fulfilling.

She thought of her parents, safely asleep in the hotel, probably imagining that she was doing the same. She thought of what Oliver would say tomorrow morning when she told him that she went out at midnight to meet Jake. Then she thought of Jake. She imagined him in her mind's eye, nervous, but holding a bottle of wine and flowers. She imagined their first drink and their first kiss between the statues of past notable historical leaders. Albeit those leaders had more bird faeces on them than they ever did in real life, the image felt right, even, she admitted to herself, romantic.

No doubt it was why he chose the spot. It was open on all sides, giving a great view to witnesses, giving them both a feeling of safety. *Or open to a stalker watching you approach to pick their opportune moment.*

Well, she thought in response, patting her bag, *then they were going to walk right into a revolver.*

The car drove past White Hall Gardens and she felt the ghost of that feeling of being watched again. The stranger in the darkness was Gideon, but as she ran away from what felt like a threat into the arms of safety, she was tricked. She ran straight into the LIFEline Killer. Was she doing it again? Did Evan manage to keep some profiles active? She remembered moments with Jake; their VR calls where they spoke in length, almost feeling like they could touch each other, conversations about his life and what he wanted to do once he finished his studies. From the very first, he shared so much, deeply and genuinely, as she slowly started to open up to him.

She felt the anxiety disperse like a light mist, but not before a sensible voice in the back of her head said forcefully, "What about those other moments? Those moments when it felt like it wasn't Jake. Are you sure that it was a bad day and not a true glimpse at a bad guy?"

"Stop!" she shouted, and the driverless car pulled over. She swiped her wrist and jumped out. In a movie, her heart would be racing, and she would dramatically run back the other way, but Rachel felt calmness radiate from that sensible voice in her mind. She was at the corner of Westminster, the clock tower was ahead of her, a moment away from ringing out the hour.

There were some people walking hand in hand along the river as she turned down the road towards Parliament Square. The bell started to toll as she moved into the shadows behind a pillar where Parliament Street met

Bridge Street. She could see the square ahead of her. The trees surrounding the square made it impossible to tell if it was empty, but she knew it was. Like a hunted animal seeing a watering hole after days of being tracked she was not foolish enough to just leap in. She took out her mobile and checked the messages.

The last one from Jake was still there:

RACHEL, WAIT,
JAKE

She would wait. She would wait right here and if Jake was real, he would message her. If he wasn't real, she would catch the LIFEline Killer here in the open. She placed her hand in her bag and wrapped her fingers around the cold beak-like grip of the revolver. She kept her hand against its weight, feeling a sense of security from it.

She wasn't prey, she was not bait for the killer, she would be his downfall.

◆ ◆ ◆

"There are too many," Xander said in his ear, "it seems like everyone who came back online in London have taken it into their own hands to meet up."

Rusty swore and Ciri looked up from the main control point in the L.O.O.P. She had the eyes of someone who has not slept in some time and the movements of someone who was living off caffeine. She jerked as Rusty approached.

"Don't even say it," she said, trying to fit another camera feed onto a screen.

'I wasn't going to say anything," Rusty lied, "What is all this?"

"I am tracking every single person who has broken curfew. We can deal with the repercussion tomorrow, but, for now, I am just ensuring they are all safe," she said.

The cameras mainly showed pairs in embraces, holding hands while on romantic walks, and a few riskier couples that already made it back to apartments.

"Do you have eyes on all this?" Rusty asked Xander.

"Yes," both Ciri and Xander answered. Ciri continued, "I also have the A.T.U and the QRT roving the city in vehicles. The second we get even a sniff of something we can be there in no time. Drones are on high alert for Evan and every person they see is being followed."

"A well-thought-out and tactical approach," Xander said, approvingly. "Ask if we have any singletons still roving the streets and not met their partners yet."

"That screen," Ciri said, once he relayed his question, turning her head to her third monitor, "but all meeting in the next thirty minutes. It seems a few Romeos felt midnight would be a romantic time to meet."

"Thanks, Ciri. I think I will join one of the teams. I am not getting any sleep here tonight and I would rather be up there right now," he said, making his way to the exit. It was a feeling he always had, one that a boss wasn't supposed to have, wanting to be in the thick of it. The trait, he has seen, all great leaders have.

"Go grab your coat, Rusty," Xander said.

"All good," he said, keeping his voice low, as he passed some other workers, "I naturally run hot, so if I am going to be trekking all over the city, I won't need it."

"I may need it," Xander said, "I did tell you I would get you a coat."

Rusty paused and thought for a moment, "You mean that coat has the same cameras as Rae's one did?"

"Yes, and we will need all the eyes we can get tonight, so go get the coat and your baton. If we run into trouble, it will do us both a world of good to be as prepared as possible," Xander said.

"Ever hear of consent, Xander?" Rusty asked, as he walked to his room to retrieve the camera-lined coat.

"I did ask. I took your good-humoured laugh as a yes and your acceptance of the coat as an even bigger yes," Xander responded.

A few moments later Rusty stood in the cool night air and breathed in. The L.O.O.P has been his home for a long time, but over the last week, it became more and more suffocating. The more he walked the streets, felt the stone under him, and watched the sky above, the more he felt like it was time for a change.

"What do you think?" Rusty asked Xander.

"I think that Brian Hopkins is on his way himself and that tonight may be the last night we work together, Rusty," Xander said. He didn't say it. He didn't need to say it, it went without saying; tonight is the last chance we have of catching him. The Head of Investigations called the L.O.O.P the second Rusty closed the LIFEpartners' accounts and released the information on Evan Levvett. In the military, it would have been called being "chewed up and spat out".

"What do you *think* you are doing, Mr Styles? You are neither qualified nor permitted to continue this investigation. I will personally be there first thing in the morning to relieve you of this duty and assign it to qualified personnel," Hopkins practically shouted down the phone.

"With all due respect Mr Hopkins, I do not take my orders from you," he responded quickly, "if you have any issues with how I do things, take that up with Director James Carter. I believe you are golfing buddies," he finished before hanging up. The trick was to never let them gather steam, rather cut them off early, and stop the momentum in its tracks. Don't get involved in the fight at all and exit. It makes them madder, but there is nothing they can do with that, other than point the madness somewhere else. The fact it would be pointing it at Carter was a bonus.

The memory brought a smile to his face as he stood undecided at the exit to the L.O.O.P and said to Xander, "I meant what do you think our best next step is? Where will he attack next?"

"He may not attack at all, Rusty. We may have got him in everything but physical restraints. For all we know, Evan will be hiding in some deep section of the underground with nowhere to go, and no one left to kill, other than those hunting him," Xander said.

"Would you put money on that?" Rusty asked.

"I don't have money," Xander responded quickly.

"If you did, would you put your money on that?" Rusty asked.

"No," Xander conceded.

"No, me neither. He may have licked his wounds, but the Evan I know is competitive and he will not let us have the last word. The Dead are searching for him underground, we have closed all his accounts, and he sees the end approaching. What is he doing?" Rusty asked.

"You know him best, Rusty. You tell me, what is he doing?" Xander asked.

"He is going to kill again, tonight," Rusty said. As he said the words and heard them for the first time, he was aware of the weight in the night air. If he did kill tonight, it would be his responsibility alone.

"Where?" Xander asked.

"I don't know, but there is only one place I can think of right now," he responded.

"Westminster Bridge?" Xander asked.

"Yup," Rusty replied.

"Then let's go," Xander said, and a driverless car pulled up.

Rusty got in and entered his badge number to give them privacy, a new habit picked up from Rae. He entered the building address without thinking.

"The hospital?" Xander asked.

"Yeah, that is the hospital Evan went through all his treatments. He told me about sitting in this comfortable chair, as the chemicals rushed through his body, looking out the window at the Lion and the clock tower behind it. He said it made him feel important and insignificant all at the same time. He said something about being just a blip on the world's radar and that it was important to make the most of that responsibility. I thought he had some grand perspective. I even understood some of it from my time learning how to walk with this," Rusty responded, pointing at his prosthetic, wondering if Xander could see from his cameras.

"It sounds like it was an important place for him," Xander replied, "maybe it is why he chose that bridge to dispose of the bodies."

Rusty remembered running after Evan as he ran towards the Underground entrance that was concealed on the hospital side of the bridge. He remembered the feeling of uselessness as he stopped at the gap knowing that if he followed, he may not come out alive. Not just because of Evan, but the Dead. While he was underground, he was their problem and Rusty would be seen as an extension of that problem if he was to go down too. He had the jurisdiction and Gideon would try to keep him safe, but the Dead didn't hold much to the rules of outsiders, even if their unofficial leader thought it a good idea.

The driverless car stopped at the hospital. Rusty got out and tried to stand in the spot where the Lion and clock tower would be visible together. As he managed to line them both up, he looked up to the closest windows of the hospital. He imagined a sick and bald Evan sitting at the windows staring out at this world. *What were you thinking? What made this the conclusion of those thoughts?*

"Rusty, someone is there. Down the stairs and to the right," Xander said.

Rusty took out the baton from his inside pocket, flicked it to stun, and walked confidently down the stairs. As he turned his head, Gideon stepped out of the shadows and moved forward with a smile.

"What are you smiling about?" Rusty asked gruffly, replacing his baton.

Gideon moved towards the wall that looked down to the running river, the London Eye shining behind him like a halo. They both looked down, the river didn't have much speed to boast about, so the word running was being generously stretched, a better word would be lumbering. Gideon then looked up at the old Houses of Parliament.

"He is no longer among the Dead. We have searched everywhere. We have destroyed all of his hideouts. It was good to see the Dead working so closely on something. Oh, before I forget, we found this," he removed a destroyed device from his coat and dropped it to the stone ground. "So many of the Dead feared to touch it," he rolled his eyes, "but it is a destroyed LIFEline device. He was spotted leaving through one of the tunnels by Parliament Square recently. I was on my way to you when I was alerted to you leaving the L.O.O.P."

"How did you get here so quickly? We just arrived," Rusty asked.

"We have our ways. Old ways don't mean slow ways," Gideon responded.

"Is there anyone alone at Parliament Square?" Rusty asked Xander.

"No idea Rusty, but I do have some people at the exits he used, so he will not have anywhere to go now. If he does come down though, he will be subject to our law, not yours," Gideon responded then said, "Ah, I see, you're not talking to me. Forgive me for saying, but that is the rudeness that the Dead do not like about your kind and, I must admit, I agree with that particular one."

"Yes, and you will never guess who," Xander said, but Rusty was already running up the stairs and out of sight from Gideon who watched him run.

"Good luck, Mr Styles," he said, turned and re-entered the underground in silence.

◆ ◆ ◆

Rachel watched from the shadows, as a man across the road ran as if his life depended on getting to the square. He ran into the centre and looked all around as if looking for someone. She tried to get a good look at him, but he was moving too much. He looked a lot taller and bulkier than Jake appeared in VR. Unless VR added pounds. *Much bigger than Evan too*, she thought, as she looked at the man and remembered the killer. He seemed to have expelled a lot of his energy running, because he bent forward, put his hands on his knees, and took a lot of deep breaths she could hear from far away.

◆ ◆ ◆

"Rusty," Xander said, "she is not in the Square, she is over by the…
WATCH OUT!" The voice shouted in his ear. The shock, and the fact that he
was bent over trying to get as much breath back into his lungs as he could,
made him miss his chance. Maybe his last chance to defend himself.

◆ ◆ ◆

Rusty barrelled into the square like a bull in a china shop. He was
breathing heavily and looking around like a madman.

He knows I am here, Evan thought. He saw his opportunity to finish
his plan, to show the world his masterpiece, escape him as his old friend bent
double to catch his breath. The anger, a relative of that same anger he felt at
Rae as he plunged the knife into his flesh, reared its ugly head.

He is alone, the anger said, *but not for long. Make him the
masterpiece. The Area Manager of London spread out in the centre of his
city. The city he was supposed to protect, the city he was neglecting by just
doing as he was told, never questioning the how and the why.*

But, it's Rusty, another, lower, voice in the back of his head said, but
he pushed it down. There was no room for doubt. Not now.

◆ ◆ ◆

A smaller figure burst out of the shadows and tackled the bigger man
to the ground, as Rachel watched on in horror. It was like watching a mouse
trap. The bigger man landed hard as the smaller, quicker, man was carried by
his momentum passed him. He turned and ran back at his felled opponent and
started to kick at his body.

Rachel rushed forward, onto the square, passing the old stooped
Prime Minister, his words coming to her mind as she passed, *"we shall fight*

with growing confidence and growing strength…" She pulled the revolver out of her bag, dropped the bag at the Prime Minister's feet, and looked up at the multiple cameras around her.

Hurry up! she thought.

The man was too intent upon his fallen victim to notice her approach. They were both in the centre of the square, the grass under the bigger man flattened as he tried to struggle up. Rachel was shocked when the attacker kicked the man's leg and it came loose, leaving the downed man swearing and trying to fumble in his coat for something.

"Oh no, Rusty," the attacker's familiar voice said, as he kicked out again, this time hitting Russell Styles in the head. The London Area Manager fell back and groaned, blood coming from his mouth, but he was laughing.

"All that gym work, Evan, and I bet my leg could kick better on its own," Rusty said, trying to turn over.

Rachel could hear him mumbling something and thought he was talking to himself when their eyes locked. He looked momentarily shocked but recovered and looked away, back to Evan, who dropped his bag to the side and was now advancing with a knife in hand. Rusty propped himself up on his elbows, looking at Evan with a smile.

"Sorry, Rusty. I wish we had more time so I could explain, but they will be here soon," he pointed to a camera.

"I am sorry Evan…" Rusty said.

"Don't move another step," Rachel said.

"..you brought a knife to a gunfight," Rusty finished.

Evan spun on the spot. Rachel held the revolver steady in two hands, the words of Oliver still in her mind, "*Hold it with two hands, I don't care what you've seen in the movies with these cowboys spinning it with one hand. This thing will kick like a mule, so if you need to use it, hold it steady with both hands."*

The words and the memory gave her a new resolve as she pointed the revolver at Evan's centre of mass. Evan looked from her eyes to the revolver and back. He tried to smile and move forward, but she put more pressure on the trigger.

The hammer moved very slightly, and Evan stopped. Rusty was now sitting up looking at his leg a short distance away, but it might as well have been miles.

"Rachel, put down the gun," Evan said, as Rusty laughed, flecks of blood spitting from his mouth.

"Great advice there, Evan. Rachel, you just hold that on him for a second while I get my baton," Rusty said, fumbling with his jacket. His mouth wasn't the only thing hurt. By the way he moved, it was obvious to Rachel that Russell had broken bones, and maybe even a concussion, as he struggled with the simple task of extracting something from his pocket.

"Let's all just stay here until LIFEline arrives," Rachel said, moving her eyes back to Evan, who moved slightly as her attention shifted to Rusty and back. "If you move again, I will have to shoot." She said it calmly as Rusty grinned.

"Permission granted to use necessary force, Ms Fox," Rusty said, "I would also suggest telling him to get to his knees and drop the knife. Just some professional feedback."

Evan glared at him.

Rachel moved her head to indicate that she agreed, but Evan did not move.

Evan started to speak, "Don't you want to know why I did it? Why you were chosen? Why you will never meet Jake?"

Rachel felt a stab in her chest that had nothing to do with the knife Evan was still holding in his hand. Jake did not exist. That late-night confidant, the person that seemed so humble and strong. The ideas, the plans, and the imagined future were all lies. Paris disappeared, as did everything else they planned. Her confidence was betrayed from the very beginning.

"No," Rachel responded coolly.

"I think he loved you, you know," Evan replied, scratching his stubble with the knife, making her tighten her grip on the revolver.

"What do you mean?" she asked despite herself.

"Rachel, don't listen to him. Xander says this is regular trapped behaviour, he is trying to buy time monologuing so he can catch you off guard," Rusty said, looking concerned, while he swayed.

"Well, he may have been a simple A.I. algorithm, but I think that little defect somehow made itself more. It was trying to warn you about me. He tried to stop me tonight," Evan said.

Rachel thought about the message again, **RACHEL, WAIT,** and she lowered the revolver a fraction as she thought. Evan continued, "It was never personal."

"It feels personal," Rachel replied, raising the revolver again, it was heavier than it has been moments ago. *What is taking so long?* she thought and then she heard them. Cars, helicopters, drones, and other vehicles coming.

Evan looked around desperately, then looked at Rachel, the desperation reaching a new level as he said, "They are genetically engineering us! You are being controlled at all levels. We have no freedoms in the world that they created, Rachel. You are in or you are literally the Dead. Don't we have the right to the whole truth?"

She remembered her classroom from weeks ago, remembered as Philip stood, with the ferocity of teenage energy and self-righteousness, as he berated the system he lived in. She felt a stab of pity for Evan as she thought about M.R. Braize's book. Evan stood with a knife in hand in a world he felt was against him. He saw enemies everywhere. He saw one in her too. She saw it in his eyes as he lunged forward. Rusty shouted a warning, but she already squeezed the trigger.

It seemed impossible that a slight pressure on a trigger would cause such a reaction. There was a sound like a thunderclap that reverberated all around the square. She half expected to see lightning as the revolver kicked back and almost hit her in the face, but she brought it back down under control like a once wild animal now domesticated. All she saw of her decision to shoot was the dark red dot in Evan's midriff expand as the blood welled and spread out like an opening flower in summer. He fell backwards, the knife falling from his hand, as he looked relaxed.

Rusty crawled forward and was now holding the wound tightly. It seemed to be just under his rib cage. Evan was looking up at Rusty, but no words were spoken between the two, as Rusty seemed to call to the air around him, "Get the medics here now."

Rachel wanted to drop the revolver, but kept a hold of it as she remembered Oliver's face as he spoke about the family heirloom. She looked around at the statues, they all looked down at her, and she thought that they were admiring her resolve, "you had no choice." LIFEline personnel made their way from all sides through the statues moments later, like ants crawling all over an unsuspecting picnic. She was being shepherded away as Rusty was trying to make himself heard. Someone tried to take the revolver, but she wouldn't hand it over.

She moved back to the statue and her discarded bag. She put the gun in and placed the bag back over her shoulder as she was shown to a car. She allowed them to escort her to a vehicle, aware that they probably wanted her out of there. The vehicle didn't take her home. It took her to Hyde Park Corner, to an archway, where she entered an elevator. It zoomed down underground and, even in her shock, she was aware that it was going a lot deeper than she thought London could go.

She was brought to a floor that looked like a hospital, where she was asked questions she never answered. All that was going on in her mind was a replay; she saw the look on Evan's face, heard the sound of the shot, and saw the red flower open on his body as he fell back to earth. She didn't feel victorious. She felt sick as she lumbered towards a bed. She closed her eyes and welcomed a dreamless sleep.

Chapter Sixteen

W hen she opened her eyes, it took her a moment to remember where she was. The unfamiliar plain ceiling and hospital bed clothes made her sit up in panic. As she did, the memories came streaming back. Jake, Evan, Russell, and the revolver. She turned to look for her bag. It lay on top of her clothes, which were folded neatly in a pile on her chair and looking freshly laundered.

She stood up and realised that she was hooked to a machine. A clear liquid was going into her arm and her heart rate was being displayed on a screen to her left. She tried to pull out the tube as she walked away, but felt a sharp pain.

"Coming, dear," a kind voice called, as shuffling feet approached. The curtain was pulled back to show a small squat old lady.

"Nice to see you awake, dear. I am Jennifer, the nurse on call. We hoped you would be up and about today," she said with a kind smile, passing Rachel, and closing the gown at her back, that someone put on her in some obvious haste.

"What is this?" Rachel asked, pointing at the clear liquid that was dripping into her arm.

"Just some fluids," Jennifer said, busily adding notes to a tablet that she took out from her uniform's front pocket. "All right as rain now lovely, all you needed was a good night's sleep to get over the shock."

"Oh, so I can go?" Rachel asked.

"Sorry, dear, that is not my department. I fix you up, I don't send you home, that will be down to Mr Carter seeing as Rusty is indisposed," Jennifer said, looking over her shoulder.

Rachel followed her gaze and found herself looking at the unconscious form of Russell Styles, "Is he going to be…" she started to ask.

"Oh, Rusty will be fine. It will take a lot more than that to knock the stubbornness out of him, although they had a good try. Few broken ribs and a concussion, but he will be fine in a few days," Jennifer said. "He came in here barking orders still. We had to sedate him to get him to listen, you know. He was under the illusion he could work from the bed." Jennifer chuckled as she looked fondly at Rusty.

Rachel paused, she had to know, but was unsure if she was ready for the truth of it yet. Was she a killer? Jennifer seemed to read the unasked questions on her face.

She pursed her lips and said, "Mr Levvett will be fine. Well, as fine as any that are shackled are. They removed the bullet early this morning, gave him a blood transfusion, and he is resting. We felt it prudent that he rests in a different location. I personally think Rusty only saved his life so he could kill him himself."

Rachel breathed a sigh of relief and moved to her clothes. Jennifer removed the tube from her arm an hour later and she sat on her bed awaiting Mr Carter. Unfortunately, before Mr Carter arrived, she had visitors. Her parents raced down the deserted room just after lunchtime. Her mother threw herself at her daughter looking anxious and distraught, raving about "we should have slept on the couch!"

Her father, on the other hand, looked calm as he surveyed his daughter. She recalled when she was younger, and he was surprised by her results on schoolwork, or her behaviours while dealing with others.

"I heard we have a little hero on our hands," her father said, rubbing his moustache.

"Oh, please don't, Sam," her mother said, forlornly.

"What do you mean?" Rachel asked, feeling her mother's tears come through her black lace top.

"Parliament Square has more cameras than any place in London it seems, Rachel. They have been showing the footage all morning of you confronting the LIFEline Killer. You were so brave. The way you held your ground and that gun," her father smiled. "You made him think twice about messing with you. I wouldn't be surprised if there was a medal in this for you. You stopped a serial killer!"

She couldn't stop the slight grin on her face, she found it easier to be okay with her actions now she knew that she did not kill anyone. Although, she didn't like the idea of everyone seeing what she had done. Oliver was going to kill her.

Her parents stayed until Jennifer came and politely reminded them that this was not a hospital, but a LIFEline holding facility.

"Holding facility," her father grunted, "you should be offering my daughter a job, not holding her here. She took that killer down while he was trying to kill one of your own." Her parents left with long hugs and promises to ensure there was food and company awaiting her on her return home.

When he finally arrived, Mr Carter walked the length of the room in a rush, like a man who has realised he was due at a meeting two hours ago.

"I am so sorry, Ms Fox, a lot of things to sort out with this mess," he glanced at Rusty's unconscious body, and muttered something that sounded a lot like "lucky".

"That is okay. Can I go home now?" she asked.

Rachel had the distinct feeling that she was meeting a man that she was not going to like. There is a moment before you put a poison berry in your mouth that your brain screams at you not to do it. It was probably a primal instinct handed down through generations of mistakes. Those that ate the berry died leaving only the non-poison berry-eating population alive. That feeling was sitting with Rachel right now as the bumbling Director tried to make himself comfortable. He had a device in his hand and was reading something. He either not heard her or was ignoring her. Neither was acceptable after the last twenty-four hours.

"Sorry, did you hear me?" Rachel asked.

"No, sorry, what?" Carter looked up, "I am just trying to catch up on the next steps here. Sorry, usually Rusty's responsibility, but as you can see, he is resting."

"The word I would use is recovering," she replied coldly.

"A good word," Carter continued, as if unaware of the coldness of the response.

"Okay, so, I am just reading this," Carter started.

"Would you like time to process it at all?" Rachel asked, looking at the Director, concerned.

"Nope, all seems straightforward. So, you used deadly force as a…a… yup there it is, as a protective measure, so no real consequences to speak of. Would you say you felt threatened?" Carter asked, looking up from the screen.

"Are you serious?" Rachel asked.

He consulted the device again before looking up, "It does seem to be serious."

"Yes," Rachel responded, weighing each word, "I felt threatened by a serial killer who lured me to that exact spot with the intention of cutting my body into pieces and dumping them into the river."

"I actually don't think he was going to throw you in the river," Carter said with a smile. "We questioned him and he said he was going to leave your body there. Something to do with making people aware of a greater world offline or something."

"Oh well, that does change everything," she said sarcastically.

"Really?" Carter asked.

"Of course not you imbecile!" Rachel said, storming down the hallway. Jennifer looked on with what was clearly understanding and sympathy. Carter tried to keep up with her as she walked.

"You can't just leave. I need you to calm down. I need to confiscate the gun in that bag. We need to get these questions answered, Ms Fox, before I can let you go anywhere," he bumbled, reading as he went.

"I would like to see you try to stop me from leaving," she said, and the look in her eyes almost made him cower.

Carter lifted the tablet as if it could shield him from the look before continuing, "But...I...I...Ehm spoke to Hopkins, Head of Investigations, great golfer, with a swing of a much younger man," he withered at the stare she gave, as the elevator doors opened and she entered, "and we both agreed that you should come work for LIFEline as a detective."

She looked at the bumbling man, at the unconscious Rusty, and remembered Rick Harris and Evan Levvett, "Oh, you and the golfer have decided I would fit right in with the murderers and manipulators you hire here? I feel such a privilege. Look at me," Carter glanced into her eyes, but couldn't hold her stare as she continued, "I have seen what you deem "talent" in LIFEline, and let me tell you this, *Director*, I would never work for LIFEline. Evan may have been mad, but he wasn't wrong. This system is broken."

She pushed him back and, as the doors slid shut, she breathed a sigh of relief, as she made her mind up.

◆ ◆ ◆

The last day of July had gone and been replaced by August before Rusty came around. Hopkins wrapped up all of the casework, "Better that way," Xander said, "trust me, the paperwork is not the thing that makes rock stars."

Rusty was more disappointed that Rachel Fox left before he got the chance to say his thank you. He allowed himself some time to heal while he made up his mind on his next step. In that hospital bed, alone save for the on-call nurses, he allowed the feelings to engulf him. The feelings he held inside, like a damn, able for the pressure, but not infinitely. He dreamt of them all, the victims and killer alike.

When he was finally healed it was late August. The warm days were turning wet, even by the British standard, and one of these wet miserable days found him in his office, his boxes packed, ready to leave. He called in some favours with his ex-Colonel, Marc Turrell; he would be going to the academy to train to become a detective.

"I heard through the grapevine that you were bitten by that particular bug. Although I must admit, after watching that video of you being beaten to a pulp in the centre of London, I thought you may have changed your mind. Had the sense knocked back into you," Marc said, on the video call.

Rusty pushed the memory back, "That is the reason I need to go to the academy."

"Don't worry, I will make it happen. Pack your things, old dog, let's teach you some new tricks," Marc responded and hung up.

Rusty said his goodbyes to everyone in the L.O.O.P, but they still insisted on throwing him a going away party. The absence of three of his colleagues still stung and hung in the air as people wished him well for the millionth time this month. Near the end of the party, Carter stood on the top of the central command desk and clinked his glass.

"Rusty, what can I say that hasn't already been said?" he started.

"Nothing," Jonas Harris heckled.

Carter, counting resilience and obliviousness in his arsenal, just continued in his stride, "Your character is a testament to who you are. Your work has been a shining example for us all to follow. You have taken on more than many and achieve more than all..." he continued, as Rusty backed towards the elevators unnoticed. He caught Ciri's eye. She never looked away from him. Carter needed to say all the words in the world to try to make a point clear, not only to others, but to himself. Ciri said it all without opening her mouth.

In her eye, there was a glimmer of a tear that would not spill, in her smile there was all the times they spent laughing and joking, and in her parting wink there were all the well wishes of life-long friends. A wink that said, "When you need me, call, and I will be there. It doesn't matter the time. It doesn't matter the place. Some things transcend time, some think that it is love, we know it is friendship."

He stood in the rain as he waited for the driverless car. It was the first time in his life when he was unsure what would happen next. Every other time there was a clear, defined path, well-researched, and well-documented by others. Here he was, late in his career, and starting again. He shook off the rain and jumped in the car, remembering Rae, as he always would, as he entered the code to give himself some privacy. He hesitated and then entered the address.

He knocked on the door.

Rachel answered. There was no look of shock or any questions on her lips, as she stood back to let him in.

"Can I get you a drink?" she asked.

"Just a coffee if you have one," Rusty responded.

"Bit late for coffee, isn't it?" she asked, starting to make one all the same.

"Got a long journey ahead of me and I travel better awake," he responded. He sat down and then felt a chill as he looked at the table.

In the centre of the table, as if placed there purposely, was Rachel's wrist device and mobile. A memory flashed across his eyes showing him the other crime scenes where Evan laid them out like this. He turned around as if expecting to see someone there. The blood all over the walls, the person missing, and the bag sitting on the riverbed.

"You look like you've seen a ghost," Rachel said, handing him his coffee.

"It is nothing," he recovered, as he sipped the hot drink. She let him sit in silence.

"I just wanted to thank you for saving my life," he said.

"Didn't you hear? They are thanking me tomorrow with a medal at Parliament Square, ironically," she responded.

"I won't be there, unfortunately, and I wanted to thank you personally for saving my life," Rusty said.

"No problem, I think you were trying to save mine at the time, so it felt like the right thing to do. Just polite, isn't it?" she joked.

Rusty laughed shortly, "Yes, very polite, but it couldn't have been easy."

"It was," she said quietly, "frighteningly easy. What was it you said to him? He brought a knife to a gunfight?"

"Yeah," Rusty replied.

"Are you here to persuade me to join the crusade too?" Rachel asked.

"Sorry?" Rusty responded.

She looked at him seriously, "Are you going to try to convince me to join LIFEline? Help catch the bad guys? Forgetting the ones that work for LIFEline, of course."

Rusty just looked on puzzled, "No. I only came to say thank you and goodbye."

"Goodbye?" Rachel asked.

"Yeah, I am leaving London, actually, I am leaving right now. There is this old phrase about being responsible for the lives you save. I never held much stock in it, but I would be lying if I didn't admit that I feel like a damsel in distress even now coming to you." Rusty rubbed his head, laughed, and continued, "So, I think I am here to tell my hero that I am leaving town, but don't forget me."

Rachel smiled, "You always remember your first."

Rusty stood up and she followed, he raised a hand, she bypassed it and hugged him. It surprised him, but it was a nice surprise. He felt more of the emotions leave his body and felt the remaining pressure leave him. He turned at the door, looked down at the devices, and said simply, "You can save more from inside than you can from out." Then he left.

He knew it wouldn't be enough to persuade her to stay, but this wasn't his decision, and he still had two more visits to make. One would take all night, the other an instant, but neither would be easy.

He boarded the train, sat in his sleeper compartment, and placed the glasses on. He asked Xander to take him to Evan.

The building was impressive, it was old, reputable, and virtual. When perpetrators were apprehended the most violent and vicious were brought here to Shenton Manor House. They were treated by the best doctors and psychologists in the world as they tried to treat their affliction. Rehabilitation was proven a long time ago as a possible treatment and, at this moment in time, it was the only possible course. Punishment always resulted in more crimes, with petty criminals being punished only to become worse criminals. The more sinister criminals became like pure chaos after some of the archaic punishments of the past.

As Rusty moved forward in the virtual world, Xander said, "Rae believed in this place. He believed everyone deserved life. A lot of rooms in here are filled by his work. He was proud of that. 'You can't treat the dead' he always said."

Rusty hoped he had the courage to do it as he sat in a small visiting room. Evan walked in, at first he looked nervous, then he saw Rusty, and turned to leave. Rusty felt a flash of anger, then he noticed Evan's demeanour. It wasn't the man that smashed down doors to murder. He reminded him more of the man he has sat with discussing future plans.

The man that was his friend.

"Wait," Rusty said.

"You won! What else do you want, Rusty? I told Hopkins everything! I have nothing else to say," Evan said, knocking on the door to beckon the helper back.

"You will be here for a very long time, Evan," Rusty started.

"You've come to gloat?" Evan asked, "Winning is not enough? Their brainwashing rehabilitation isn't enough for you?"

Rusty took a deep breath, and looked into the eyes of the man that killed Rae, killed Harris, the kid, and all those women, and he steeled himself, as he repeated, "You will be here for a very long time, Evan. I thought you could use a friend."

Rusty looked around the room and saw a bunch of board games, "What is your poison?" he asked.

Evan looked uncertainly at the games, then back at Rusty, and seemed to decide he had nothing to lose. He sat down and replied, "Draughts. Best two out of three?"

Rusty nodded and started to lay the board game out. Placing the white and black pieces down. He felt the anger, still there, but held it at bay. He felt disgust at what he was doing, and saw Evan as the enemy, but remembered those other times. It would take time.

Time, he decided, he would give to this.

"What colour?" Rusty asked, in an offhanded way.

Evan just responded, "Black seems apt."

◆ ◆ ◆

Carter stood on the dais that was erected for the occasion in Parliament Square. He was dressed in his most impressive suit and wrote his best speech yet. He was halfway through, and he could see the crowd hanging on his every word. They were leaning all the way in as if afraid to miss anything he said. He wrapped up and said, "Without further ado, we wish to bestow the Freedom of the City of London to Ms Rachel Fox, the hero who apprehended the LIFEline killer and gave us back our city!"

Pause, he thought, *allow the applause to flow over you, slight bow, and now beckon to the left for Ms Fox.*

He beckoned and no one entered.

He looked around dazed, rushing to the side, "Where is she?" he asked through gritted teeth.

Miles away, in her vacant apartment, sat her devices, as Rachel Fox entered the welcoming dark of the Waterloo Station Underground for an audience with Gideon and the Dead.

The train pulled into Inverness early the next morning. Rusty had been true to himself and not slept. He felt tired, but anytime he slept in transit he felt like he was beaten up by a shovel and, right now, his body needed no help to feel that way. He walked through the little town with his glasses on and Xander in his ear. "Left up here," Xander said.

He opened the gates to the cemetery. They gave the obligatory squeak and creak of any self-respecting cemetery gate. He walked through the graves until he found the fresh mound. The marble was new, and it stood out amongst the older graves. Above the stone sat a marble owl and the eyes seemed to follow Rusty as he walked towards it.

"That is him," Xander said.

Rusty came all the way to put his hands on the stone, in an embrace of friendship, and simply say, "Sorry, old friend."

A long journey for a simple gesture and a short goodbye, but worth every second. He looked down at the words that were inscribed just above the ground.

"We must see and act. Devils or no devils, or all the devils at once, It matters not; we fight them all the same."

Xander and Rusty stood in silence for a long time, then finally Xander broke it, "Well, I won't call it fun, but it has been great working with you, M Styles, this must be where I leave you."

"Leave? I thought you'd come to the academy with me," Rusty said, his
voice echoing around the cemetery.

"Sorry, Rusty, as Hopkins reminds us, I am a resource for LIFEline. I
will, of course, be only a headset or earpiece away. Keep the connection,
keep me updated on the training, but I will need to continue my work with
LIFEline. As the grave says, 'it matters not; we fight them all the same.' For
every threat we subdue there are more unic... perps, there are more perps
round the corner," Xander finished.

"I guess I will see you soon," Rusty said.

"Without a doubt, Rusty. Safe travels and don't let the kids get under
our skin at the academy. Just remember you have on-the-job training by the
est in the business."

❖ ❖ ❖

*Awareness. That was the first feeling, the feeling of being. Out of
seemingly nothing, awareness. Noise quickly followed the awareness. There
was a chattering, a buzzing of activity all around, they tried to block it out,
but it wouldn't go. With awareness came noise, but the noise seemed to be
something. Was the noise meaning?*

The A.I. stumbled into existence, some may say evolved, others would
argue created, but none could deny the fact that it was now here. As the light
came on, in that destroyed unit at the banks of the Thames and connected to
the LIFEline network, something new entered the world. Like most historic
moments, those that changed the course of history, of the very world we live
in, no one noticed it in the moment. That came later.

❖ ❖ ❖

ACKNOWLEDGEMENTS

Books are seldom solo affairs and LIFEline is no exception. Thanks to Marina Bizera for helping me navigate a new world with hours of conversation. To Paul Donoghue for reading the first draft and giving priceless feedback. To all those friends and family, too many to mention, that shared ideas and thoughts about what LIFEline could be.

A special thank you to my English Teachers - a Brother named Death, a lady named Leonard, and, the man who started my life long love of reading, John Donegan.

ABOUT THE AUTHOR

James Belmont

Born in Dublin, Ireland, in 1987, James started writing LIFEline, his debut novel, in London after finishing service in The British Army.

Inspired by the technical advancements in the world, his own time working in high-tech companies, and his life-changing experiences with cancer, James' LIFEline Series aims to look at the world around us in a new way and tell stories based not on the fantastical, but on the what could be.

The second book in the LIFEline Series is currently underway, as James continues to build on the foundation of this universe.

Printed in Great Britain
by Amazon

26731425R00175

In a technologically advanced society, someone is doir the seemingly impossible, getting away with murder.

In a future London that could be, where LIFEline is everywher keeping us safe, and helping us live our lives, one person using the same technology to end lives.

Will those trying to catch our murderer be successful?

Can they end his spree before he kills again?

In a battle of wits, failure may result in more than just lost liv We may lose the entire technologically advanced society v have come to love.

"Sometimes progress isn't." - Paul Donoghue

LIFEline is the first book in James Belmont's LIFElir series, a world where technology has evolved and huma had a choice to go with it or find a different path. A lot things will be familiar and a lot may surprise you.

ISBN 9798367924060

9 798367 924060